TO STIR A FAE'S PASSION

A Novel of Love and Magic

Book 3

NADINE MUTAS

Cover Design by Najla Qamber Designs
www.najlaqamberdesigns.com

Editing by Faith Freewoman, Demon for Details Manuscript Editing

ISBN-13: 978-1546474487
ISBN-10: 154647448X

For Sergej, my real-life hero

ACKNOWLEDGMENTS

I need to thank the people who continually make it possible for me to pursue my dream: Sergej, Mama, and the great ladies (and one gent) from my toddler's daycare. Seriously, I couldn't have done this without daycare, folks.

Also, coffee. I love you, and the lies you tell me about how productive I'll be today.

My awesome editor Faith, with endless patience and understanding for the special circumstances of a writer with young kids. And for excellent edits, of course.

Najla Qamber, for bringing my books to life with beautiful covers.

And many, many thanks to you, my dear readers, for sticking with me even when my releases are scheduled so far apart you could grow out a bad dye job. Not that I did that, or anything. Ahem.

TO STIR A
FAE'S PASSION

1

Isa's list of *Things I'm Loath to Do* featured a select few items, and dropping off a fugitive at the fae court ranked right under scraping fox poop off her shoes.

The splendor of the royal palace alone rubbed her the wrong way, the fine livery of the guards so unsuited to actual combat, the shining marble and stone so polished it barely sang to her anymore. Not to mention the gold and silver adorning the doors. A small splinter of that would pay for a new bow and more arrows than she could shoot in a month.

But the stares were the worst. The finest of the fae gathered at the court, sycophants basking in the grandeur of the royals, blissed out among the riches of Faerie. Things *they* were loath to do? Being reminded that not all of Faerie lived this life of luxury, that some actually needed to *work* to survive.

However, for all that Isa hated those cold stares directed at her—the despised reminder—she relished how she ruined those faeries' day by daring to walk among them.

So, when she brought her latest fugitive back to the royal court to serve his sentence, she did enjoy the fact she had to drag him through gleaming halls of jewels and precious stone right up to the throne room.

Highborn fae sniffed while she passed them, curled their lips at her dirty attire—she'd chased the escaped faery through muddy wetlands, and hadn't bothered to change, all the better to scandalize the royals—and muttered sophisticated insults at her. She allowed herself a smile hidden by her *talôr*, the cloth covering the lower half of her face.

When she arrived at the massive double doors leading into the throne room, the guards blocked her way.

"You will hand your capture over to us, hunter," one of them said, so proud and uppity in his beautiful uniform. The one with serious design flaws, from the tightness across the shoulders that would impede his ability to move freely in a fight, to how it allowed no room for even the lightest of armors to protect his vulnerable spots.

Idiots. Complacent, that's what the royal court had become. Thought themselves so safe within the borders of Faerie, so settled and smug in their power, they'd neglected to keep their weapons sharp and their minds even sharper.

She brought the fugitive to heel next to her with a yank on his magical leash. "My contract is with the king, and only with him. His Highness signed it, not you, nor any other guard. Therefore, I will only surrender the capture to His Majesty, and receive my reward from him personally as well."

The taller of the two fae guards narrowed his eyes. Oh, how he wanted to deny her entrance. It was written all over his handsome blue face, but agreements among fae were considered sacred, and had to be followed word for word. With a clenched jaw, he stepped aside and allowed her through. The escaped fae grunted when she yanked him into the throne room behind her.

Ah, splendid. Nearly the entire court was assembled. Conversation ceased when she marched into the middle of the massive hall, stopped in front of the dais with the two intricately carved thrones, and bent her knee before the royal couple and the noble fae. Hissed whispers floated over to her. *Bounty hunter scum. Reeks of humans. So obscene.*

Isa squared her shoulders, lifted her chin, and focused on the reward for this job. *It's good money, it's good money,* she repeated to herself, over and over. She'd long ago shed any shame over her profession, and outside of the royal court, she rarely encountered prejudice like this. She was good at what she did, and to hell with those who looked down on her because of it. And yet, something about the combined force of the disdainful stares of those noble fae stung her despite her determination to ignore them.

When the king bade her rise, she stood and released the escaped faery from the magical leash, forcing him to face the thrones. He'd been a real prick to her all the way back into Faerie, and had spit on her more times than she could count. If she began this mission with the slightest scrap of sympathy for him, he thoroughly trashed it with his vulgar taunts, not to mention the attempted bite attack. She didn't care what he did to incur the royals' wrath, to make them pay a lovely sum to a lowborn bounty hunter to track him down and haul him back from the humanlands. Not that she usually wondered, or even asked, about the subjects she was tasked to retrieve, but in his case, she honestly couldn't care any less.

"Bounty hunter," the king intoned, his blue eyes striking in a brown face just a little darker than Isa's own complexion, his long blond hair elegantly parted around his pointed ears.

"Your majesty." Isa bowed. "I present to you the fugitive you tasked me to capture and bring before you. I humbly request to receive the agreed-upon reward."

"Ah, yes."

The king waved a hand, and a guard hurried forward and dragged the whimpering fugitive to the side. The highest of the highborn fae then tossed a satchel toward Isa. It landed with a metallic clink at her feet. She snatched it off the floor, opened it and started to count the coin, when the king spoke again.

"You are dismissed. Begone."

With a bow, she moved toward the doors, still counting the money. A spasm clutched her limbs, a hot flash of piercing pain fired up her nerves. The hand that sorted through the coins twitched and numbed. She paused, breathed through her nose, and forced herself to hold her hand still.

Not...yet...

Focused on curling her fingers into her palm. She shook from the effort. Sweat broke out on her skin. Seconds ticked by, but she managed to make a fist, to fight back the debilitating numbness until she felt her hand again.

Not...yet...

The curse was acting up again. Sooner than she expected. With a sharp shake of her head, she refused to consider the implications.

Not...yet...

She finished counting the money instead. Her stomach curled in on itself. Her pulse sped up. Heat washed over her.

Suppressing a growl, she turned back to the dais. "Your Majesty."

He barely spared her a glance.

"Your Highness." She cleared her throat, spoke louder. "This is not the sum we agreed on."

The king's deep blue eyes focused on her, as did the queen, sitting beside him in her exquisitely fancy dress, her moss-green skin radiant in the light of the chandeliers, her red locks adorned with her sparkling crown. Boredom lurked in her gaze, as well as a finely-honed cruelty, and it was she who replied to Isa's accusation.

"There has been an amendment to the contract. The

reward has been adjusted."

Isa exhaled through her nose. Her pulse pounded in her ears. "With all due respect, my lady, that is illegal."

"Against the law, yes?" The queen leaned forward. "Pray tell me, *sayunai*, who is it that makes the law?"

It had been a long time since someone had referred to Isa with that term, a name for bounty hunters that wasn't *quite* an insult, but carried enough of a sneering undertone that it felt like one.

"You are welcome to file a complaint about your remuneration," the king chimed in, his smirk revealing the knowledge that Isa would do no such thing.

And he was right. She knew when to cut her losses and run. Filing a complaint would lead nowhere, might even eat up more money than she'd get out of the process in the end.

"No, thank you," she murmured, clutched the satchel and strode toward the exit.

She was almost at the threshold when the double doors slammed shut with a bang that reverberated in the lofty hall. Stunned, Isa swiveled around, her hand already hovering over the dagger at her thigh, her eyes darting toward the royal dais and the guards.

But they looked just as baffled as she felt.

Bang, bang, bang.

Three more doors along the walls of the throne room slammed shut as well. Agitated whispers ran through the ranks of the two dozen or so highborn fae in attendance. Before anyone could move, a storm of rage and hatred blasted through the one remaining open door, which closed behind the intruder in the very next instant.

With a gasp, Isa backed up against the wall, the hand that had reached for her dagger now flattened against the smooth surface of the stone. As soon as she touched it, she called upon her magic, and it sang to the stone, flowing over and through her until she merged with the marble at her back. She wasn't really part of the wall, of course, just concealed so well that, for everyone else, she'd become invisible.

Whatever was about to happen here, it was going to be ugly, and she wanted no part of it.

Magic swelled in the air to deafening levels, and the storm in the middle of the throne room raged on, swirling, howling, whipping, and then collapsed in on itself with a whoosh that rang in Isa's ears. The lone figure of a male fae emerged out of the lingering cloud of darkness—and murder whispered about his vibrating form like mist gathering upon graves.

The king took one look at the intruder and yelled at his guards to arrest the threat...those feeble, arrogant, complacent guards, whose last serious battle might well have been hundreds of years ago.

Still plastered to the wall, Isa could only watch in horrified paralysis while the royal guards met their match—and their deaths.

The intruder moved like liquid, like lightning, there and gone again in the span of a heartbeat, wielding his slim sword with lethal efficiency. The guards around him fell like flies. Panic surged in the room, and the noble fae rushed to the doors, rattled on the handles—in vain. Magic locked all the exits.

The blood of the guards spilled over the gleaming stone floor, saturated the air with its thick, coppery scent. Hissing, the king threw out his arm toward the attacker, but whatever power he'd meant to hurl fizzled out when the intruder blocked the magic with a flick of his hand.

"You killed her!" the attacker bellowed. "You murdered them both!" He took a step toward the dais, where the king and queen sat in horrified paralysis. "Their blood is on your hands. Now I'll drench this room in *your* blood. This is for Roana!"

With a roar, the intruder launched himself at the royal pair. The queen jumped to the side and threw a dagger at the attacker. It penetrated his chest, yet didn't slow him at all. As if forged from the fires of wrath, the intruder seemed unfazed by any of the king and queen's defensive moves. Neither magic nor weapons deterred him. Within seconds, he decapitated the king and shoved his sword through the queen's eye. She twitched once, and collapsed in a lifeless heap. The intruder planted his foot on her face and pulled his sword out of her head.

Without so much as a pause, he went for the rest of the noble fae huddling against the walls and in the corners. He slashed and ripped and stabbed, blood sprayed, screams filled the room, fear and darkness descending until Isa couldn't breathe anymore.

He was down to the last remaining faery, a female

already lying on the floor, holding her injured side, but still alive. When he raised his sword to deliver the death blow, the fae rasped, "Your child lives…"

The intruder hesitated, halted his downward strike.

"Your son…" the fae coughed. "He's…alive."

A sound escaped from the attacker's throat, so anguished, so broken, it reminded Isa of the rabid wolf she once had to kill in an act of mercy. The intruder lowered his sword, his chest heaving with his labored breaths.

"How?" His single question was half a growl, half a whisper.

The female fae shuddered, her light brown skin reduced to a sick pallor. "I…smuggled him out. Exchanged him… Witch family…" She coughed again. "Murray."

The attacker's sword clattered on the floor. He went down on his knees in front of the fae. "Why?"

"Roana…" The fae lifted her head to look directly at the intruder, her face wracked with pain. "She was my friend." Old magic echoed in her words…so much love, so much devotion it made Isa shiver.

The attacker gingerly propped the fae up against the wall, fumbled over her wounds for a moment, his hands shaking. "You'll live," he said hoarsely. "Your injuries aren't fatal."

He fidgeted for a few more seconds before he grasped his sword and stood abruptly. Looking up, he seemed to calculate something for an instant. In the next second, he called upon power that tasted of the earth, of green and thriving things. The floor rumbled, broke apart in front of him, and branches shot out of the hole. They twined around him, enfolded and surrounded him, and then they rose, rose, rose, lifting him up to the lofty ceiling, where starlight twinkled through high-arched windows at the top, right under the dome of the throne room. As soon as he reached those windows, the intruder jumped off the branches, through the glass pane, and into the dark of the night.

Isa shook so hard her hand almost slipped off the stone wall, which would have exposed her presence. She couldn't leave now. She had to wait for the guards to break through the magically locked doors—which should open soon, now the intruder and his magic were gone. She could then try to sneak out through the open exits.

If they saw her here, she'd be implicated in the massacre. Who'd believe a lowborn bounty hunter when she told them about an attacker with powers beyond anything she'd seen in recent times and how he slaughtered the entire royal court in the span of a few heartbeats? No, they'd assume she played a part in it, and no fair trial would await her.

While the magic securing the doors still worked—guards shouted outside, rattled the handles, in vain—something stirred among the carnage. One of the fallen fae rose on unsteady legs, clearly injured, yet able to crawl-walk over to the female fae propped against the wall.

Two. There were two survivors. Plus Isa, merged

with the stone.

The other wounded fae—a male, his skin a golden glow underneath the blood painting him in gory strokes, his hair probably silver—sank down in front of the female fae.

"The witch family's name," he said in a low voice, "is Murray?"

The female eyed him, hesitated.

He pulled out a dagger, plunged it into one of her wounds. She uttered a gurgling scream.

"Yes?" he asked.

"Yes," she hissed. "Murray."

"Good."

And he slit her throat.

Isa flinched, pushed her back harder against the wall in an instinctive urge to sink into the stone, to reinforce her cloaking. Her heart thudded against her ribcage, its drumbeat pounding in her head. Sweat coated the hand she held pressed against the stone, praying it would continue to keep her hidden, and safe.

The magic in the air, the one barring the doors, eased, then vanished. The male fae—a member of the royal court, judging by his expensive tunic—lay down next to the female he just killed, and when the doors burst open and guards streamed inside, he groaned and cried out for help.

In the flurry of agitation while the guards inspected the room and carried the male fae out, Isa inched closer to one of the open side doors, keeping her hand on the wall and herself hidden in stone. She timed it right, made it out when no one was looking—the doors were wood adorned with gold, nothing she could work her magic on, so she had to make herself visible to sneak out—and immediately plastered her hand against the stone again once she was out of the room.

She walked as fast as she could without losing contact with the walls, until she was far away enough from the throne room that she wouldn't arouse suspicion. And then she *ran*. Because for the first time in twenty-six years, she had hope, real *hope* of surviving this curse. She just had to find the changeling.

Problem was, she wasn't the only one looking for him.

2

"Ladies first." Basil Murray bowed and, with a courtly gesture, indicated the dark oak door to his family's kitchen.

"Cut the crap." His twin sister Lily—recently turned into a demon by a wacko suitor who then deservedly met a most violent death—shook her head and took a step back. "You go ahead."

"Don't be a wuss."

"You're the one who's being a sissy."

"Am not. You're—" Basil sighed, pinched the bridge of his nose. "What are we, ten? This is ridiculous."

"I agree." Lily crossed her arms, her black curls sliding over her bare shoulders, her light skin now adorned with her demon markings. He still wasn't used to it, and he was startled every time he saw the swirling lines, or noticed their color change from dark brown to fading henna, depending on Lily's energy level.

"Which is why you should just go in and talk first," Lily added. "After all, you've always been so much more mature than me." She batted her eyelashes at him and gave him an innocent and slightly pouty smile.

Basil shot her a dark look. "That trick only works on your mate, sis."

She blew a lock of her hair to the side. "Was worth a try."

He stared at her. She stared back. He gestured toward the closed door, and the daunting task looming behind it. She gestured right back at him, silently telling him *no fucking way*.

He inhaled through his nose, exhaled through his mouth. "It seems we're at an impasse. No other choice."

She nodded sagely. "On three?"

"On three."

Lily went into fighting position. He mirrored her pose.

"One," he said.

"Two..."

"Three."

They both struck at the same time. His outstretched hand, palm down, against Lily's hand, curled to a fist.

"Yes!" He pumped his fist, then pointed at his sister. "Paper beats rock."

She rolled her eyes. "All right, all right. I'll go first and do the talking. But there's gonna be hell to pay if you don't back me up, mister."

"Right here behind you," he muttered.

Lily took a deep breath, and for a second she looked like she wanted to bolt. He flung open the door and shoved her in the kitchen.

"Ouch, Baz!" She shut her mouth and stopped slapping at him when Hazel turned around. "Oh, hi, Mom. Um, do you have a minute? Baz and I want to talk to you."

Hazel's chocolate-colored eyes took them both in, her face ever so radiant, so full of warmth and love and all things cozy that made up a *home*. Where Aunt Isabel had often been stern, unyielding—a general determined to steel you through the use of rough handling—Hazel had never been anything but the soft comfort of unconditional, maternal love. Even during the years when Father was still alive—which brought Basil back to the present.

He cleared his throat. "Yes. Let's sit down."

Hazel frowned a little but nodded. "Sure."

They settled at the small table in the breakfast nook, in front of the bay window overlooking the expansive backyard of the Murray mansion.

"What do you want to talk about?" Hazel asked.

"Umm..." Lily fidgeted in her seat. "It's just that recently, I've gotten to thinking. After I mated with Alek. There were some things I'd never realized, stuff in my past...in our past... I mean, our family—" She shifted her weight. "Um. Baz?"

He sighed, sent his twin a sideways glance, which of course she understood as if he'd said it out loud, and shot him back a look that clearly said, *Nu-uh, I did my part. I did talk first. Now you go.* And knowing her, he also knew he had to pick up the convo now.

"What Lil's trying to say, rather ineloquently—ouch!" He glared at Lily, and rubbed his shin where she had kicked him, hard. "She's kind of had commitment issues that go back to her childhood. She realized the problem when Alek was courting her, and we talked about it, and we think it's from seeing...your relationship with our father."

Hazel went very still.

Basil pushed forward before he lost the nerve. "Thing is, we—that is, you, and both of us—never actually discussed it. But it's always been this huge, taboo subject hanging over our heads, and we think it's time we tackle it. Talk it through. So we can let it go."

He'd grabbed an apple from the crystal fruit bowl, and was peeling off the sticker label on it, his attention meticulously on the tangible, practical task that was easy to accomplish, not on the mess of emotions so difficult to untangle.

Hazel cleared her throat. Her voice was measured when she spoke. "What, exactly, do you want to talk about?"

Lily was fidgeting again. "The way Dad treated you..."

Dad. Yeah, Robert had been a dad to Lily, all right. To Basil, though... And that was part of it, wasn't it?

"He was an abusive asshole to you, Mom." He couldn't suppress the gruff edge to his voice, from the too-long-buried hurt and anger now rising to the surface. If his father hadn't died when Baz was still a meager, weak fifteen-year-old who was only slowly growing into his gangly long limbs…if Basil had been stronger, or had more power…all that hurt and anger and righteous protectiveness would have erupted one day, and his father might have died by *Basil's* hand instead of Aunt Isabel's.

"Language," Hazel snapped.

"Sorry," he muttered. "But it's true. He had control issues, and was a jealous freak who treated you like shi —like garbage. Did you think we didn't notice? He didn't even try to be subtle about it."

And while Father never laid a hand on Hazel, he intimidated and manipulated and verbally abused her until she became a cowering little mouse in his presence, until she wouldn't even leave the house without his express permission. The change in Hazel after Robert died was astonishing. She was a new woman, a glowing, vibrant version of the meek mother they'd known all their lives.

"Mom," Lily said gently, leaning forward to stroke her shoulder before straightening again. "I found you crying so many times. You'd always say it wasn't his fault, and you'd make excuses for him, but the way he spoke to you… He *hurt* you. And yet you always defended him, told us that love requires compromise and concessions. And I…I started thinking, that's what love is. That it makes you just take everything, no matter how bad, without complaining. That it robs you of your will to stand up for yourself."

She paused, looked down at her hands on the table. "It almost cost me the love of my life. I would have missed out on Alek if I hadn't realized how twisted my perception of love was."

Hazel made a small noise, took Lily's hand in hers, and squeezed.

"It wasn't right." Basil knew his voice was hard, his anger about the past too great for him to even pretend to be diplomatic. "His behavior, the way he talked to you, shamed you in front of us—how you let him treat you like a...like a despised slave..."

"Let?" Hazel narrowed her eyes at him, eyes the exact same color as his own, seemingly the only link he had to his family in terms of appearance.

"Why didn't you stop him?"

"*Baz.*" Lily kicked his shin again.

"No. I want answers." He focused on his mom. "You know what I mean. Aunt Isabel said the same thing. You never stood up to him. You never—"

"How dare you." Quiet, so quiet, but Hazel's voice carried thunderous anger. "How dare you imply it was my fault. I'll not have you speak to me like that."

She rose, her chair screeching on the parquet.

Lily reached out, took her hand. "Mom, please. That's not what we—of course it wasn't your fault. He was the one being shitty toward you." A sharp glance from Hazel had her adding, "Sorry. Wrong, his behavior was wrong. You didn't deserve that."

Something flickered over Hazel's face, a shadow darkening her features for a second.

"Wait." Basil leaned forward. "Wait. Mom—did you think you deserved his treatment?"

"Of course not." But she looked down, to the side—a lie. She bristled at the implication that she was partly at fault for allowing Robert's behavior, but somehow, somewhere in her heart, her mind, she did believe it... or maybe she believed she had triggered it? Believed she'd done something to make him *start* treating her like crap?

Lily saw it too. Her demon senses allowed her to read auras exceptionally well—something he envied her, his own perception as dull as any human's, born without magic as he was—and whatever she read in Hazel's energy pattern made her gasp.

"Mom...why would you feel guilty? Why would—"

"Because," Basil interrupted her quietly, "I'm not his son."

Hazel flinched. Lily whipped her head around, stared at him slack-jawed. True, they'd entertained the theory some years ago, but they dropped it when Hazel yelled at them for even considering it. It hadn't come up in the years since, which explained Lily's surprise.

Basil, however, never let it go. His looks were just so different from the rest of the family, and he didn't really resemble Hazel's husband, or his relatives. Black hair, creamy white skin, and blue eyes ran in the Murray family, and Lily was the perfect example, was almost the spitting image of her late Aunt Isabel. Hazel's brown eyes were due to her own father's, and one could argue that Basil had inherited his eye color from her.

But his blond hair had no precedent in either family. Hazel's husband had light brown hair, and all his relatives' hair was even darker. Basil's skin glowed with a light tan, as if he sunbathed regularly, when both Hazel and her husband had very light skin. It made sense to Basil that he must be the product of an affair.

The fact that he and Lily were twins made the biological explanation a bit trickier, but not impossible. Basil read up on it, back when he and Lily first started joking about not sharing the same father.

A twin pair of a boy and girl was always fraternal, meaning they didn't develop from one egg, but from two separate ones, each fertilized by a different sperm cell. And since during ovulation eggs were fertile for up to twelve hours, and since sperm was able to survive for up to seven days in the uterus and fallopian tubes, if a woman had a twin-egg ovulation, and slept with two men within the couple of days leading up to her ovulation, each of the men *could* father one of the twins.

Yep, Basil sure had been thorough with his research. Doubts about your parentage could do that to you.

He'd just never scrounged up the courage to outright ask his mom about it. Not until now.

"Am I right?" His voice wavered just a little bit. He swallowed. When she didn't say anything right away, he carefully put all the apples he'd divested of their label stickers back in the crystal bowl, one by one.

His mom opened her mouth, closed it. "How can

you ask me that?"

"Just tell me. Robert's dead, so he doesn't care anymore."

"*Basil.*"

"Mom."

She cringed, turned to look out the window into the dark backyard.

"Please," he said through gritted teeth, shedding his pride, desperate, so desperate for a final answer to the burning question that—

Something popped around him. Like a bubble surrounding him had burst, or that strange opening of your ears when adjusting to pressure. A wave of sensations flooded him, and his senses sharpened, attuned to his surroundings with so much detail, so much input, that his brain short-circuited for a moment.

Hazel gasped, swiveled around, and her eyes widened when she looked at him. "Yes," she blurted out, almost as if she thought she had to say it fast to say it at all. "You're not his son."

She exhaled on another gasp, her face lost all color, and she sank down on the chair again, her hands covering her mouth. "Dear gods above and beyond…"

Basil was still reeling from whatever the hell had just happened to him, but—he could think about it in a minute. Right now, he forced himself to take a deep breath and said, "Thank you. I mean, I think I always knew, but to hear you—"

Hazel met his gaze and shook her head, her dark

eyes glistening with unshed tears. "And I'm not your mother."

3

Stunned silence.

Basil's heart could have stopped beating, and he wouldn't have noticed. He was that numb.

"The what with the who and the how?" Lily asked, her voice squeaky high.

His mom sobbed.

No, not his mom. The thought echoed around his brain, so clinical, so rational, seemingly unattached to any emotion. *Not my mother.*

When he recovered the ability to speak, he could only utter a single word. "How?"

Hazel inhaled on a shudder, sniffed, blew her nose on the tissue Lily handed her. "You're a changeling. A fae changeling. Exchanged after birth." She closed her eyes and whispered, "Oh, gods, I can finally say it."

"You couldn't before?"

She shook her head. "A spell. She put a silence spell on me. It remained in place all these years, and I could never tell a soul…"

Basil's ears pounded. He rubbed his temples, trying

to alleviate the pressure building in his skull. A skulking, yet-unnamable sensation crept along his bones, made his heart race and his skin crawl. "She?"

"The fae who exchanged you. She never told me her name."

"Okay, whoa," Lily said, holding up her hands. "Let's take a step back here and start from the top. Mom, please tell us—wait, you are *my* mom, right?"

Hazel swallowed, smiled. "Yes, baby."

The tightness in Lily's shoulders eased, she leaned back in her chair, and waved one hand. "From the top, please."

A deep breath, then Hazel said, "Well, the beginning isn't much different from what you've both been told about how you were born."

Like most children, they wanted to hear the story at one point, and because it was so adventurous, they wanted to keep hearing it again and again for several years. The suspenseful tale featured a broken-down car on the side of a country road late at night, and a miraculously accident-free twin birth in the back of said car.

Unlike most other deliveries in the witch community, Hazel didn't have the support of her fellow witches, didn't even have doctors or nurses there in the event of an emergency. It had always seemed incredibly lucky that Hazel was able to deliver healthy twins out on the road with only the help of her husband.

Evidently it had, in fact, been more than "luck."

"And at which point does the thrilling tale of our

birth deviate from what actually happened?" He couldn't help the reproach seeping into his tone. He rationally knew if Hazel had been spelled into silence, that she literally had no choice, hadn't been *able* to tell him. And *yet*...betrayal was a niggling, uncomfortable feeling festering in his bones.

Hazel touched her neck, avoided his gaze. "After the car broke down and the labor pains got worse, a female fae appeared. She carried a bundle in her arms, proclaimed she didn't mean us harm. I was in so much pain, I couldn't have used my magic against her if I wanted to. I was worried about the delivery—a twin birth, without help... Back then we didn't have cell phones, couldn't call for an ambulance, and we didn't know if anyone would come down this stretch of road. We hadn't seen another car in an hour.

"The fae offered help with the delivery. Scared as I was, I accepted. With her assistance, I delivered two healthy baby girls. Robert was overjoyed. But what he didn't know, what I feared, was that with faeries, help always comes at a price. When a fae does you a favor, and you accept it, be prepared for it to cost you. And as soon as I took my baby girls in my arms, the fae claimed her favor.

"She picked up the bundle which she'd left on the front passenger seat while she helped me with the delivery. It turned out to be another baby, a newborn male fae. She had smuggled him out of Faerie in order to save his life. Or at least it's what she told me. And what better place to hide him outside of Faerie than in the middle of a witch family? She said it would provide him with the best protection—from whatever enemies he might have. She never told us that much, only that both parents were dead and the child was in danger. Her favor was as simple as it was heartbreaking. She asked me to take in the newborn male fae and raise him as my own son, in exchange for one of the twin girls I had carried next to my heart for nine months."

Hazel rubbed the heel of her palm against her chest, and her chin trembled.

"I pleaded with her. I begged her. I told her I would take him in, I would raise him as my son, but please, please don't take one of my baby girls. I told her I was more than willing to comply, to repay her favor, but without giving up one of my girls.

"She didn't listen. She insisted on taking one of my daughters back with her into Faerie, as a hostage. She said it was to make sure I would take good care of the male changeling, and as long as I kept him safe, my daughter in Faerie would be safe as well. No matter how much I pleaded with her, she wouldn't budge. She made me…"

Hazel's voice broke. Her shoulders shook, and she stifled a sob.

Lily grasped her mom's hand again, tears shimmering in her eyes as well. "Mom…"

Hazel shuddered. "She made me *choose*. She made me pick which one of the girls to give her to take back into Faerie. How could I make that decision? How can anyone make that kind of decision? That agony, that heartbreak, I wouldn't wish upon my worst enemy. No matter how much I hate Juneau, I would not want her to have to make such a decision. Not a day goes by that I don't relive that awful, impossible choice."

Hazel sniffed, her throat working as she swallowed, and she fell silent for a long, heavy moment. Neither Lily nor Basil prodded her to continue with her story.

"After I made the choice," Hazel finally began again, "the fae took the girl I gave her and handed me the male fae baby instead. Robert was furious. He was as distraught as I am. I told the fae it would be hard for me to pass off a male baby in the witch community. I explained that, naturally, witches always have female offspring. She just looked at me and said, 'You will find a way to make it work.' Before she left, she laid a spell on both me and Robert. On Robert, she placed an oblivion charm. She thought it better to erase his memories of what had happened instead of putting a silence spell on him as well.

"I pleaded with her again. But again, she didn't listen. Her spell on him would ensure he wouldn't remember the exchange had taken place. He would only remember helping me deliver the babies in the car. Maybe she thought it would be harder on him if he knew the male baby wasn't his. By making him forget, she might have figured he would fully accept the baby as his own son.

"Then she laid another spell on me. It was powerful magic. For twenty-six years, I have been unable to tell a single soul about what had actually happened that night. I couldn't even tell Robert. I wanted to, so many times. Especially after he started..." Her brows drew together, and she looked down on the table.

"He suspected, didn't he?" Basil asked quietly. "That's why he was so insanely jealous?"

Hazel gave a shaky nod. "At first, the oblivion spell seemed to be working well. But over time...I think the fae's magic poisoned his mind. You know, he wasn't that way...before."

She looked up then, met Basil's eyes, then Lily's, so much pain carved into her gentle features. "We were happy. He'd always treated me like his queen, and he was a decent, good man. The spell changed him. Made him suspicious. He started having doubts about you, started looking at me differently. He even asked me directly once, but when I denied having had an affair, he only got angrier. He didn't believe me. He sensed I was hiding something from him, and I literally could not tell him the truth. The fae magic corrupted his mind, and he got worse and worse. All those things he said...it wasn't like him. He would *never* have treated me like that."

"And you still loved him, didn't you?" Lily's voice was soft.

Hazel gave a bitter laugh. "Love is a stubborn thing. It can cling to you even when you *know* it's wrong, twisted."

"Did you try to break the spell the fae put on him?" Basil asked. "So he'd understand what happened?"

"I thought about it, yes. I researched as much as I could, but fae magic is very different from witch magic. Everything I found describing how to break fae spells said I could possibly do just as much damage as good. And those passages referred to simple fae magic, not one as intricate as an oblivion spell on a human mind. There was a very real risk of me scrambling his brain into madness."

She paused, her mouth pressing into a thin line. "You've seen what Maeve's magic did to her father. That's the kind of damage we're talking about."

Basil cringed. Maeve MacKenna's powers kicked in when she was eight years old, in an explosion of unmitigated magic so unfettered, so destructive, that it killed both her older sister Moira and her mother—and psychically maimed her father, irrevocably damaging his mind to the point he remained catatonic to this day.

"Okay," Lily said, rubbing her hands over her face. "How is it that we never realized Basil is a fae? He has a human energy pattern—"

She stopped, looked at him, her brows knitting together. "Used to have. It's…changed. Your aura is… fae now. How…?"

"Glamour," Hazel said quietly. "The fae put a glamour on him to mask his identity. She hid his innate magic signature, and made him look more human."

"Kind of clumsy," Basil murmured. When both Lily and Hazel looked at him in question, he explained, "Well, if she had the means to change my appearance, why didn't she make sure I looked more like Robert?"

He gestured toward his blond hair.

"Ah." Hazel's expression vacillated between wry amusement and regret. "At the time the fae met us to do the exchange, Robert's hair *was* blond. He'd been dyeing it for a couple of weeks. He was going through a phase..." She sighed. "Well, the fae apparently didn't know it wasn't his real hair color, and I guess she figured she could leave your hair naturally blond."

Lily kept squinting at him with narrowed eyes. "If he's fae..." she said, "why aren't his ears pointed?"

"What?" Basil touched his ears, felt the usual roundness at the edge. "Hey, you're right. These are still human."

Hazel frowned. "I'm not sure. They should be... Maybe the glamour hasn't yet lifted all the way."

"Hm." Lily tilted her head, then shook it. "Okay, that's something we can figure out later. Let's get back to the basics. Baz is not my brother—not even half?"

"Not by blood, no."

The sting in his chest was the first emotion he felt since the revelation began. It was finally starting to sink in. Lily wasn't his sister. They weren't actually twins. The girl he grew up with, the person closest to him, the one who always understood him intuitively— because he thought they shared this special twin bond. It was all a lie.

And his mom—he glanced at Hazel again—wasn't actually his mom. The hurt in his chest spread, a crawling sensation of loss and betrayal that tainted every memory of his childhood with doubt and alienation. Was everything a lie? Had she ever truly loved him? Or had she acted out of obligation, to keep protecting the daughter she'd lost—her real child?

His pulse sped up. His breath came faster and faster, until he was light-headed.

"Baz..." Hazel reached for him.

He shot to his feet, so fast the chair screeched in protest, and turned to the French doors to look out at the dark backyard.

Lily, always so perceptive, so attuned to his feelings, so good at understanding what he needed, muttered something soothing and reassuring to Hazel to keep her from approaching him.

He watched their reflections in the glass of the doors, how Hazel nodded, took Lily's hand.

It hurt all the more.

4

"Okay then," Lily went on, her voice at normal level, "but I do have a sister. A twin. And she's somewhere in Faerie?"

"Yes."

"How do you know she's...alive?"

"I can feel her." Hazel tapped her chest with her fist. "It's the same link I have to you, the one all witches in a family have to each other. I've felt her all this time..."

Lily sat back in her chair, her shoulders drooping, her gaze turning inward. "I can't feel her."

Hazel touched her face, pushed one of Lily's black locks behind her ear. "It's because you're not a witch any longer."

Lily's flinch was barely noticeable, a tiny reminder that she was still in the process of getting used to her new demon nature. "But, I can't remember ever feeling any link to her before. I mean, with Baz I figured I don't feel a link because he's not a witch." She cringed and shot him an apologetic look before focusing on her mom again. "That's what you always said, right? But shouldn't I have felt some link to my real sister when I was still a witch?"

Hazel considered it for a moment. "Maybe you did feel something, but you weren't aware of it at the time. After all, you didn't know you had another family member out there. So maybe there *was* something, but you didn't recognize it. You weren't expecting to feel anything."

Lily frowned. "I guess..."

While Lily was still pondering the implications, Basil decided to rejoin the conversation. He turned to the table again and asked, "Why now? Why can you suddenly speak of it after all this time? Why has my glamour been lifted now?"

Hazel tilted her head to the side and frowned. "That's a good question. Come to think of it, the fae would only lift the glamour and the spell on me if she wanted to come back and claim you. That's the only thing that makes sense. I would have expected her to show up here and *then* rescind her magic. It doesn't seem logical for her to remove the glamour and the spell before coming here. Unless..." Hazel's eyes suddenly went wide, her face ashen. "Oh no..."

"What?" Lily asked.

"What if...?" Hazel raised her trembling hand to her mouth. "What if the reason the spell and the glamour have been lifted is because the fae who cast them both is dead?"

Lily and Basil exchanged a glance.

"Okay..." Basil said slowly. "That would be

unfortunate, I guess, because it means she can't tell me more about my fae family and all that, right?"

"It's not just that." Hazel balled her hand to a fist. "What about Rose?"

"The who, now?" Lily asked.

"Your twin sister." She shook her head as if to clear it. "Right, I haven't told you yet. I named her Rose, right before the fae took her."

Pieces visibly clicked together in Lily's head. She sat up straighter. "Oh. Of course—if the fae who took her into Faerie and who was responsible for her over there died, then..."

"...Rose could be in danger," finished Basil.

Hazel nodded, rubbed her forehead. "At the very least, it means her fate is uncertain. Before, I could count on the promise of the fae who took her that she would be taken care of. She'd make sure to protect Rose and keep her alive. But now...Rose may have lost the only fae who guaranteed her safety in Faerie."

Lily's face hardened. "We need to get her out."

Hazel met her look for a moment, and something passed between mother and daughter. Basil felt that sting again and involuntarily took a small, quiet step back.

"Yes," Hazel said, dark eyes glittering with resolve. "We need to find her and bring her home. The fae who took her is dead. I have kept my promise all these years, and now our deal is null and void. I deserve to get my daughter back." She thought for a few seconds. "We need a fae to take us into Faerie."

"Why?" Lily asked.

"Faerie's borders are magically sealed, only allowing fae and lower life forms to cross over. Fae can take humans, witches, or otherworld creatures over the border, so we need a fae to grant us passage. They're just so hard to find outside of Faerie…"

"Umm, hello? Basil's a fae? He can take us."

Both pairs of eyes focused on him.

"I'll do it," he said, without missing a beat.

Hazel shook her head. "No, sweetie."

The endearment cut something tender within him, leaving behind the same taint that spoiled all the memories of his *mom* now. *Not my mom, not my mom.* He clenched his jaw.

"From all we know," Hazel continued, "granting passage is not just the physical act of a fae taking non-fae over the border. Some sort of invocation of fae magic is needed, and you…" She didn't finish, but the message was clear.

He didn't know any fae magic. He might possess fae powers now, but he didn't have the tiniest clue how to use them.

"Can't we look it up? Ask around?" Lily put both elbows on the table, leaned forward.

"There's nothing in our books about that sort of fae invocation, at least not that I remember. Back when I was looking for a way to break the oblivion spell on Robert, I did intensive research about all things fae magic, not just in our library, but those of other witch families as well. I never found any information about the details of a border crossing invocation." She rubbed her temples. "No, we'll need to find another fae who's willing to take us into Faerie."

And it could take days, if not longer. Time Rose might not have, depending on her situation over there.

"I can ask Alek," Lily said, "and he can tap his resources through Arawn's network. Maybe he can point us to a fae, and then Baz can learn along the way."

As one of the enforcers of the Demon Lord, Lily's mate Alek had access to information and contacts among the otherworld community that eluded the witches. Still, even with Alek's help, finding another fae would be time-consuming.

I could go alone.

The thought whispered through him, rising up out of the darker corners of his heart, his mind, where a primitive need sat and festered. All his life, he'd been the odd one out, the rare male born to a witch line, the one without powers, in need of protection. Sure, he'd long shared the position of being the magic-less anomaly with Maeve, whose powers were bound inside her after her lethal outburst at the age of eight, and knowing he wasn't the only one had helped him get through his darkest hours.

He once mentioned to Merle, Maeve's older sister and one of his best friends, that he'd made his peace with his lack of magic. Truth was, a part of him had never gotten over it. Maybe if his family let him contribute more, if they allowed him to participate in their work as much as his human strength enabled him to, he wouldn't have felt so left out. So *coddled*.

But as it was, he had to fight for every scrap of independence and agency along the way. Hazel would even have barred him from the mission to rescue Lily when she was kidnapped a couple of weeks ago if Merle hadn't stepped up and vouched for him.

He was tired of having to ask, to beg, to argue for them to accept him in their ranks. Tired of being considered weak and vulnerable.

Well, he wasn't that anymore, right? He did have powers now, he just needed to learn how to wield them. What better place to gain knowledge about how to be a fae than in Faerie? He could go look for Rose and discover his powers along the way. If he managed to find her and bring her back, Hazel and the others would *have* to acknowledge him as their equal.

Resolve set, he backed away quietly. Hazel and Lily were so busy discussing the details of the rescue mission, they didn't notice his retreat.

He decided not to tell them about his plan. Doing so would only trigger the usual arguments, making it harder to get away. They'd never let him go alone. Knowing they had such little faith in him hurt. He should probably be used to it by now, but all these revelations left him raw, his emotions strung like a taut rope, his heart aching.

They thought he couldn't do it alone. He'd prove them wrong.

~~~

Sling backpack packed with essentials: *Check*. Bow: *Check*. Quiver full of arrows: *Check*. Half a dozen knives and daggers strapped to his body: *Check*. Combat gear: *Check*. Nerves…nerves? *And we have a runner.*

Basil sighed, rubbed his sternum over the twin strips of his sling backpack and the quiver, trying to alleviate the pressure there. He had an uneasy feeling it wasn't caused by the weight he carried. Well, at least not the physical one.

He'd just finished packing everything together, had pulled on his boots, and was ready to sneak out of his room when the door opened and a petite redhead peeked in.

Maeve.

He opened his mouth to say something, but she beat him to it.

"You're going alone, aren't you?" Her voice was still so husky, hadn't recovered even yet. Probably never would. It had been months since her rescue, and Merle and Hazel had worked all the healing magic on her they were capable of. Some things, though, not even magic could erase. Like the memories she now had to live with for the rest of her life…

"You heard us?" he asked.

She nodded. "I always knew you were more."

When she gave him a small smile, the vicious scar that ran across her face twisted, a violent reminder of what she'd been through. Despite the best efforts of the healer witches in the community, who were able to minimize or even remove most of the scars on her body, the remnant of the deep cut crossing her face remained. Like the hoarseness from screaming for days on end during her torture.

He was so proud of her for pushing through, holding her head up high, in defiance of what had been done to her.

"Well," he said, "looks like neither one of us is as powerless as we thought."

Maeve looked to the side. "At least you can access your powers."

"I don't know..." He shrugged. "It feels like *something* has been knocked loose, but it's not like I suddenly have all this awesome magic at my fingertips. It's more like a...low-level hum I couldn't hear before. But I have no idea what to do with it."

"You'll figure it out, I'm sure."

"Thanks."

Always, she'd believed in him. Unlike his family, and his friends in the witch community, to whom he'd been a walking liability. Even before her abduction, Maeve was quiet, not one to display enthusiasm, but she never made him feel like he was lacking anything.

Which was probably the reason he had a crush on her for the longest time.

He never told anyone, not even Lily, because Maeve...Maeve was almost family. He'd grown up with her, and just like he considered Merle a sister, his feelings for Maeve had long been those of a brother for his younger sibling. When it changed…he'd been too confused for a while to act on it, couldn't bring himself to take a step that would irrevocably alter their relationship and how others perceived them.

And then—Maeve was kidnapped, held captive for days, tortured…raped. When she came back, when he saw how deep her scars ran—the mental ones, because the physical ones wouldn't have bothered him—he figured the last thing she wanted to deal with was the revelation that her childhood friend wanted to be more than her big brother. He saw how she flinched in the presence of a male—any male—those tiny tells she couldn't manage to hide, no matter how much she seemed to be trying to shake it.

He wouldn't add to her anxiety, no way, nohow.

Instead he settled on being there for her in the non-sexual, big brother kind of way she knew and felt comfortable with, and, as the months went by, his feelings for her changed yet again. What had been a desire in its kindling form morphed into something deeper, going beyond the physical, the bond they'd always shared now evolving from big brother-little sister to a more equal footing of…true *friends*.

Maeve fidgeted with her loose, comfortable sweater for a moment, her eyes downcast. Then, in a move that surprised the hell out of him, she stepped forward, into his personal space, and hugged him.

His heartbeat faltered. Not because the gesture sparked anything like the desire he once felt for her, but because he knew how much this simple touch meant for her—for her recovery. In all the months since her rescue, she'd never let any male this close to her, had avoided touch unless she was with Merle, Lily, and Hazel. For her to take this step, to initiate an embrace with a man…

He blinked rapidly, clearing his eyes. Leaning down, he kissed the top of her head. When she broke the hug, she wiped at her eyes quickly.

"Come back, yes?"

He swallowed hard. "That's the plan."

5

Basil closed and locked his car before trudging down a dirt path leading farther into the dark woods. He'd taken Highway 26 east from Portland to Mount Hood Village, and followed the country roads south from there as far as possible, closer and closer to the pull he first began to feel in Mount Hood Village. Faerie's border called to him.

He'd already known that Faerie lay somewhere between Mount Hood and Mount Jefferson, and from the parts of the discussion he overheard before he left Hazel and Lily behind, he learned that the closest entrance reachable by car was located south of Mount Hood Village. The country road came to a halt at this dirt path, which must be the one leading into Faerie.

Now he needed to hike the rest of the way.

Apparently, this sanctuary of the fae was one of many across the world, and, unlike what old human folklore depicted, it wasn't actually a pocket of alternate reality. Faerie wasn't so much a different plane of existence that happened to overlay the human world—with the non-fae reality existing at the same time in the same place—but more of a...reservation, for lack of a better word. An area of the state of Oregon that was fae territory, and didn't allow any non-fae inside.

Not that humans knew it was there. They had no clue, and were repelled from the area by the fae magic worked into the borders. No human settlements existed within Faerie's territory, and on human maps, it was simply marked as a huge swath of nature reserve.

According to the bit of history Hazel taught Basil and Lily while they were growing up, fae had once lived among humans the way most otherworld creatures and witches still did. As the human population grew, however, spreading across the lands with their iron and their penchant for destroying what they didn't understand, the fae feared they would one day be overrun, and so chose to establish safe harbors for their kind, and to retreat behind their magical borders.

To most otherworld creatures, fae were considered isolationist, suspicious of outsiders, and content to keep to themselves in the fae sanctuaries around the world, known as Faeries.

Basil sighed. Naturally, his secret heritage turned out to be that of a paranoid people who didn't play well with others.

The pull he felt deep in his bones became stronger and stronger with every step he took on the path. Any human would have been compelled to turn around by now, courtesy of the repellent aspect of the border magic. His pulse sped up, his mood lifted. This was real. He was fae, was more than human. How often had he wished for this? Had dreamed of some shocking revelation that would give him the kind of powers he craved? After Maeve's abduction uncovered the truth behind her apparent lack of magic—that her powers were actually bound inside her, a tightly kept family secret that not even Merle had known—Basil's hope that he, too, was somehow more than the weak, powerless male descendant of a witch line had been infused with new strength.

Excitement pounded through his veins. Magic crackled in the air. He was getting closer.

One more step—and he felt it. He passed through an invisible wall, its energy sizzling over his skin, raising the hairs all over his body. He stopped right beyond the border and took a deep breath of the chilly, humid night air.

A fairy flitted past him, leaving trails of sparkling magic behind her. The tiny, winged fae creatures were more common outside of Faerie than their larger, wingless counterparts. Culturally, they seemed to be closer to pixies and brownies, and thus often lived close to those colonies in the human world.

The fairy flew to a tree a couple yards away—which was illuminated by garlands of gently glowing light bubbles, highlighting tiny platforms, walkways, and entrances to what appeared to be a fairy tree house.

Basil grinned, breathless with joy. This was amazing.

The tree and its illumination hadn't been visible from outside the border, a testament to Faerie's glamour skills. The dirt path he'd been following was now neatly paved with cobblestones, and much broader.

He started down the road with a spring in his step.

Five minutes into his journey into Faerie, a muffled scream sounded from somewhere to the left of the road. He tensed, paused, listened into the dark. Beyond the sounds of a nightly forest, there was the distinct noise of a struggle.

He only hesitated a second, then veered off the path and into the underbrush, toward the sound. Taking care to remain as quiet as possible, he moved quickly over the moss-covered ground, and, almost as an afterthought, noticing his night vision was far better than it used to be. He could discern twigs and stones and holes in the ground when before it would all have been steeped in shadows. Courtesy of his new fae powers?

Thanks to his apparently heightened senses, he managed to approach the sounds of struggle while staying inhumanly quiet, moving through the woods as silently as a nighttime predator. Close to the source of the noise, he drew one of the arrows from his quiver, nocked it on his bow.

There.

On the ground a few feet away, two shapes seemed fused in a fight. He could make out the form of a person, pinned to the forest floor by…a mountain lion? *Holy crap.*

Basil blinked, and stealthily moved closer. The person uttered another muffled cry, convulsed in obvious pain. The mountain lion had its claws sunk into the torso of its prey, its jaw clamped over the person's neck in a feline predator killing bite.

He'd seen enough.

Exhaling, he released the arrow. With a lethal swoosh, it shot toward the puma, and it pierced its head with a thunk. The big cat twitched, its slackening muscles loosening its grip on the prey, and collapsed.

He rushed over to the injured person. A female fae, dark skin, pointed ears, black hair pulled into a braid. She was still convulsing, as if caught in an epileptic seizure. Her armor seemed to have partly saved her from the cougar attack—through the holes in the leather and fabric of her tunic-style clothing ripped by the puma's claws, some sort of metal shimmered, like a chainmail. Her neck, which should have been mauled by the lion, only showed minimal injuries from the puma's fangs. Apparently, the cat had only just positioned its jaws for the killing bite when Basil interrupted.

Carefully, he turned the fae on her side so she wouldn't choke, then made sure no sharp objects were close to her. From what he learned in first aid, there wasn't anything more one could do to help someone having a seizure except wait it out.

But damn if it didn't make his blood boil to see someone in pain like that and be unable to give them relief.

He crouched down next to her, balled his hands to fists. After about another minute, the convulsions subsided. The fae calmed, except for her heavy breathing. Her chest rose and fell rapidly, but her face lost its expression of agony, and her features softened, revealing a stunning beauty.

It struck Basil like an electric zing to his heart. The lines of her face—elegant, quintessentially feminine— would have inspired artists of all eras to immortalize her in stone and canvas and song. When she opened her eyes, luminous gray met his gaze, aglow in the dark of the night.

He forgot to breathe for a heartbeat, for an eternity.

She asked something in a language he didn't understand. Dammit, of course. He'd forgotten the fact that fae would have their own language—which he didn't speak. Having a fae guide to interpret definitely would have been smart.

"I'm sorry," he said. "I don't understand you. I just... Are you okay? That bite wound may need stitches. I have a first aid kit in here..." *Stop babbling, idiot.*

The fae frowned, sat up and touched her neck. "Bite?" she asked in English.

"The mountain lion. It got ahold of your neck, was going to crush your trachea."

The fae cringed and turned to where he pointed, and when she saw the dead cat, her shoulders hunched, and her mouth turned down. "You didn't have to kill her."

"Um, she was going to kill *you*."

Laying a hand on the puma's head, behind the arrow protruding from between its eyes, the fae muttered something in her language. "You could have shot at her in warning," she said in English. "She would have fled."

"I…" Great, now he felt miserable for killing the cat. "Sorry, I guess. Well, at least I saved your life."

The fae flinched as if he'd slapped her. She whipped her head around, fixed him to the spot with a glare that could have shredded his guts. She cursed violently in her language, shot to her feet, and then cursed some more.

Inappropriate as it was, hearing her swear in that husky voice of hers, her face alight with passionate anger, made his body react with a wholly different form of passion. *Quit it.* Not the right time to be having lurid, explicit fae fantasies.

"Uh, you're not suicidal, are you?" he asked. "I didn't thwart any plans of yours for death by cougar, did I?"

She rounded on him, her slate-gray eyes throwing sparks. "No." Grudgingly, as if it cost her, she added, "Your assistance is appreciated."

"O…kay." Then why was she so angry?

She closed her eyes, tightened her mouth, and bowed a little. "I owe you a life debt."

Aha. "And…you'd rather you didn't."

"I don't have time for this." She bent to pick up something—a bow, and a quiver full of arrows.

Huh. She was an archer, too.

Well, it made sense, considering that otherworld creatures, including witches, couldn't use firearms. The magic running through their veins somehow interfered with the technology of modern guns, so they had to resort to weapons of simple mechanics, like a bow and arrow or swords.

The fae strapped the quiver to her back, her movements jerky and impatient.

"Do you have somewhere else to be?" He rose to his feet as well.

She sighed. "Yes. I have to find someone, and I don't have the time to be following you around."

"So don't." He sure wouldn't mind her company and getting to know her better, plus she could act as his interpreter, but if she had to run an urgent errand, he wouldn't keep her.

She shot him a look that was halfway between incredulous and annoyed, and full-on adorable. "You're funny."

"What?"

She frowned. "I'm bound to you now. I have to save your life in return, or else I'll be struck down by magic." She shook her head. "Why do I even have to explain this to you? You're fae, aren't you?"

"Umm…yes. Yes, I am. But it's…complicated."

She narrowed her gorgeous eyes, tilted her head as she regarded his head. "Your ears… Where did you say you come from?"

"I didn't." He hesitated, considered it for a few seconds, decided that if she was bound to protect him, she might come in handy on his quest to find Rose. He could use an ally, an insider with knowledge of Faerie —and how to use fae powers. "I'm from the human world. Portland, to be precise. I'm fae, but I was raised by witches. I'm here to find the baby who was taken into Faerie when I was exchanged. My name is Basil Murray."

Even in the dark of the forest, he clearly saw all color leave her face. Eyes wide, mouth agape, she stumbled back. Her bow thudded on the ground. Her knees gave out. He rushed forward just in time to catch her as she lost consciousness, sagged in his arms.

6

Whispers in the darkness…voices drifting in and out…

…curse you, Isa of Stone, for death to find you through slow-crawling pain…

…could not break your curse…stall it, for some years, at most…

…if the one who cast it does not rescind the curse, it can only be broken by killing the curser…or the last of her line…

Isa came to with a start and a gasp. Sights and sounds of the nightmare still lingered.

No, wait. Not a nightmare. Memories.

She opened her eyes, focusing on the shape of the young male hovering over her, his golden blond hair a spark in the dark of the night. *Changeling…*

Reality rushed back, slapped Isa in the face with all the harshness of an icy winter draft. She'd found the changeling, all right. Roana's child, the last of her line, the key to breaking her curse. The person she needed to kill—and the one person to whom she was now bound with a life debt.

Could the Fates truly be this cruel? Could her lot in

life be any more miserable? As impossible as it was, Isa had to protect Basil Murray, and save his life to repay her debt to him—only so she could then turn around and kill him. Because as long as she owed him this debt, she couldn't take his life. Fae magic was merciless, bound by strict rules, and she'd risk her immediate death if she violated her obligation to protect him by harming him herself.

"Are you all right?" Basil asked, his brown eyes—glowing gently in the darkness—full of concern.

"Yes, I'm fine." Isa sat up, and her head immediately punished her for it. She flinched.

"You look like you've seen a ghost."

"Something like that." Ghosts of the past, for sure. A past that came back to bite her in the butt.

"You know," Basil said with a sheepish grin, "this is the first time a woman has swooned for me. I gotta tell you, it's not as glamorous as they say it is."

That spark of humor in his eyes was infectious. She absolutely wasn't in the mood to laugh, or even smile. And yet, despite herself, a small grin sneaked its way onto her face.

"I don't mean to pry or anything, but do you have a medical condition I should know about? Since you're responsible for my safety and all."

She frowned. "What do you mean?"

"Well," Basil said, gesturing at the ground where he'd found her, "it looked like you had a seizure earlier."

"Oh. That." She shrugged, rose to her feet. Dusting

herself off, she avoided facing him. "It's nothing serious."

"Looked pretty serious to me."

Isa sighed. "You don't need to concern yourself with that. It just...happens sometimes. I can handle it."

She wasn't going to tell him about the curse. To do so would be tantamount to suicide. She had to walk a fine line between acting friendly enough for him to trust her, to let her come along and protect him, and not letting herself open up to him too much. Something about him drew her in, something irresistibly likable, and yet she couldn't afford to *like* him. Considering what her plans for him entailed.

"What's your name?"

She jerked around to look at him. Right. She hadn't introduced herself yet. "Isa," she said before her brain caught up and she realized it might have been smarter to give him a false name. *Blast.*

He gave her a dazzling smile, triggering unwelcome fairy flutters in her stomach.

"All right," she said, and turned away from the sunshine of that smile. "Tell me about your changeling history. Since I am now stuck with protecting you for the time being, I may as well know how you came here and what you seek. I could help you find it while I'm waiting for the opportunity to save your life." *And then end it.* She gritted her teeth.

"Okay. The short version is that, apparently, I was born in Faerie, but smuggled out to Portland by a fae female who exchanged me for a witch baby in order to protect me. I don't know what I needed protection from, because the fae who exchanged me never actually told my mom—well, I guess I should say *adoptive* mother—about her real reasons for smuggling me out of Faerie. The fae who exchanged me put a glamour spell on me to hide my fae appearance and powers, and she also put a silence spell on my adoptive mother." He shrugged, one corner of his mouth tugging up in a half-smile. "Basically I grew up thinking I was nothing more than a powerless male born to a witch line, an anomaly without an explanation."

The hint of bitterness in his tone let her know a whole host of things he *wasn't* saying.

"My adoptive mother, Hazel Murray, actually had *two* babies the night I was exchanged. The fae who swapped me took one of Hazel's twin girls back with her into Faerie as a hostage, to ensure Hazel would protect me and raise me as her own. And I only learned about this a couple of hours ago. For some reason, the glamour on me and the silence spell on Hazel were lifted, and we think the most logical reason for the spells' disappearance is the fae who exchanged me and worked the magic is dead. And since fae are nearly immortal, it's very likely the one who smuggled me out was murdered. Which in turn means the daughter who was taken into Faerie—her name is Rose—may be in danger."

"Because she will be without protection," Isa muttered.

Basil nodded. "Exactly. We have to assume Rose has had a protector since the day she was brought into Faerie. That she has been taken care of all this time, but now the fae who brought her here has died, we can't be sure she's still being taken care of. That's why I'm here, in a nutshell. I need to find Rose. And I need to bring her back to Portland, to Hazel."

Isa frowned. "Why have you come alone? Where is your adoptive mother?"

At her question, Basil's face hardened almost invisibly. "It would have taken her too long to find another fae to take her into Faerie. I was able to go right away. I'm sure once she finds a fae to take her across the border, Hazel will follow, probably with more backup. But it can't hurt for me to go first and try to find Rose as soon as possible."

"I see."

And she did. His drive to prove himself was visible to the naked eye, pouring off him in waves. Well, she would not rebuke him for it. His need to go it alone played into her hands. This way she had him without the protection of his family, could win his trust, and bide her time until she saw an opportunity to save his life—only to take it the very next moment.

An inexplicable ache spread in her chest. She breathed past it, reminding herself this was it. This was her chance, finally, to break her curse, to save her own life.

"I can help you search for Rose," Isa said, as much to distract herself as to drive the mission forward.

"Thank you." That dazzling smile lit his face again, lighting Isa's veins with prickling sunshine.

He tilted his head and regarded her with disconcerting warmth. "Hey, maybe you could help me with my fae powers, too. I can feel something different in me, like a humming presence that wasn't there before…or maybe it was muted. But even though I know it's there, I have no idea what to do with it. I don't even know how to access this power. I've tried a little, but I keep hitting some sort of block or wall. Is there something I need to do to unlock my powers as a fae?"

Isa considered it. She studied him closely, her attention snagging on his humanly rounded ears. If his glamour had indeed been lifted, his appearance and his powers should be those of a fae or… She frowned.

Well, yes, then again, considering who his father was, it would make sense that his ears weren't those of the fae. As for his powers, his paternal heritage could also play a part in his inability to unlock them. "I'll try to teach you. It's possible you just haven't tapped into it deeply enough, but I can try to show you."

Basil's shoulders relaxed and he took a deep breath. "I appreciate it."

She held up a finger. "I will help you, yes. But know this—you will owe me a favor in return."

Basil frowned. "What do you mean? Don't you owe *me* a life debt?"

"Sure I do." Isa shrugged. "But that debt will be paid when I save your life. Now, helping you with anything else, like finding your lost adoptive sister, or unlocking your powers, is another matter. Since you already thanked me, and thus accepted my offer of help, you are now bound to me with a favor of your own."

Isa expected him to be angry, resentful of the way she sneaked that favor in there. But he surprised her. The corners of his mouth lifted in a sly grin that did all sorts of unwelcome things to her need for detachment.

"All right, all right. I can admit when I've been had. My adoptive mother warned me to watch out for favors when dealing with fae, and that thanking them would make me beholden to them. I guess I should have paid more attention." He tapped his forehead with his fingers and saluted her.

Isa blinked, baffled by his reaction. He just seemed to take everything in stride, didn't he? He was so unlike anyone else she'd ever met.

"Just one thing: The favor will not end my life, enslave me, or do either of those things to a person close to me."

Ah, this she could handle. She cocked a brow. "Negotiating?"

One corner of his mouth tipped up. "Let's just say a friend of mine recently had to learn the hard way how to cover all bases with open favors."

She inclined her head. "Accepted." Ending his life would not require her to collect a favor... This was just additional security. She cleared her throat. "Regarding your search for your lost adoptive sister..."

"Rose."

"Yes, Rose. I was thinking…her exchange wouldn't have been well-known."

Basil came to attention. "Right. Because if the fae *smuggled* me out to hide me, she wouldn't advertise the fact she'd done an exchange."

Isa nodded. "If she wanted to spirit you away from danger, she'd have kept the entire thing a secret. If she brought back a human baby—"

"Witch," Basil interrupted her. "The baby was from a witch family."

"Close enough," Isa muttered, waving a hand. "If she brought back a non-fae baby as a changeling to be raised here, and didn't hide that fact, people would ask whom she exchanged for that baby. When the fae who were after you realized you were gone, they'd definitely have gone looking for any changeling swap made recently, and they would have come across the one with Rose. Unless the fae hid it well."

Basil exhaled through his nose, his mouth pressed into a thin line. "Which means it'll be extremely difficult to find any hints about Rose's exchange."

Isa was silent for a moment, pondering. She had no stake in his quest, had no reason to stick around until he actually found Rose. All she wanted was to bide her time until she could save his life and then break her curse. She could lead him on a merry chase through Faerie, pretending to help him look for clues of his lost adoptive sister, without ever getting him any closer to his goal.

And yet… "I know someone who might know more."

Hope sparked in his eyes. "You do?"

"Well," she shrugged, "I'm good at finding people. I have some resources, contacts we can tap for information. There is no such thing as the perfect crime, and word always gets out about everything. You just have to know where to look for rumors and gossip, and whom to bribe and charm into giving up more than they intended to."

He bowed and made an extravagant flourish with his hand. "Lead the way."

She nodded. "I suggest we stop at an inn and spend the night. It's on the way to my contact. It's getting late, and it's been a long day for me. We can catch some sleep, and start fresh in the morning."

Basil let out a heavy breath. "If it's on the way, sure. To be honest, it's been a long, hard day for me, too." He shrugged one shoulder. "You know, the whole finding-out-I'm-adopted-and-not-actually-a-human-without-powers-but-a-fae-with-an-unknown-parental-history-and-a-lost-adoptive-sister thing."

Despite herself, Isa had to smile. She jerked her head in the direction of the path leading farther into Faerie, and started walking. Basil fell into step with her.

"If it's any consolation," she offered, "you're taking this rather well. I'm not sure what I would do if faced with such life-altering revelations."

"Maybe it's because I think I always knew, in a way. Finding out the very thing I have always wanted, I have always dreamed about, is actually true, hasn't felt like a disruption of my life, but rather like a missing puzzle piece has fallen into place, you know? It's like my life up until this point always felt a little off, a little odd. Learning about this whole changeling thing, it just makes sense. I feel like...yes, this is what's been missing. This is what my life should have been all along." He shrugged, and winked at her with a half-smile that sent heat shooting up to her cheeks. "Why don't you tell me about yourself?"

She almost missed a step, rushed to hide her stumble. "Me? What about me?"

"I'm just curious. You're actually the first fae I've ever met. I'd like to know about you. Your life, your world, what's it like to be a fae? What do you do for a living? Where do you live?"

"Um..."

No one had ever asked her such questions. No one had ever looked at her with this focus, this intensity, as if he genuinely wanted to know about her. As if he was truly interested in *her*, as if her life mattered to him. What a novel feeling.

She didn't quite know how to respond to his questions, his forthright interest in her. She wasn't well versed in social interaction, and it had been a long time since she simply chatted with someone. Not giving him an answer at all was rude, however. She had to say *something*, even if it was some lie wrapped in half-truths.

"I'm a bounty hunter," she blurted out.

His eyes widened.

Her hand twitched with the urge to slap her

forehead. *Why, Isa, why?* What had gotten into her? Telling him the truth… *Oh, go ahead and spill the rest of your life story, why don't you?* She was usually so good at evasive answers and protecting her privacy.

"A bounty hunter? For real?" His expression was one of gleaming interest. "Now, when you say bounty hunter, do you mean as in a *Star Wars* Boba Fett bounty hunter, or more along the lines of modern-day bounty hunters who supplement law enforcement?"

She frowned at him. "I'm not sure I understand the first part of your question. Who's *Star Wars*?"

"Who's—" He stopped dead in his tracks, slapped one hand over his heart, absolute bafflement written in every line of his face. "You don't know *Star Wars*?"

"Uh…should I? I mean, I spent some time in the humanlands here and there over the years, and I know a little bit about human culture, but I'm not fully on top of things…" She studied him closely. "Are you all right?"

Basil took a deep breath, closed his eyes briefly. "Sure. I just need a minute." Shaking his head, he started walking again. "I recognize the weight of my responsibility here, you know." He glanced at her, his expression as serious as someone swearing an oath. "Passing on this sacred knowledge…" He nodded sagely. "This unique opportunity to teach a young *Padawan* all about the awesomeness that is *Star Wars*, and the fabulous tale of the Skywalkers."

"Oh, it's a tale? Is it some sort of human mythology?"

The corners of his mouth twitched, and the sparkle in his eyes almost did her in. "Yes. Yes, it is."

She paused, tilted her head. "You are jesting."

He raised his hands, palms toward her. "I am not. Jedi are a recognized religious group among the humans. And believe me, I take my *Star Wars* references *very* seriously."

She pursed her lips, wry amusement bubbling in her bloodstream, so unexpected, unfamiliar. And yet...not at all unwelcome. "All right then. Are you a Jedi?"

His laughter was like the crack in the clouds that let sunshine spill forth. "Ah, I wish. Don't tell anybody, but I do pretend I'm using the Force whenever I walk through a set of automatic sliding doors." He flicked his hand and made a swooshing sound.

Her belly fluttered with lighthearted joy.

"Okay," Basil said, as they continued walking, "I'll initiate you into the world of *Star Wars* after you explain a bit more about your bounty hunter job. How, exactly, do you work? Who do you bring in, and why, and who hires you?" He gestured with one hand. "I'm pathologically nosy, so I need to know *all the things.*"

She shrugged. "Mostly criminals. Sometimes, when a fae commits a crime, they get the bright idea to outrun the law by fleeing Faerie. Bounty hunters like me are often tasked to go outside our borders, follow the trail of the escaped fae, and bring them back to face justice."

"Is there no fae police or military to do that?"

"No, not really. There is a bit of a...military, if you want to call it that, but they don't usually bother to go outside of Faerie just to find an escaped criminal and bring him or her to justice. If it is someone important enough, they will hire a bounty hunter to get it done. That's what I do. Like I said, I'm good at finding people."

"I guess then it's especially lucky I ran into you." That damnably attractive smile of his lit up his face again. "Seeing as I need help with finding Rose, and the first fae I encounter just happens to be perfect for that."

Lucky... That was a matter of perspective, wasn't it? What was one fae's luck could be another's tragedy. In a way, of course, she *was* lucky she had found the changeling she was looking for so easily. If it weren't for that pesky life debt she owed him...

They'd reached the main road, illuminated here and there by floating will-o'-the-wisps.

Basil gazed up at the stretch of starlit sky visible between the towering heights of the firs left and right of the road, put his hands on his hips, and asked, "What was the hardest case you ever had to bring in?"

Isa bit off her reply before it left her mouth, but it echoed in her head, and in the darkest corners of her heart.

Your mother.

7

Merle sneaked down the hall of her family's old Victorian house, peeking around corners, listening... anticipating. Silence greeted her. It seemed like no one else was around. She knew better.

They always lurked. Lay in wait for her, watching her, ready to pounce on her when she least expected it. And she always, always, squealed. Damn embarrassing, that.

Not this time, they won't make me squeak this—

A clawed ball of fur attacked her legs out of nowhere right before strong arms swept her off her feet and hoisted her over a muscled shoulder—and of course she damn straight squealed at the top of her lungs.

"Rhun! Dammit!" She pummeled her demon husband's back—to no visible effect whatsoever—while Sauron, the Kitten from Hell, dashed away with glee.

"You. Are. Impossible." She underscored each word with a swat at Rhun's shoulders, though the overall seriousness of the message kind of got lost in the fit of giggles she couldn't suppress any longer.

"Hmm. Yes. Yes, I am." Rhun patted her butt, and then languorously stroked down her thighs—and up again until his fingers rubbed against the pulse at her core, caressed her through the fabric of her jeans. "And you adore me exactly like this, little witch."

She moaned and dug her fingers in his T-shirt. Exquisite pleasure rippled through her in waves, and she wiggled her hips, pressed against his hand, trying to increase the sensation. He made a low sound of approval and nipped at her butt.

"Rhun," she managed to say after a moment—through the haze of desire clouding her brain—"put me down." Her body wailed in protest at the idea, but —"I need to mix a decoction. Low energy. Need to— oh, gods, *Rhun!*"

Muscles spasming with a sudden explosion of pure pleasure, she let out a sound somewhere between a moan and a sigh, and then sagged on his shoulder, limp and sated.

She sort of came to her senses again when he put her down on a stool at the kitchen island and gave her a kiss of heartbreaking tenderness.

"Which ingredients do you need?" he asked her with a smirk.

"Damn sneaky demon," she muttered, though her reprimand had no edge at all.

She told him which herbs to get from the pantry, instructed in him how to chop them and slowly simmer them in water until they were thoroughly decocted. As the tangy smell filled the kitchen, she scrunched up her nose, already dreading the taste of the muddy result.

"I just came from Hazel's." She sighed, rubbing her forehead with one hand. "It seems like Basil took off on his own. He didn't even say good-bye, just...left. His gear and weapons are gone, like his car."

Rhun turned from supervising the simmering decoction and met her eyes. "You think he went into Faerie?"

"It's the most likely scenario, considering it's what they were talking about. Hazel's distraught. She blames herself—"

"How so?" Rhun interrupted her. "Didn't you say she had a silence spell on her, so she couldn't tell him anything before?" After Lily called Merle earlier tonight with the shell-shocking news about Basil's real identity and her lost twin sister in Faerie, Merle brought Rhun into the loop as well.

"Yeah, but she feels like she could have handled the revelation better. She's afraid it turned out to be more about Rose, and that maybe Basil felt rejected, and like she didn't have the mind to reassure him..."

"She worries too much."

She shook her head. "I don't think so. She has a point. I mean, Basil ran off by himself right after he found out. And just put yourself in her shoes...what if something happens to Basil over there? What if he took off because he felt he needed to prove something, and he'll..." Her breath hitched, and the lump in her throat choked the rest of her sentence.

Rhun crossed his arms, leaning against the kitchen island with his hips. "You really think he can't take care of himself?"

"It's not that," Merle said on a heavy breath. "It's just…there's strength in numbers. He shouldn't have gone alone."

He tilted his head in a conceding gesture. "Now what?"

"Now we're all scrambling to find a fae who can take us into Faerie so we can look for Baz and Rose."

"We?" Her darling demon cocked a brow. "Please don't tell me you're part of a proposed rescue mission for Blondie and the Lost Twin."

She narrowed her eyes at him. "So what if I am? Are you going to bark at me and tell me to stay home like a good housewife?"

He pursed his lips. "Aside from the fact that you should know better, and not accuse me of chauvinism when I'm the first person to believe in your skills and your ability to fight…"

She cringed.

"…what my skepticism was actually in reference to is what your participation in the rescue mission in La-La-Land would mean for the little spat you and Hazel are having with Juneau and her witches."

At his mention of the Elder witch who'd provoked a rift in the formerly united witch community, Merle's hackles rose, her power buzzing to the surface. Juneau's misguided and reactionary persecution of Lily after she was turned into a demon—through no fault of her own—was a dangerous travesty.

Merle clenched her jaw. "What about it?"

"Well, you and Hazel are the linchpins of the opposition against Juneau, right? Sure, you've got other witches on your side, but you two, you're the cornerstones of the movement against her. What do you think is going to happen when Juneau realizes both of you have left for an open-ended trip into Faerie?"

Her breath stuck in her throat. "Oh, gods. You're right. I can't leave. Why didn't I see it before? If word gets out that we're both gone, it'll weaken our side in her eyes…"

"…and she'll swoop in and strike."

"Ugh. That bitch." She closed her eyes, let her head fall back for a moment.

"Getting feisty, little witch?" He moved to the stove and ladled out a cup of the finished brew.

She took the mug he handed her and sipped on the decoction, made a face and said, "You should use less mold."

He grinned at her echo of what he once said to her, after they just met, and, damn, but his smirk hadn't lost any of its appeal. "Bottoms up."

Bracing herself, she downed half the cup of Mountain Dirt before having to pause and shudder at the taste.

"I can ask my contacts, see if anyone knows a fae." He laid both hands on her shoulders, massaged her neck and her nape, grounding her with his touch.

She sighed. "That would be great. Thank you."

Closing her eyes, she leaned forward, resting her head against Rhun's chest. As always, the feel of him soothed her to the depths of her soul, calmed her restlessness, shifted everything back into focus. She inhaled a good noseful of his scent and hummed with contentment.

"I'm so damn tired," she whispered.

His arms came around her, stroking her back. "The magic you've been doing for Arawn?"

She grimaced at the thought of the Demon Lord, that rotten bastard who had the right to call on her magic at will, courtesy of an ill-fated deal Merle struck with him to keep him from claiming her sister Maeve. "Yeah. You know what he made me do this time? He had me change the freaking color of his stupid fireflies. Wanted them red. Fireflies! I had to fumble around for hours until I got the spell right, and all the while he sat there in wolf form, watching me with a grin on his face. And let me tell you, a grinning wolf is not a comforting sight."

Rhun's muscles tensed under her touch, and his growing irritation vibrated along their mating bond, a dull throb deep within her.

"He's using up your magic for meaningless shit." It was a growl filled with dark, dark anger.

"And laughing his ass off at the show."

Stepping back, he pinned her with a steely look. "Tell him to go fuck himself. This has gone on long enough.

It's time you put an end to it."

She snorted. "Yeah, right. Don't you think I'd do that in a heartbeat if I had a choice?"

"But you do." He glared at her. "You can tell him it's over. End the deal."

"Oh, sure, and I'll just go tell my baby sister that I'm throwing her to the wolves." Or *wolf*, in that case.

"So you'd rather—"

"I'm not discussing this, Rhun."

He looked like she'd slapped him. A muscle ticked in his jaw. "One of these days," he said slowly, quietly, "I'm going to hog-tie you, go to Arawn, and end the deal for you."

Blood beginning to boil, she glared at him. "You do that, and I will unleash a world of hurt on you that will make your time in the Shadows seem like a five-star vacation."

They stared at each other for a good ten seconds, then they both growled, "Fine!" and turned away.

Seething, she stomped over to the counter, snatched the bread, and started making a sandwich. Gods, she was hungry. And exhausted. And so, so angry at that stubborn demon husband of hers, who was currently rearranging the dishes in the cabinets in some OCD-compliant order, no doubt working off his frustration. The bread suffered from some frustration of her own, what with the way she almost butchered it.

Going through the fridge, she pulled out a bunch of stuff to put on the sandwich, all the while furiously thinking, brooding, fuming with what in her opinion was clearly justified anger.

He couldn't honestly expect her to give up on her sister, not after all she'd been through. Only a few months had passed since Merle rescued Maeve, and Maeve still suffered from the trauma of her abduction and torture at the hands of a demon. Merle's stomach turned when she thought back to how she had to ask Arawn for help in finding Maeve's captor, and how Arawn's price for his assistance was an open favor… which he claimed later, after Maeve's rescue, by demanding Merle surrender magical custody over Maeve to him and let him take her baby sister.

Bruised and hurting from the race to save Maeve, and from seeing the open wounds in Maeve's psyche, Merle had desperately bargained with the Demon Lord once more to keep Arawn from claiming her right away. So she ended up locked in a deal with Arawn— she granted him free use of her magic as long as he didn't come to take away Maeve.

And she had to keep it up, because the thought of the Demon Lord dragging Maeve off to the heart of his dark dominion soured her blood. Why couldn't Rhun see that she had to hold on to this last chance of keeping Maeve safe, that it was simply not an option to surrender her baby sister to a being like Arawn if there was still a way around it?

Grinding her teeth, Merle barely kept herself from squeezing the honey bottle to death—and then she froze. She stared at the sandwich in front of her, a dizzying suspicion crawling up her spine. Mentally doing some math, she then put the honey down on the counter with shaking hands, heart pounding a thousand times a minute.

"Rhun," she whispered.

Pausing with a mug in his hands, he met her eyes, then followed her glance to the sandwich—which consisted of bread with peanut butter, cheese, bacon and pickles, topped with honey. He frowned, looked at her face again, before his attention dropped to her hand, which was resting on her abdomen.

His eyes widened. The mug slipped from his grasp, fell to the floor, shattered. Suddenly Rhun was in front of her, his hands cupping her face, his lips on hers, searing, possessive, kissing the hell out of her while the mating bond between them pulsed with a tangle of white-hot emotions. Excitement, fear, protectiveness, and, above and beyond all, a love that went so deep, it fucking broke her heart.

Swallowing a sob of bittersweet happiness, she wound her arms around his neck, kissing him back with all the passion she felt for him. She jumped up and wrapped her legs around his hips, and he caught her, set her down on the counter with utmost care, stroking her face. Resting his forehead against hers, he closed his eyes, his hand warm as it curved over her belly. There was a hush of awe about him, and it was so damn beautiful she wanted to cry.

For the longest time they remained like this, Rhun's one hand tangled in her hair, his other resting on her belly, her arms around his neck, fingers digging into the silk of his hair. He smiled as he met her gaze.

"I'm sorry I yelled at you," they both said at the same time, and she giggled, giddy and high on an overload of happy hormones.

"Are you really...?" he whispered.

"Yes." She gave a shaky nod. "I can feel it. A tiny spark."

Rhun's smile brightened until it was blinding. "We're going to have a little witch volcano."

8

Your mother.

The unspoken words whispered through Isa's mind, and brought back memories of what had indeed been the hardest case Isa ever worked.

"Please, please, I beg you. Search your heart, find some mercy." Tears streamed down the fae's face, her eyes huge and round and imploring as she looked up at Isa. "Please let me go."

The magical leash in Isa's hand burned into her skin, even though the power was calibrated not to affect Isa herself. And yet she burned. Her hand trembled. If Isa had even a shred of compassion in her heart, she would release the faery, would grant her the freedom she so desperately craved. But alas, the heart the fae had spoken of was made of stone.

"Come with me," Isa said, her voice as cold as the marble that sang to her.

Basil's voice drew her back into the present. With a start, she looked over at him.

"I'm sorry, what did you say?"

"I was just asking about the hardest case you ever

had." His brows drew together over those gorgeous brown eyes. "But hey, if it's too personal a question, forget I asked."

Isa swallowed hard, pushed back the feeling of an irrevocable, heavy mistake. "Well, I guess it's a tie between the one fae I had to chase up Mount Hood— all the way up—and the other fae, who fled into the sewers of Portland. And yes, I had to chase him through pipes full of human waste."

Basil choked out a laugh. "I don't even want to imagine how long it took to wash off."

Isa grinned, glad he accepted her diversion at face value, bought into her implication that *hard* had been a matter of physically taxing versus emotionally devastating. Because even with a heart of stone, dragging Basil's mother back into Faerie almost broke Isa.

It was wrong, she knew that. All these years of suffering, all the pain, the looming specter of her own death, it was only fair, wasn't it? Didn't she deserve it? Had the curse not been the just reward for declining to do what had been so obviously right? Yes, maybe she deserved to suffer.

Isa took a deep breath, closed her eyes, and shook herself. Shook off the maudlin feelings of self-recrimination, and reminded herself of what had been her reality ever since she was a little girl. How could she have made the right decision, or even known what was right? How could she have known how to care for anyone else, how could she have put the welfare of anyone else before her own needs, when no one had ever done the same for her?

She had to claw and fight for every scrap of food and shelter while she was growing up. She struggled through a childhood intent on seeing her die rather than succeed, and she made her way out by herself. No one helped her. No one cared. She never had the luxury of caring for someone else more than she cared about staying alive, so declining to listen to the pleas of one desperate fae had just been par for the course.

She made a mistake, she suffered for it, but what was done, was done. Breaking the curse would be her chance to start fresh.

"Your turn, Basil," she said, shutting down the internal clamor of doubts and what-ifs, "tell me your tale of the one who walks the sky."

His laugh warmed her, chased away the chill of the night and the shadows of the past. And, oh, he looked so delighted, so full of joy, like a coyote pup with something new to play with.

By the time they reached the Treetop Inn, she was thoroughly immersed in the story of Luke, Leia, and Han, and their struggle against the evil Empire.

"You have to tell me how they'll make it out of that trash compactor," Isa said to him as they approached the treehouse.

"Sure," he muttered absent-mindedly, his eyes glued to the towering structure in front of them, the stairs and walkways, the walls, parts of the roof, windows and decorations, all worked around and into and through the copse of grand firs ahead of them.

Isa tilted her head, studied Basil's reaction, and then looked at the inn, tried to see it with his eyes. Yes, for someone who had never beheld an elaborate faery treehouse before, this must be wondrous. She tended to forget how different human architecture was from that of the fae.

All around them, fae creatures were moving to and fro, coming and going, the inn being a popular meeting place for their kind. This commotion, however, went beyond the usual bustle of the lodge. Whispers rose and fell while fae sped past, an air of urgency and trepidation about them.

What was going—?

Just that second, a snippet of dialogue floated over to her. "…royal court. All of them. Dead…"

Isa inhaled sharply. *Right.* News of the slaughter hadn't reached the outskirts of Faerie when she passed here a couple of hours ago, but it sure was on everyone's lips now. Her stomach curdled at the thought of what the future might hold, considering the power vacuum created by the gruesome murders. Well, whatever change might be ahead, she'd weather it like she did everything else in life. She'd survived worse.

Provided, however, she could break her curse.

She slanted a look at the one thing standing between her and survival.

"This is amazing," Basil whispered.

"Just do me a favor and try not to leave your mouth hanging open," Isa said in a low voice, leaning into him.

Basil straightened, threw a glance at her, and closed his mouth with an audible click. Isa looked down at the ground and bit her lip to keep from grinning. To no avail. She ascended the stairs ahead of Basil with a not-unwelcome smile on her face.

The wide staircase encircling the massive girth of the main tree holding up the Treetop Inn was illuminated by will-o'-the-wisps, like the main road. The old wood planks creaked under her feet as she took the stairs up, up, farther up, until they reached the main landing a good thirty feet above the ground. A few fae mingled on the large platform in front of the entrance to the inn, but Isa ignored them, and signaled Basil to follow her into the main house.

Inside, a live band in the corner played upbeat music, and a few smaller fae creatures danced in front of the bar, either oblivious to or uncaring about the slaughter of their royals. The rest of the room was packed with patrons. Despite the heightened buzz of agitation caused by the news of the throne room massacre, the crowd promised anonymity, just as Isa preferred. She rarely stayed in less-frequented establishments, for fear of drawing too much attention, a result of a life lived on the fringes of society, always braced for the next kick.

She approached the front desk while muttering to Basil, "Let me do the talking. You don't speak Fae, and insisting on speaking English would be weird. We don't want to draw unnecessary attention."

Basil nodded, then gasped, his face all shocked. "Wait, does that mean I can't wear my Legolas outfit around here?"

Isa blinked, stopped short. "What's a legolas?"

His grin was positively mischievous. He winked at her, bumped her shoulder gently with his. "Methinks I'll have to show you a couple of movies to bring you up to speed on human culture."

"Another religious tale?"

His eyes crinkled at the corners while he chuckled. "Yes."

Her heart inexplicably beating faster and lighter, Isa stepped up to the front desk and conferred with the main host, a stout female fae with skin resembling the white- and green-flecked pattern of red alder bark, and hair the color of young moss. Isa paid for a room for the night and signaled Basil, who followed her out of the main house and over the platform, past the mingling fae, up another flight of stairs, to one of the single rooms nestled in the upper branches.

She opened the door with the silver key—not iron, the despised metal not to be found anywhere in Faerie —and held the door while Basil entered. Shutting it behind him, she turned around and scanned the room, noting all the exits and entry points for a possible threat.

It would do.

Basil let out a breath, put his hands on his waist. "I can't believe it. This is...amazing architecture." He spread his arms wide. "Do all fae live like this?"

Isa deposited her weapons in the corner with the bunk bed, so her bow and arrows would be within easy reach while she slept. "No, not all of us. Fae architecture actually differs according to the fae's element."

"What do you mean?"

"Well, since you asked me to teach you about fae powers, here's your first lesson. No two faeries' powers are exactly the same. But some of us have ties to the same element. Some parts of nature...sing to us, to our own power. Some fae have an affinity for water, for example, while others can manipulate fire."

"In other words, fae magic is elemental magic?"

"Not quite, but close. Our magic is not limited to elemental magic, or rather that there's one element we prefer. A water fae, for example, will be strongest in the presence of water, and the core of her talent will be in manipulating water, and anything to do with water. But she may have magic that has nothing to do with water as well."

"That means a water fae would still be able to work a spell on someone's mind, right?"

Isa nodded. "Yes, kind of like that. The elemental part of our magic is the part we are born with. It's the magic we barely need to study, since it comes naturally. Now, other types of magic, those similar to the magic witches wield, those types we have to spend time to learn, just like witches. Our powers are still far below those of witches, but we are able to learn and wield some magic that goes beyond our natural element."

"What's your element?" Basil's eyes held a speculative gleam.

Inexplicably, she felt the urge to tease him, to be playful. She marveled at the feeling. "Why don't you take a guess?"

The spark in his eyes, the hint of a smile on his face, both deepened, spread into an expression of interest and appreciation that caught her off guard. He took a step closer, studied her from head to toe and back up again, lingering over the feminine places of her body—which grew hot and sensitive, as if in answer to his visual examination.

The intensity of his regard, the unabashed interest, seared through the layers of her clothes, made her suddenly aware of the overwhelming *maleness* so close to her. He leaned in, inhaled deeply, as if trying to sample her very essence. She shivered in response, struggled not to sway forward, into him.

"I'd say," he murmured in a voice pitched so low, so seductive, it invoked images far too intimate in nature, "it's not fire, or water."

Unable to raise her voice to speak, she just shook her head, mesmerized by his presence.

He tilted his head and studied her face so closely, she had to lock her knees so she wouldn't tremble. "Earth?"

She exhaled on a gasp. Her heart skipped a beat.

"Am I close?"

Far too close. But not in terms of guessing her element. His heat brushed against her skin, his scent wrapped around her—he smelled like warm earth caressed by rain, touched by an intriguing dark note. Her pulse sped up, her breath caught in her throat, and desire uncurled in her lower belly. Insidious, unwelcome—she hadn't wanted a male in years, had been too preoccupied with stalling her curse, and now was not the time to reawaken a long-buried need.

So instead of an answer—or any of the disastrous, traitorous ideas her newly invigorated libido came up with about how to respond to his interest in her—she called to the stone around her, drew the pieces she found close, raised them up and swirled them in the air —and then let go so they could rain down on Basil.

9

Basil ducked as small pebbles hailed down on him, covered his head with his hands, and backed away. Squinting at the mischievous fae in front of him, he watched the last of her gravel missiles hit the wooden floor.

He lowered his hands, cocked a brow. "Did you just stone me?"

She had the good grace to look a little rueful. "I let them fall softly. If I wanted to hurt you, I'd have pelted you with them."

He rubbed a spot on his head where one of the pebbles had hit him not-so-softly. "You know, I imagined the first time I got stoned would be more relaxing than this."

She frowned. "Relaxing? Isn't stoning a method of capital punishment among humans? How can it be relaxing?"

"No, I meant—never mind." He grimaced. *Time to change the subject.* "Okay, so your element is earth. And the fae who built this"—he waved his hands at the impressive treehouse structure—"their element is wood, I gather?"

"Correct." She inclined her head, and a lock of her smooth black hair slid over her pointed ear.

"But since your affinity is for earth, wouldn't you feel more comfortable in a ground dwelling?"

The small smile that stole across her face made his heart beat faster. "You're quite perceptive. But my element isn't precisely *earth*. It's stone. Which is related to earth, same as wood." At his frown, she elaborated. "Some of the elements for which fae have an affinity are related to each other, some are not. Fire is its own element, with no relation to others. Earth, on the other hand, is—in a way—a base element from which other, more refined elements originated. Earth gave birth to stone, metal, and wood. Which means earth fae can manipulate those three to a certain extent, but most of their power lies in controlling earth. Stone fae are strongest when surrounded by rocks and mountains, but they also feel at home in earth or forest dwellings, because stone is linked with those elements."

"And because you're a stone fae, you don't have a problem staying in fae houses made of wood."

She winked at him, and her playful expression hit him right in his heart. He could see it now, could see her element in her gray eyes, the stoic nature of the stones she could bend to her will mirrored in the depths of her calm attitude. Would her character have jagged edges, too, like rocks breaking off a cliff? Which parts of her personality would resemble the smoothness of pebbles polished by years of friction, which parts would be rough and cutting, like fractures forged under pressure? He marveled at the drive, his intense curiosity to learn about her, to explore what made up the pieces of her soul, her heart, her mind.

Plenty of time to find out. Searching for Rose was shaping up to be a complicated endeavor with an unknowable timeline, but at least he had good company. Isa was more than he could have hoped for in a guide through Faerie—not only was she an invaluable resource, and pledged to protect his life, she was easily the most beautiful female he'd ever laid eyes on.

When she smiled, her slate-gray eyes sparkled with surprising mischief, her full lips tempting him to caress them with his own. First time he kissed her—yep, he'd already made plans to do so the second she welcomed that move—he'd take his time and drown in the taste, the feel of her. There was something to be said for the first kiss with a new lover, and he'd enjoy the hell out of that moment.

And lovers they would be. He'd never been one to hem and haw about pursuing a girl—with the exception of Maeve, where the closeness of their families put a damper on his usual straightforwardness. Apart from that, he always jumped in with both feet when he was attracted to a female, because what was the use of life if you didn't go for what you wanted, no-holds-barred, relishing the way love would steal your breath before you even knew you were falling?

He wanted her, wanted to see if that buzz in his veins when she was near, that charge in the air between them, that subtle pull in his chest when he looked at her, would develop into the *more* he could almost taste.

But there was something else he wanted to try first.

He peered at her. "Now I know what your element is, can you help me find out about mine?"

"Sure. It shouldn't be too hard. Let's sit."

They settled on cushions on the floor.

"All right," Isa said, "let's see which element you feel most drawn to. Try wood first. We are surrounded by it, so it should be easy for you to connect."

He frowned. "Okay, how exactly do I do that?"

Isa shrugged. "Try closing your eyes, rest your hand on the wood beside you, and just feel it. If it is your element, you should sense a sort of pull toward it. Or rather, you should hear it…singing, for lack of a better word." She shook her head. "I promise, you'll know when you feel it."

"Okay." *Here goes nothing.*

Basil took a deep breath, closed his eyes, and laid his hand on the wooden plank floor beside him. He spread his fingers, feeling the texture of the wood, the unevenness of the material. After growing up among witches, seeing all the magic they were capable of, he shouldn't feel so foolish waiting for an object to sing to him. Nothing happened. The wood didn't greet him as an old friend, or anything along those lines. It was just dead.

He opened his eyes and shook his head.

"Nothing?" Isa asked.

"Absolutely nothing."

"Very well. Let's try—oh, what the hell—stone."

"You think our elements could be the same?" He cocked an eyebrow.

"I don't know. We'll see."

She grabbed one of the pebbles still lying on the floor and held it out to him. He took the small stone from her hand, the contact of their skin sending an electric buzz up his arm and into other parts of his body.

"Same procedure." Isa inclined her head, nodded at the pebble in his hand.

Again Basil closed his eyes and tried to connect with the element he was touching. Again, nothing happened.

With a sigh, he tossed the pebble aside.

Isa tapped a finger against her mouth, pondering. "I wonder..." She got up, and half-turned to him. "I'll be right back." She walked out of the room, leaving the door slightly ajar. A minute later, she reappeared, holding something in her hand. She closed the door and sat down opposite him again.

"Here, take this."

He opened his hand to accept what she was holding out to him. When the cool earth touched his skin, an involuntary shiver ran down his spine.

"Earth?" He glanced at Isa's face.

"Try it."

And he did. Closing his eyes, he reached out to the

element in his hand, listening, waiting. At first there was nothing. Just like with the wood and the stone, he didn't feel anything.

He was about to toss the earth out the window with a frustrated sigh, when...he heard it. A low-level hum, not unlike the one he experienced after his glamour was lifted. Only this one came from outside him, from the earth in his palm.

His mouth fell open of its own accord. His heart beat faster. Could it be? He went deeper into himself, opened himself to the buzzing melody inside him. He strained to hear more of the other melody, too, the one coming from his hand. And yes, they were one and the same.

"That's it, isn't it?" Isa said breathlessly.

He opened his eyes, met her gaze of sparkling gray. He nodded, not quite able to put into words what he was feeling.

A gorgeous smile lit up her face. She leaned forward, inched closer to him. "All right. Now, I want you to connect with it more deeply. You're probably hearing two melodies, right?"

Again he nodded silently.

Isa seemed just as eager as he was to tap into his powers. A euphoric thrill flooded him, and goose bumps whispered over his skin at the tenuous bond forming between them, the shared delight.

"Try to connect those melodies," she told him.

"How?"

"Imagine it's like...tying two threads together, at the

most logical point. Visualize it. Once you've done that, you should be able to direct the melody, and thus affect the earth."

He strained to listen to the hum resonating in him, to the corresponding almost-music coming from the element in his hand. They did...seem to overlap here and there. If only he could grasp the parts where they should connect, he might be able to knot them together. But every time he went to grab either thread, it slipped through his mental fingers.

Minutes ticked by. He lost count of how many times he tried. All the while Isa sat opposite him, patiently waiting for him to achieve something that probably came naturally to fae toddlers. Heat rose up to his neck and face, choking him like a too-tight collar. The hum in him faded, as did the melody from the earth on his palm, drowned out by his own heartbeat and the rush of blood in his ears.

His stomach hardened, and he shook his head once, balled his hand to a fist and crushed the bits of soil. "It's no use," he said and got to his feet, marched over to one of the windows, opened it, and threw out the dirt.

~~~

Basil remained standing there, his back turned to Isa, and stared out the window, hands on his hips. The frustration rolling off him was palpable, tinged with a dejection that saddened her. He'd been so hopeful, so anxious to connect with his powers, and…she'd felt it, too. With him. For him. She'd breathed his anticipation and joy as if it was her own, and his disappointment now cut her keenly, as if *she* had failed at something that was dear to *her*.

"I'm sorry," she whispered.

She walked over to him, and, driven by an impulse she couldn't name, laid her hand on his shoulder. He took a deep breath, closed his eyes, and shifted infinitesimally closer, the move seeming almost subconscious.

"Maybe," she ventured, "some of the glamour hasn't lifted yet, and it impairs your ability to tap into your powers. Let's give it some time. I'm sure you'll figure it out soon."

He nodded, turned toward her, and the move brought her hand from his shoulder to his upper chest. For some insidious reason, she found herself incapable of drawing back, her gaze glued to his face, to his eyes, the dazzling melange of shades of brown illuminated by the low light crystals scattered around the room. She saw it now, the earth in him. The kaleidoscope of his irises featured all the hues found in the soil, from lighter ochre to umber to burnt sienna to flecks of near-black.

The gleaming gold of his hair contrasted starkly with the dark of his eyes, complementing a face of masculine grace that was so finely drawn, its beauty so honed, it almost hurt to behold it. A gift from his fae genes, for sure.

Those mesmerizing eyes dropped to her mouth, and his intent lit the colors of his irises with an inner glow, warmed them until they glittered. That kind of focus...

She inhaled sharply, and every feminine part of her sat up at attention, basked in his overt appreciation.

When he slowly lifted his hand to her face, she didn't flinch, didn't retreat, rooted to the spot by the irrational, uncontrollable desire to welcome his touch. He brushed his thumb over her lower lip, so gently, so reverently, his gaze still locked on her mouth. Her pulse raced, her thoughts a scattered mess.

He leaned down toward her, stopped with his lips a mere inch from hers, his breath caressing her skin, his scent a heady embrace.

"Tell me you want this," he murmured.

"If I didn't," she whispered back, "you would have already been pelted with pebbles."

He laughed, so close to her mouth that his delight sank into her pores, lit up the darkness within her.

And then he kissed her.

The first touch of his lips on hers was the faintest caress, featherlight, a sweet hello. She breathed him in while a need—long-tamed and laid to sleep—awoke and stretched, reaching out for more. His next touch seemed to echo her awakening desire, his response unmistakable in the pressure of his lips on hers, the warmth of his hands as he rested them on her waist.

She met him eagerly, and when she opened her mouth against his, he licked at her, grazed his teeth over her lower lip, bit her tenderly. He inhaled her gasp, went back to kissing her before she could react, exploring her as one might sample and savor a delicacy. Pulling her closer, he seemed to drink her in, absorbing her every response, as if kissing her until she forgot her own name was his sole purpose in life.

Every shiver, each sigh, any lick of her tongue against his, appeared to fuel his determination to make sure his name was branded on every last cell in her body. His hands cupped her face, his fingers sliding into her hair, as he angled her head to kiss her even more fully, until she couldn't say whether she'd ever been kissed before, until everything fell away beyond his heat stroking her senses, his taste sinking into her soul.

He devoted himself fully to this moment, as if he had all the time in the world, nothing but time for *her*. By the gods—no one, *no one*, had ever treated her this way. He kissed her like nothing he tasted for the rest of his life would ever caress his senses the way their kiss did.

The desire he kindled burned her from the inside out, setting her very bones on fire. For *him*. Breath heavy and fast, she pressed herself against him, her hands sliding up the hard planes of his chest, over his neck and into the silk of his hair. Desperate. She was desperate for more touch, more sensation, needed to *feel* him. And yet he held her still, kept his focus on kissing her, as if intent on driving her insane by giving her enough to make her smolder, yet too little to let her combust.

When she uttered a sound between a whimper and a

frustrated growl, he laughed. *Laughed* against her mouth, rested his forehead on hers, his hands still cradling her face. The intimacy of that gesture hit her hard, smashed through the fog of need and passion in her brain. What in the woods' darkest pits was she doing? This was wrong on so many levels. He was the very last male she should lust after.

With a hitch in her breath, she drew back, her eyes downcast, and turned away from him. "We should go to bed. I'll take the top bunk, you'll take the bottom one. We leave at dawn."

She didn't look back, didn't dare check for his reaction. The heavy silence that followed her statement was indication enough. She could only hope he wouldn't press her for an explanation.

No way could she tell him the sinister truth behind her need to keep him at arm's length.

10

The morning light streaming in from the living room windows painted Rhun's face in a golden glow, made his pale blue-green eyes shine even more brightly. Plopping down on the couch next to him, Merle sighed.

"It's not fair," she said.

"What's that?"

"How blindingly beautiful you are." She gestured wildly in his general direction.

That damn, sneakily hot-as-hell smirk of his curled his mouth, lit his eyes.

"Of course," she added, just to take him down a notch, "you often temper the ethereal quality of your looks by opening your mouth and shooting off a sarcastic remark that makes me want to strangle you, so there *is* some balance."

"I'm offended," Rhun declared, glaring at her.

"Oh? Why?"

"My sarcastic remarks only make you want to *strangle* me? That's so mild and unimaginative. What happened to wanting to eviscerate me after beating me to a pulp? Do I need to step up my game? Because clearly I'm not annoying you enough anymore." He crossed his arms and pouted.

She snickered and smacked his shoulder. "I may yet use that spoon I've been threatening you with."

One side of his mouth tipped up, and his eyes sparked with interest. "That's more like it."

"I've been wondering," she said after a pause, sobering, "about this witch-demon hybrid thing." She waved at her belly. "I'm a little worried about it, to be honest. I don't know what to expect. How much of her will be demon, how much witch? What will her powers be like?" She looked up at him. "Her needs? I didn't find any precedent to go by..."

"I did." He shrugged at her inquisitive look. "I did some research among my kind. Turns out there was a case of a mating between a *bluotezzer* demon and a witch some eighty years ago, in Europe. She was expelled from her community, which is probably why you didn't find anything in your archives."

Merle growled, irate at the thought of another witch being ostracized just because she fell in love with a demon. Those damn bigoted, narrow-minded, hateful —

"Yes to all of that," he said, nodding at what had to be a murderous expression on her face. "Anyway, the couple had three children, all of them daughters."

"The witch gene."

"Yep, seems like it." His free hand came up to twirl a

lock of her hair around his fingers. "They had witch powers."

"But…?" Merle prodded. His tone definitely indicated a *but*.

"They were part demon, too." He met her eyes. "They needed to satisfy one of the nourishment needs of my species, but only one, and always the same one, for the rest of their lives."

Merle blew out a breath. That wasn't so bad. "Well, then I hope they'll only have to take pleasure."

Rhun bristled, his aura blazing. "Well, I damn sure hope they won't! If it was up to me, they'd have to take pain."

She stared at him, baffled.

"We are talking," Rhun growled in response to her scowl, "about *my daughters*. They will never—*ever*—take pleasure from a male. They will be cute little witch volcanoes for their entire lives, and the only thing they'll ever do to males is cause them pain. Are we clear?"

Merle stared at him a moment longer, trying to maintain a straight face, until she couldn't fight it anymore. She burst out laughing. Flopping down face-first on the couch, she laughed and laughed and laughed, coming up once, thinking she could sober up and stop.

One look at Rhun's disgruntled expression had her wheezing with laughter again. She barely noticed when he left the couch and stalked out of the room, muttering something sounding like "not funny" under his breath.

"Oh, come on," Merle said, getting up and following Rhun out of the living room. "You have to admit—"

Sudden pain made her break off mid-sentence and double over. Searing fire shot along her nerves, and she cried out, falling to her knees, the pain of hitting the hardwood floors just a blip compared to the agony wracking her whole body.

Dammit, not now.

Rhun was at her side in an instant, his hands warm on her clammy skin. "Merle? What is it?"

"The...balance..." Had it been this long already? Hadn't she just paid back recently?

Rhun cursed. "All right, little witch. I've got you."

He lifted her, his arms under her knees and behind her back, cuddling her close while he carried her back into the living room to set her gently on the couch. She barely noticed. Her back was bowed, her skin on fire, explosive pressure building in her core. The Powers That Be were merciless in demanding she pay back for the magic she'd used, the energy she'd drawn from the layers of the world to supplement her own brand of witch powers. It was the responsibility and curse of all the heads of witch families—the greater the gift, the greater the cost.

Her skin split. One by one, gashes opened up all over her, and she was bleeding magic. Her power-drenched blood dissolved in the air on a sigh of the Powers That Be, those forces holding the world together. She cried out. Sweat slicked her skin, her stomach turned, her jaw locked, and she dug her fingers into the fabric of the couch.

"I'm right here, little witch. I've got you. It'll be over soon." Rhun's voice was steady, his tone infused with reassuring confidence, but his hands—they shook while they stroked her, as he cradled her head with the utmost care.

Merle had her eyes closed, couldn't see Rhun's expression, could barely feel his presence at the other end of their mating bond, her entire consciousness dominated by the pain wracking her. She could only hope and pray that this time upholding the balance wouldn't take long.

"It's okay, Merle mine. You'll be okay, you're strong —" Rhun's voice broke off, and something in it, an echo along the mating bond, made Merle snap to attention, even in the midst of the agony razing her body and mind.

She opened her eyes, focused on Rhun, and her heart skipped a beat as she saw his expression. He was white as a sheet, horror in his eyes.

"Rhun..." she ground out past the pain that was so debilitating she all but wanted to lose consciousness. "What...is it?"

She followed his look to the cushion underneath her hips—and the bright red stain spreading across the beige fabric.

Her heart stopped. Her stomach—already in turmoil —made a dive for the ground. She felt it now, through the pain and the magic leaving her body...the wet warmth between her thighs…

The baby…

~~~

Rhun stared at the pool of blood spreading underneath Merle's hips. She was wearing black jeans, so he hadn't noticed, had thought the blood he smelled was from the gashes on her body, her payback to the Powers That Be. He hadn't noticed she was bleeding somewhere else…

"Rhun…" Merle cried out again, and then she sagged against the cushions, her mind lost to darkness.

Through their mating bond, Rhun could see, feel, sense her slipping into unconsciousness. And just before the link to her went numb as she fainted, he felt a weakening which promised to break everything inside him—the spark of life in Merle's belly flickered, dimmed.

No.

Heart hammering a thousand beats a minute, he shot to his feet. It was day, his demon powers muted, but even at night he wouldn't have the magic to heal her. His demon species' powers weren't of the healing kind. There was nothing he could do for her, or their baby. He jumped to pick up his phone from the table. Browsed through the contacts, dialed the number, and waited, with bated breath, his soul shattering into a million pieces.

"Hello?"

He'd never been so relieved to hear that voice. "Hazel, you need to come here ASAP."

"What's going—"

"Get the fuck over here right now."

He hung up, crammed the phone in his pocket, and rushed over to Merle's side again. As he did not so long ago—and yet it seemed like a lifetime had passed —he closed his eyes, his hand wrapped tightly around Merle's, and prayed to the Powers That Be, to those gods he'd shunned all his life, and who had nevertheless heard his fervent pleas when he had begged them to take pain and magic from him instead. They'd done it once, they could do it again.

So he prayed, and prayed, and fucking prayed. *Take it from me... Take my blood, take my magic... Spare her. Take it from me instead...*

Nothing happened. Nothing but more gashes opening up all over Merle's body, more of her blood, her magic, pouring out, widening the pool of angry red on the couch cushion.

No! No, you fuckers. Take it from me.

He sat on the couch, pulled Merle onto his lap, and rocked her, holding her tightly in his arms, feeling the life drain from her body—both lives.

He didn't know how long he sat there, how long he rocked the ravaged body of his witch, of his unborn child inside her, before the front door burst open, and in stormed the intimidating force of a concerned Elder witch.

"She's pregnant," Rhun called out. "She's paying

pack to the Powers That Be, and I think she's losing the baby."

"Give her to me." Hazel ran to Merle's side, took her from Rhun's arms.

Cradling Merle in one arm, she laid her hand on Merle's abdomen, closed her eyes and murmured words of magic, the meaning of which flew right past Rhun's tortured mind. A glow formed around Hazel, visible to his eyes even with his dulled daytime senses.

The Elder witch worked her magic like a madwoman, the glow around her blinding in its intensity. The gashes on Merle's body closed, and she stopped bleeding magic. Had her other bleeding been stopped as well? Rhun couldn't tell, because the air was drenched with the smell of blood to the point that —with his dulled daytime senses—he couldn't discern whether there was any fresh blood. Merle's skin was so white the freckles on her face stood out starkly.

He couldn't read her aura, and he couldn't feel anything from her. Rhun's only way to tell how Merle was doing was through their mating bond, and that link lay silent. He didn't dare ask Hazel how she was doing, for fear of interrupting her focus. He had to wait, he had to fucking wait for Hazel to be finished with whatever she was doing for his mate before she could tell him whether Merle and the baby would be okay.

The minutes ticked by. It seemed like forever. He swore his heart couldn't beat this fast for such a long time without exploding in his chest.

Sweat broke out on Hazel's forehead, her face scrunched up as if she was struggling. She kept muttering spells, most of them in Sanskrit, the ancient language used for many charms. And Rhun didn't understand a single word of it. He couldn't tell if she was making progress.

Then, finally, Hazel took a shaky breath, and withdrew her hand from Merle's abdomen. She was shaking all over. Rhun got up, and knelt next to his mate. Hazel opened her eyes and looked at him, the white around her irises bloodshot, with dark circles under her eyes that hadn't been there when she arrived. She seemed to have aged years within a matter of minutes.

"Is she...?" croaked Rhun, unable to ask aloud what he most feared.

Hazel signaled for him to take Merle from her arms, and he did so without a moment's hesitation. Cradling his fiery witch volcano against his chest, he looked at the elder witch in trepidation.

"She will be fine," Hazel said, her voice weaker than Rhun had ever heard it. "And I managed to save the baby. The bleeding has stopped, and, from what I can tell, the pregnancy is stable again."

Rhun sagged against the couch, exhaling an enormous sigh of relief. He closed his eyes and rested his forehead against Merle's.

~~~

When Merle came to, she was enveloped in the heat of Rhun's arms, cradled by his love. The mating bond pulsed with his concern for her, feeding her strength. Her eyes fluttered open to behold a face of stark male beauty, set in harsh lines of worry and anger. When he noticed she was awake, the hard mask of his features softened, taking on that special expression he only ever showed when he beheld her.

"Merle mine..." A low murmur, pitched for her ears alone.

"The baby..." But even as she said it, she sensed the tiny spark inside her, felt its life glowing, growing, taking root. "Oh, thank the gods..."

"The gods have nothing to do with this one," Rhun growled. "In fact, if it weren't for Hazel, your precious gods would have taken our child's life, along with your magic."

"Hazel..." She frowned, sat up a little in his arms, looked around.

"Here." The Elder witch, as dear to Merle as an aunt by blood, leaned closer and grasped Merle's hand, squeezed. "I'm still here. It's only been a few minutes."

"You fucking scared me, little witch," Rhun rasped. "If Hazel hadn't been able to come so quickly..."

Hazel shook her head. "Merle would have survived." Her unflinching stare slammed into Merle's, a haunting truth written in it. "But your baby wouldn't have."

Merle's hand instinctively covered her abdomen. "How...? Why did this happen? Paying back hurts, yes, and it's always a burden, but it shouldn't end anyone's life."

Hazel's brows drew together. "I'm not sure. I've been thinking a little while you were recovering... It's always the oldest living witch who becomes head of her family, and as far back as I can remember, I've only ever seen witches who were past childbearing age take that position. It's the natural order of things.

"Which means that it should never be an issue that the head of a family—with the obligation to uphold the balance of magic—would become pregnant, and the pregnancy be at risk because of the excruciating process of paying back. I have never heard of a case like this, but then again, there wouldn't be many. It is so very unusual for a witch of Merle's age to be the oldest surviving member of her family and have to take the leading position. I have to look into this, see if I can find any precedents in our history."

"I will research in our library, too," Merle said, a sinking feeling of foreboding churning in her gut. "I never thought..."

"Merle." Hazel's tone was so, so quiet, as if she was unwilling to fully voice what was on her mind. "Even without having done any further research on this, I can already tell you that the next time you have to pay back to the Powers That Be for the magic you've been using, I might not be able to save the baby. Even now it was a close call. There was a moment..." She took an unsteady breath, closed her eyes for a brief second. "I just barely managed to save her. As far as I can see, upholding the balance jeopardizes your pregnancy, and unless you stop using magic right now, and avoid using magic for the rest of the pregnancy, this baby very likely will not survive."

It took a moment. Then the words hit Merle, crashed through the numbness saturating her mind, her heart, her soul, and smashed her nascent bud of hope. *Stop using magic…* To do so would mean—

"It's time to end the deal with Arawn, then." Rhun's anger vibrated along the mating bond, underlaid with a terror so profound it shredded Merle's tenuous grasp on her composure.

"No." A whisper, a desperate rebuttal.

Rhun shifted on the couch to face her, his eyes glittering cold. "The deal with him means you have to put your magic at his disposal, and he's been taking advantage of it—a lot, and mostly for trivial shit. As long as you keep the deal with him, you'll have to keep using your magic, which means you'll have to pay back to the Powers That Be." His neck muscles corded, and his nostrils flared. "Which means our baby will die."

Merle shook her head, feeling too much for her cracking heart to keep in. "I can't," she rasped. "I can't just send Maeve to that…that monster." Tears clouded her vision as she looked at her mate, her husband, her lover. "Don't ask me to make that decision."

Rhun made as if to say something, but she laid her hand over his mouth. "Please…not now. I can't do this right now." She turned to Hazel, who still sat in her chair, cloaked in awkward silence. "Does Maeve know?"

Hazel shook her head. "She's gone to the movies with Keira, Lenora, and Anjali. She had her phone turned off, so I couldn't reach her."

"Don't tell her." Merle's voice was as husky as her baby sister's, her throat tight with anguish. "Don't say a word to her about the pregnancy and the risk. I... need to think before I discuss it with her."

Hazel hesitated, shifted her weight on the chair, but then she nodded. "Sure. We'll look into this, Merle. We'll find a way to make it work."

A muscle ticked along Rhun's jaw. "You better do it fast. Considering the rate at which Arawn has been using her magic, we have about a week before she has to pay back again."

11

The midday sun filtered through the canopy of trees, painting a lazily moving filigree of gold on the forest floor. Birdsong and the rustle of animals in the undergrowth surrounded Basil as he followed the fae in front of him down the path, the comforting sounds of the woods a stark contrast to the silence of his traveling companion.

Isa had barely spoken a word to him all morning, had reverted to being his professionally distant guide and protector in Faerie. Gone were all traces of the desire she showed him last night, of the lust and longing he felt in her kiss. He hadn't imagined it, had he? She *had* welcomed his kiss, had responded in kind, revealing a streak of fiery passion underneath her usually calm facade.

She wanted him, that much was clear after last night. Desire such as she displayed didn't just fizzle out over a few hours. For whatever reason, she was reluctant to admit her attraction to him, and put up a front of indifference, acted as if nothing happened.

Well, now. That didn't mean all hope was lost. The possibility of winning her affection was worth fighting for. At the very least, it was worth another shot, another attempt to find out if those doubts of hers would truly keep her from acting on her desire for him, or if they'd dissipate when she got to know him better. He'd barely begun courting her, so he'd give her more time, would respect her boundaries—while at the same time making sure she knew, felt, *believed* that he appreciated her, and would love to make her his.

If she truly didn't want him, if she rejected him completely, he'd back off, of course. But until she told him to go to hell, he planned to do his damnedest to woo her off her feet.

"By the way, who is your source?" he asked, referring to the fae they planned to tap for information about Rose. They'd been hiking for a few hours now, drawing close—according to Isa—to the informant's dwelling.

Isa threw a quick glance at him as he caught up with her. "He's a collector of rare and extraordinary objects. Buys and sells all sorts of things that are hard to come by, which means he often hears the strangest rumors from people all over Faerie and beyond. Chances are he picked up something about a witch changeling. Or knows someone else who might have heard."

"Do you think he might have something to eat, too?"

She blinked, stopped short. "You're hungry? Didn't you just eat a whole bag of dried meat? And two apples?"

"Well, yes, but that was a snack. We *are* going to have lunch soon, aren't we?"

"You had two breakfasts. Two!"

"Which is the way it should be. Just ask any hobbit."

"Any what?"

He sighed, closed his eyes, and shook his head. "Seriously, we are going to have to watch *so* many movies."

Something flickered through her slate gray eyes, there and gone again within a heartbeat. "I'll see if I can bag a rabbit later."

She resumed walking, and he followed, his attention inexorably drawn to her hips, to the firmness of her butt, so deliciously revealed by the tight fabric of her pants. Her legs were elegantly muscled, a testament to her active lifestyle, to the strength of a hunter. He indulged himself in blissful visions of how those legs would feel wrapped around his hips...or his shoulders...while he dove in and tasted her. Would she squeeze him tight, pull him closer? Would her thigh muscles quiver and flex in response to his licks? Would she be sensitive in the dip at the juncture of her thighs?

His body hardened, desire pumping hot through his veins. He wanted to explore her, every tiny bit of her. He wanted to learn what made her sigh, moan, which touch made her writhe, what move would make her look at him with eyes turned to candescent silver by the force of her desire. And what would she do to *him* when he gave her free rein?

By the gods, he'd never felt such a powerful craving

for a female before. The little taste of her he sampled when they kissed? It had kicked off an avalanche of need, a longing so strong it bordered on addiction.

He took deep breaths of the chilly forest air to clear his head and cool his desire, savored the fragrance of the most recent rain shower. Winter in the Pacific Northwest meant lots of moisture and mild temperatures, which he didn't mind at all. He'd take months of rain over snow and ice any day.

The path opened onto a meadow, lush green, and rolling out toward wooded hills. A hawk's cry echoed across the glade, and Isa stopped abruptly. Her face turned toward the sky, she smiled, then whistled a melody. The hawk cried again, almost as if in answer. Basil blinked when she held out her arm, and a few seconds later the bird of prey swooped down and settled on the wrist guard on her forearm.

Isa murmured something in her language to the hawk, her face graced with an indulgent smile. The bird tilted its head, and when Isa touched its beak, caressed its feathers, the raptor nibbled at her hand in what was clearly a display of avian affection.

"Uh, I assume you two know each other?" he asked, one eyebrow raised.

"We sure do." Isa used two fingers to gently groom the bird's plumage. "This is Kîna. I saved her when she was a fledgling. Her parents were killed during a storm, when another tree fell on the nest, and Kîna barely survived. I was in between hunting projects and had some time on my hands, so I took her in and fed her until she got big enough to take care of herself. She's been my friend ever since." Those eyes of stone glowed with warmth while she regarded the raptor. "Seventeen years, and she still finds me every few weeks, and joins me when I'm hunting."

"Seventeen years? I didn't know hawks could live that long."

"That, and longer. Fates willing, she'll be my friend for years to come yet." She blinked, and a sudden darkness swept over her face. She peered at him from underneath her lashes, then quickly looked away. A muttered word in her language prompted Kîna to push off her arm and take off with powerful flaps of her wings.

"She's beautiful," he said quietly while he watched the graceful flight of the raptor.

"If you are nice, I'll ask her to hunt for you." She started walking again. "Something tells me you won't be satisfied with a rabbit for lunch."

Oh, he could be more than *nice* to her. If only she let him... "I'm forever at your service, milady."

She paused, turned to him. "Don't ever say that to a fae unless you plan to enslave yourself. Be very careful how you speak. Fae take a lot of things literally, and many will hold you to an oath like that."

He let out a breath, nodded. "Point taken."

They started back on their trek, the hawk circling high above them, and thirty minutes later they reached a cottage set at the edge of a small lake.

"Let me do the talking," Isa told him as they

approached the front door, which featured intricate metal ornaments.

Before she even raised her hand to knock, the door swung open, revealing a tall, slender fae male with skin the color of pewter. He was half-bald, the other side of his head covered with long hair of gleaming silver. Numerous metal piercings adorned his nose, eyebrows, lips, and pointed ears.

His golden eyes flicked from Isa to Basil, studying him for a few seconds before he focused on Isa again and said something in Fae. She responded, waved at Basil, said some more, and part of her answer must have caught the fae's attention, because a calculating spark lit his eyes, and he beckoned for them both to enter.

The main room was packed with objects of every size and origin, so many, and so wildly assorted, it reminded Basil of the Room of Hidden Things in *Harry Potter*. The opposite wall was barely visible behind the piles and towers of valuables and collectibles.

"I understand you wish to find something rare and special," the fae said in English, his voice a deep bass with a metallic echo. The piercings in his lips moved as he smiled. "I happen to have a soft spot for such things."

"Not a thing," Isa said. "A person."

The fae raised his silver brows. "And who would that be?"

"A changeling, brought into Faerie many years ago. A witch baby, to be precise. Her exchange may well have been hidden."

Narrowing his eyes, the fae murmured, "A witch… That is indeed rare. We do not usually dare anger them thus."

"Have you heard anything about a witch living among us? About a witch baby brought here? The swap would have happened more than two decades ago."

"Hmm." The fae stroked his chin, tapped his lips. "I think…I might have heard…" He made a frustrated sound. "Alas, my mind is not what it used to be. If only something could…jog my memory." He tilted his head, smiled at Isa.

She sighed. "Name your price, Hathôm."

"I want the dagger strapped to this one's lower back." He indicated Basil with a nod. "The one with the blade of palladium."

Basil raised his brows. "Your element is metal, I take it?"

"Quite obviously so." The fae smiled and waved at his silver hair, gold eyes, and the abundance of piercings on his face.

"That dagger is worth a lot of money," Basil said.

"As is the information stored in here." The fae tapped his head.

Basil gnashed his teeth and fisted and opened his hand before drawing the dagger out of its sheath. He offered the blade to the fae, hilt first. "I promise you this dagger in exchange for all the information you have about the witch changeling."

Hathôm inclined his head. "Deal."

The dagger moved in Basil's hand, and he let go, watched as it floated toward the fae. Hathôm gently grasped the hilt, caressed the polished silver of its palladium blade. A pang pierced Basil's heart. That dagger had been a gift for his eighteenth birthday. From Hazel. Though he could handle steel blades, he'd always preferred weapons made from other metals. Knowing what he did now about his true ancestry, it made sense—iron weakened fae.

And another thing occurred to him...Hazel must have known, too, that he'd have issues with iron and, to a lesser degree, with steel. So the dagger made of palladium—a metal related to platinum, but much lighter and thus making it a perfect weapon to carry strapped to his body at all times—had been, in fact, not just an expensive gift, but a thoughtful one as well.

"The information," Isa interrupted Basil's conflicted pondering.

Hathôm snapped out of his admiration of the valuable blade. "Yes. Of course. I heard about a witch changeling, many years ago, from a trusted source. He said he saw her, a girl with raven hair and the aura of a witch, hidden away by a fae couple. He chanced upon them, and barely made it away without the girl's keepers blasting him with magic. They seemed so belligerent he didn't want to pursue the matter further, and he only confided in me after..." A grin jingled the piercings on his mouth. "...an evening of indulging in the best of my royal wine."

"Did he say where he saw her?"

Hathôm shook his head. "But I will give you his name and address, for the value of this blade."

"Agreed," Basil said.

"He is called Rinnar of Stone, and he lives in Lam'il."

Isa inclined her head to Hathôm. "Your intel is worth the dagger."

Basil took note how she didn't *thank* the fae and yet managed to convey her appreciation for a bargain kept. Ah, the subtleties of fae protocol…

Hathôm bowed his head to her. "We part in goodwill, Isa of Stone."

"We part in goodwill, Hathôm of Metal."

When the door closed behind them and they'd walked out of earshot of the cottage, Basil turned to her, raised one eyebrow. "Isa of Stone?"

"That is my full name."

"A fae's last name is their element?"

"Correct."

"Then I would be—"

"Basil of Earth," Isa said with a smile. "Yes."

"I like it." His excitement fizzled out quickly, however, as his thoughts turned darker. "I wonder what my real mother would have named me. Or maybe she did, but it was never passed on."

Isa studied him, her expression inscrutable. "Do you feel Hazel wasn't real? As a mother?"

Well, hell. She'd picked up on the nuance in his tone, the underlying bitterness. He sighed. "She took care of me, yes. But how much of that was true affection on her part? What if she acted mostly out of obligation? What if, deep down, she resented me for being the wrong child? How many times did she wish the fae who swapped me for her daughter would return and take me back, so she could have her real child again? My father—*adoptive* father—was an ass to me most of the time, and now I can't even be sure my mom—" He broke off.

Isa was silent for a few seconds. "You love her, though. Hazel. You wouldn't be this upset if you didn't care about her."

"Yeah," he said quietly.

"Which must mean she treated you well. You've believed her to be loving all this time, no?"

"Sure, but—"

"Then you are luckier than you realize. I would have killed to have someone love me like that when I was a child, someone with a heart so big that they're still able to show me love even after losing their baby."

His breath caught painfully in his chest. He stopped, looked fully at her. "Who raised you?"

She kept walking, face turned away from him. "I did."

It fucking broke his heart.

He swallowed, caught up with her again. "You were alone? For how long?"

She shrugged. "My parents died when I was five. I barely remember them. I've gotten by on my own ever since."

"Wait—what? Five? You've survived alone since you

were *five years old*?"

"I didn't have any other family. No one else wanted me. Those who *did* show an interest in me…well, I quickly learned their motives were less than loving. So I avoided adult fae and learned to hunt."

Vicious rage heated his blood. "Did they—" He clamped his mouth shut, shook his head. "I shouldn't ask."

A side glance from those sparkling gray eyes. "A few tried. They paid for it."

"With their lives, I hope?"

Her smirk was positively wicked. "With their testicles."

"Can fae grow back body parts?"

Her smile widened until she showed teeth. "No."

"Good." Grim satisfaction wound itself around his heart, even though a part of him itched to track down those fae and do some more major damage.

Isa uttered a choked sound, and stopped abruptly. With her hand fisted over her chest, the knuckles flashing white, she wheezed, her face ashen.

His heart skipped a beat. "What's wrong?"

Muscles twitched in her face, and her neck corded, sweat coating her paled skin. With a cry, she fell to her knees, balling her other hand to a fist, too, biting into it.

"Isa!" He crouched next to her, his mouth gone dry as desert sand.

"S-seizure," she hissed, panting. "Ugh!"

She doubled over, and he caught her before she hit the dirt.

"I've got you." He pulled her close, but she slapped at him.

"No. I'll be...all right."

Veins stood out starkly on her skin, which had lost its usual warm tone, taken on a sick pallor. Tears gathered in her eyes, and she blinked furiously while breathing fast and shallow, keeping her chin up.

"I don't...need..." She bared her gritted teeth while she panted through what had to be an excruciating wave of pain.

"Yes, you do." He drew her closer, careful not to hold her so tight that it hurt her more. "And you'll let me." He leaned down, spoke in her ear. "Allowing someone to care for you is not weakness, Isa. You don't have to suffer alone. I'm here, I've got you, and I'll help you through this. *Let* me."

With a shuddering breath, and a broken sound in the back of her throat, she closed her eyes, grabbed his shirt, and buried her face against his shoulder. Basil exhaled roughly, stroked her back, and murmured words of encouragement and healing.

He held her through a storm of convulsions, through muffled screams that pierced his soul, through tides of agony so violent, so palpable, he could taste them with every breath. He channeled his despair about his helplessness into unflinching emotional support, into the steady strength of his embrace, poured every ounce of his desire to see her free from pain into the words he whispered in her ear.

When the last of Isa's seizure subsided, leaving her

trembling in his arms, her skin sweat-slick and cold to the touch, he rested his forehead on top of her head, and fought to keep his limbs from trembling along with hers.

Her breath hitched, and she pushed against his chest. He released her, and she came to her feet, staggered to a tree, which she grabbed for purchase.

Eyes downcast, she took a deep breath and said, "Thank you. Your help pays for the favor you owed me for my assistance in guiding you through Faerie and searching for Rose." She inclined her head and turned away.

"What the—" Basil huffed, stood up. "Not everything has to be measured in favors, Isa. I gave my help freely."

"Are you saying you'd rather be beholden to me still?" She peered at him, her warm brown tan returning slowly.

He sighed, linked his hands behind his head. "No, but that's not the point. It's just... Why does it have to be about paying a price? Why not just accept it as kindness?"

She dusted herself off, righted her clothes. "Because asking yourself 'what will this cost me' is the smartest way to stay alive."

"And the fastest way to a life spent alone."

She flinched as if he'd slapped her.

Shit. Basil rubbed a hand over his face. "Look, I didn't mean—"

"Yes, you did. And it's just as well. I appreciate frank

words more than polite lies."

He sighed. "All I'm saying is, there's another way to look at life. Kindness doesn't have to be bought. It shouldn't be."

"You and I," she said quietly, "have lived very different lives, then."

His heart splintered a little at the resignation in her tone. He let out a breath that hurt his lungs, and asked, "What is it you're suffering from?"

"I beg your pardon?"

"Your seizures. What causes them?"

She shrugged, turned her head away. "Nothing important."

"Nu-uh." He stepped in her line of sight again. "You already gave me that spiel. I want to know the truth. How bad is it?"

She wouldn't meet his gaze. "It's curable."

"And you haven't cured it yet because…?" He raised his brows.

A muscle feathered along her jaw, and she shook her head a little. "You saved my life. I need to repay my debt first."

"What? No. We are not traipsing around Faerie with you being attacked by seizures when there's a way to heal you. We'll get your cure, and then we'll go on."

Her throat worked as she swallowed. She finally met his eyes, and the glint in hers made him cringe. "And what about Rose? Did you not say she's likely in danger? You'll just abandon her to her fate?"

He cursed and gripped the nape of his neck. His

stomach was knotted tight, his muscles twitchy with irritation. "You're right. We need to find her first."

"Besides," Isa said, "blood debts such as this must be paid before anything else. Even if it weren't for Rose, I would have to wait until after I save your life to cure my condition."

"That's messed up." He shook his head. "Your health is more important than repaying a favor."

Her chin trembled before she pressed her mouth into a grim line. "Magic doesn't care."

She walked on ahead of him, and he couldn't shake the impression that she'd really meant to say...

No one cares.

~~~

"And this one here," Basil said, pointing at a faint scar on his chin, "I got when Lily decked me after I filled her toothpaste tube with wasabi." He chuckled and ducked to evade a fairy flitting past as he and Isa maneuvered down the busy main street of Lam'il. "It took me several hours to prepare the tube so she wouldn't notice it'd been tampered with. So worth it just to hear her screech when she brushed her teeth."

Isa couldn't help grinning. "She was right to hit you for that."

"Yep. But she took revenge beyond that. When I got dressed the next morning, this horrible itch started in my pants." He slanted a look at her. "She'd dusted my underwear with magical itching powder. I had to shower ten times—*ten*—to get it to stop."

Isa covered her mouth with her hand, a choked chuckle escaping her. "It's a miracle you two didn't kill each other growing up."

"Nah." He shrugged one shoulder. "It was all in good fun. For all the pranks we pulled, we always had each other's back. We shared all our secrets, talked about everything. I had best friends all throughout school, but Lily and I were even closer. Being twins, we —" His sunny expression darkened, like the shadow of clouds blotting out the light. He cleared his throat. "Yeah, so much about that."

"What?"

"It was all a lie, too, wasn't it? We're not twins. I always thought…" He shook his head. "It just hurts."

"Why?"

He faced her, his brows pulling together. "What do you mean, why?"

"Does it change your relationship, knowing you're not of the same blood?"

"Well…"

"When you think about it," Isa ventured, "the bond you two formed is all the more remarkable for not being sparked by a twin relation. You grew up to be so close, not because you shared the same womb, or a blood link, or some sort of psychic twin connection. No, it is because the two of you *forged* it, all on your own. Because you truly care and trust and love each other as family. And that doesn't change now, does it? If your bond did not form because of a blood relation, then the realization that you are adopted cannot weaken it. Lily will always be your sister."

"Damn, you're good at this."

"At what?"

A smile that threatened to turn her knees to rubber. "Calling me out on my bullshit."

She shrugged and averted her eyes, her neck and face flushing. "I call things as I see them, and I don't mince words."

"I like that in a woman." The warm appreciation of his gaze on her made her skin prickle. "Usually Lily's the one to talk sense into me, but I gotta say, I much prefer having you set me straight."

She chanced a glance at him—which was a mistake. The playful wink he sent her zinged right into her bloodstream, causing all sorts of unwelcome tingles.

Along with the surge of desire came a pang of yearning so intense she nearly missed a step—yearning not just for the kind of affection Basil offered, but for the bonds he shared with others. He had loved ones in his life, family and friends, a network of support he could fall back on. Something she never had. His anecdotes and tales painted a picture of people willing to fight for him, to die for him, even if it had to be spelled out for him amid his current doubts.

No one would ever have sacrificed anything for Isa.

...the fastest way to a life spent alone...

Basil's blunt statement echoed in her mind, touched on all the sore spots in her soul, speaking truth to the stubborn illusion she held on to, too afraid to let go.

What must it be like to be part of a larger whole, to be surrounded by people who loved her? She'd never know, would she? Because a network like that, it wasn't built on favors.

Throat raw and aching, she swallowed, jerked her head toward an alley a few paces ahead. "This way."

Rinnar of Stone lived in a mess of a house in a side street off the main road, or rather, the house appeared neglected from the outside, but surprised with splendor within. The fae they sought let them in after they stood waiting for ten minutes, and only after Isa pushed a note through a slit in the door.

"What did you write on it?" Basil asked her in a whisper while Rinnar hurried down the hall ahead of them, past mosaics inlaid in the walls, over expensive-looking rugs, and underneath several chandeliers of glittering crystals.

"That Hathôm received a valuable dagger of palladium for referring us to him," Isa replied in a tone low enough that Rinnar wouldn't hear her, "and that he won't be happy if we may have to return and ask for it back since we didn't even get to meet his source."

Basil chuckled. "Glad your trick worked."

"It usually does with paranoid chumps."

The fae led them into a parlor with gilded mirrors, the finest upholstery on the chairs, and a grandfather clock tick-tocking away in a corner.

"Your house is beautiful," Isa said in English, in an attempt to build some goodwill with the jumpy fae.

"Right." Rinnar turned around to face them, his

hands fidgeting in front of his plump belly. "What ya want?"

So much for polite chit-chat.

"Information."

Rinnar scoffed, moving around the room, straightening things that didn't need straightening. "Don't everybody?"

Isa inclined her head. "Hathôm told us you know of a witch changeling who was brought into Faerie many years ago. We wish to know where you saw her, and anything else you know of her whereabouts."

The twitchy fae paused for a second in rearranging a vase on the mantel above the marble fireplace, and eyed Isa. "Was long ago. Not sure I remember."

Basil shifted his weight next to her, and she gave him a subtle sign with her hand to stand down. "Why don't you recount what you do remember, and maybe the rest of it will come back to you?"

"Why you want to find her?"

Isa took a breath while she measured her words. "She doesn't belong here. It is time for her to go home."

"Why you care?"

"Her mother wants her back."

"She's a changeling," Rinnar said with a shrug, as if that explained everything.

"She's my sister," Basil snarled.

The fae twitched and leveled his attention on Basil for the first time, narrowing his eyes at his ears. "You half human? Give me your blood."

Isa tensed while Basil shook his head.

"I'm fae," he said. "But the witch changeling is the daughter of my adoptive mother. Tell us where you saw her."

Rinnar frowned. "You don't look full fae. You don't feel full fae." With a shake of his head, he added, "Never you mind what you are. Give me bit of your blood, and I tell you what I know."

Isa took a step toward the fae. "No blood will be given. Do not overestimate the value of your intel."

When Rinnar opened his mouth as if to argue, Isa hissed at him. The fae cringed and drew back.

Reordering the crystal bowls on the low table in front of the couch, he said, "You want to know, you pay well. If not blood, then what? Things changing in Faerie. I need security."

Basil shot her a look. "The dagger was the most valuable thing I carry," he whispered. He grasped the nape of his neck with one hand. "Maybe I should just give him my—"

"No." Isa glanced around the luxurious interior, the abundance of precious jewels and shiny noble metals, the high quality of fabric and workmanship in the furniture. With a heavy feeling in her guts, she dove into one of her pockets, pulled out the ruby that would have paid for a brand-new set of armor.

"Here." She held the gemstone out to Rinnar. "This will do."

The fae's face lit up as he beheld the ruby. He made a move for it, but Isa pulled her hand back at the last second.

"Provided," she said, "your intel does give us an exact location. Swear on this stone that you saw her, and that you're telling us the true location."

Rinnar's eyes glittered with avarice. "I swear I tell you truth. I swear on the bloodstone."

Isa nodded and handed him the jewel. "Deal."

The fae snatched the stone and cradled it to his chest. "I saw the witch changeling near the Sar'oa lake. A fae couple had her. They chased me away. Never went back, and don't want no trouble with them."

"Where exactly near Sar'oa?"

"Close to village of Tamnar. Hike from Tamnar toward the lake, one hour, and you find a house in a clearing."

Isa inclined her head. "Be well, Rinnar of Stone."

"Yes, yes." Rinnar shooed them out with a wave of his hand. "Be well."

They walked back through the lavishly decorated hall, Basil's excitement a palpable force. He was all but jumping out of his skin with agitation, and when he turned to her once outside, his eyes sparkled.

"This is it, right? We might be just one step away from finding Rose."

"Or not." For his sake, she wished she could share his enthusiasm, but life had taught her to be less optimistic. "I don't want to smash your hopes, but be prepared for this not to work out. We might have to keep searching."

He released a heavy breath while they made their

way back to the main street. "I am. This is still the best lead we've had so far, and I'd have to be dead not to be thrilled about it." He paused and frowned. "I've been meaning to ask—what did Rinnar mean when he said, 'Things changing in Faerie'?"

Her nerves fluttered, and she took great care to keep looking ahead. "There has been...a disruption of power."

"How so?"

She cleared her throat, which felt far too dry. "Recently, the entire royal court of Faerie was murdered."

Basil halted abruptly. "What?"

She signaled for him to keep moving, and he did.

"How...who..." He shook his head as if to clear it. "What the fuck happened?"

She grimaced. Oh, the tightrope she was walking... "From what I heard, a single attacker entered the throne room and slaughtered them all. The king, the queen, their noble fae..."

"Wait a second." Basil stopped again, grabbed her arm and turned her to face him. "How recently?"

She hesitated. "The night you came to Faerie."

He blinked, his mouth opening. "Holy shit. Do you think the fae who exchanged me was in there? If she was murdered that night, it would explain why my glamour and the spell on Hazel were lifted."

Damn, he was fast. Such an agile mind...

"It's possible," she conceded. "However, Faerie is big, and she could well have lived—and died—

somewhere else."

"Sure. But I don't believe in coincidences, and this smacks of being connected somehow." He frowned, started walking again when she indicated they keep going. "Did they catch the murderer?"

"No."

"Who's in charge now in Faerie?"

She lifted one shoulder in a shrug. "There are some generals who have stepped in to keep the peace while…" A heavy exhale. "I guess they have to find someone who's next of kin to the royals but wasn't in the throne room. Some distant relative, maybe? I don't know."

She peered at Basil out of the corner of her eye. If not for his mixed heritage, *he* would qualify to contend for the throne. Provided he lived… Which, considering her plans, he wouldn't, so it was a moot point.

Shaking off that line of thinking, she continued, "But there is talk about someone completely new taking over. Some are saying it's time for fresh blood. A new line of royals, not related to the old ones."

Basil was silent for a moment. "That's going to be messy."

Again, he'd grasped it, his mind truly quick on the uptake.

She sighed. "Yeah. It's quite possible there'll be some sort of civil war if this escalates. The military might keep some of it in check, but if there's discord among the generals regarding whose claim to support, Faerie will bleed."

"Damn." He shook his head. "The fae who slaughtered the court sure did some major damage. What's their motive, if not to usurp the throne?"

Isa raised her brows. "Well...let's put it this way—every single member of the royal court had blood on their hands, and—as the humans say—an entire graveyard in their closet."

Basil snorted, then caught himself. "Skeletons."

"What?"

"The idiom is 'skeletons in the closet.'" His grin made her stomach flip.

"Right." She cleared her throat. "The fae nobility has been corrupted by cruelty over time, and all of them had more than one skeleton in their closets. Enough to give plenty of people plenty of reasons to take bloody revenge."

"Are you saying they all deserved to die?"

"No." Her chest drew tight with the knowledge she was among those with blood on their hands. Or, at least she'd helped the royal fae bloody *their* hands. Still, the sins of her past paled in comparison to the rotting darkness that had pervaded the court.

"I didn't wish for them to die," she said, her gaze on the intricate wood carvings in the facade of a house up ahead. "But I don't mourn them either."

Basil exhaled through his nose. "Considering the threat of unrest here in Faerie, I'd say it's even more urgent to get Rose out."

Isa nodded. "Then let's pick up the pace."

12

"I can't believe Faerie is this big." Basil stopped and leaned against a tree.

Isa halted as well, and sat down on the trunk of a fallen fir. Her feet ached. Even though she was used to traveling long distances on foot when she was in pursuit of a fugitive, she still felt the toll of the day's hiking keenly.

"We do sort of…expand the territory a little," she admitted.

"What?" Basil stopped with his water bottle—made of some lightweight metal, from what she could tell—halfway to his mouth.

"Well, Faerie has the habit of…growing. But not outward. It's more of a mirroring and folding of space, while nominally staying within the borders that were once set."

"So…it's like a TARDIS?"

"A what?"

"So many movies, so many shows…" he muttered to himself, rubbing a hand over his face. Focusing on her, he said, "It's bigger on the inside than it looks from the outside."

"Yes." She grinned. "That's a good way of putting it."

He took a swig from his water and offered her some as well. "All right, how much longer until we reach that village?"

She drank a bit, calculated in her head. "I'd say probably another five hours."

"Good gawds." He banged his head against the tree.

Eyeing the rising moon, she said, "We could rest for the night. We've been hiking all day, but we still have quite some distance to cover. I don't think it's a good idea to keep going right now."

He let out a heavy breath. "Yeah, I sure am beat. Sleep does sound good."

"I saw what looked like a cave not too long ago. We can double back and see if we can camp there. It'll be good to have a roof above us in case it rains." The next settlement was too far away, but they did have enough gear with them to spend the night in the woods in relative comfort.

"Sure." Basil fell into step beside her while she backtracked. "We'll have—"

"Dinner, yes. For the second time."

He bumped his shoulder against hers. "You know me so well, Isa of Stone."

It occurred to her that, yes, she did. To bide their time, eager to distract herself from maudlin pondering, she'd asked Basil to tell her about himself during the long hours of their hike, and he'd obliged with the cheerful openness that was as much a part of him as the gold silk of his hair—which her fingers still remembered, a sensory memory she was constantly tempted to repeat. Over the course of the day, she had to physically restrain herself from reaching out and touching him again so many times, had to curl her fingers into her palm instead, hard enough to snap herself out of the wave of need riding her.

Every time Basil tried to shift the conversation to her, she managed to derail him by following up on something he said with another, more specific question about him, and he took the bait, seemed delighted that she showed such interest in him.

She would have felt bad about deceiving him... except she wasn't. Not anymore. The more she learned about him, the more she wanted him to keep talking. She found herself entranced by his voice, by the calm yet serene way he spoke about his life, and she wanted to know even more about how he saw the world. She'd always been better at listening than talking anyway, and yet she'd never before met anyone she wanted to listen to for more than an hour.

Basil, however, could talk to her all day, and she didn't mind it one bit. In fact, she soaked it all up, and relished the way listening to him calmed her thoughts.

Now, as they sat at the mouth of the cave in front of the crackling fire, her belly full of the stew Basil prepared—damn, but that male could cook up something delicious, even in such meager surroundings as a cave out in the woods—she was caught unawares when he leveled the full force of his quiet attention on her and asked, "When was the last time you laughed?"

Blinking, her mind slow in coming back from late-night idleness, she opened her mouth, closed it, glancing around the cave...anywhere except him.

Basil shook his head. "Too long ago, then."

It was true. She couldn't even remember the last time she laughed out loud.

He sat with one leg stretched out in front of him, the other cocked up, had his elbow on his raised knee and put his chin on his hand, looking at her with such disconcerting, thoughtful, *caring* focus, it rattled her.

"Tell me," he said with a smile that set her nerves aflutter, "what makes you laugh?"

The way he regarded her...so unapologetically interested in her, as if he truly cared about her as a person, a friend...a lover—if she let him. The affection in his gaze hurt her heart, not because it was wrong, or unappreciated, but because it touched upon long-neglected parts of her, and like a muscle that hadn't been used in a while, the feelings he stirred in her ached from being activated after years—decades—of disuse. His attention made her feel special, treasured, as if she was someone worth looking at, listening to... caring about.

Quickly shaking off those feelings before they pulled her under, she cleared her throat and said, "The hardest I've ever laughed..." She broke off, grimaced and shifted her weight. "No, I can't tell you. It's too embarrassing."

Basil perked up. "Well, now you've *got* to tell me. No teasing. Spit it out."

She took a breath, looked down at her hands. "There was this cat…"

A giggle bubbled up from some half-forgotten corner of her heart, and interrupted her. She tried to stifle the laughter with a hand over her mouth, and forced herself to continue, but barely managed two more words before the full memory washed over her and laid waste to her composure.

She laughed so hard she was gasping for breath, with tears running down her face and her body tingling, nerve endings alive with delight, her chest light even as she struggled to draw in air in between her giggles.

"I'd urge you to calm down and tell the whole story," Basil said with a chuckle, "but to be honest, just watching you laugh this hard is way more fun."

"All right," she choked out, catching her breath while waving her hands in wait-a-minute signal, "all right. When I was out in the humanlands on a case, I once saw this cat sitting on a porch. I went to pet it."

She wiped tears from her cheeks. "It was very majestic-looking and dignified, but then…" She stifled another bout of giggles. "…it had to sneeze"—giggles erupted from her again—"and…" Flopping down on her sleeping mat, she succumbed to belly-aching laughter.

Basil started chuckling along with her. "And?"

"—it farted, at the same time." She had to laugh so hard, her entire body shook, every muscle sore and tingling.

Basil choked out a laugh of his own. "It *snarted*?"

"Snart?" She wiped at her eyes.

He grinned. "Sneeze-fart. It's a thing."

More giggles burst forth, and she nodded, caught her breath. "Yes," she said, with the very best straight face she could muster. "The majestic cat snarted."

"I can't believe it." He shook his head, still smiling. "Serious Isa is amused by fart humor."

"I know," she wheezed. "It's so silly."

"I like silly," Basil said with a wink. "In fact, nothing's too silly for me. My favorite movie is *Spaceballs*."

Still snickering and wiping her face, she said, "I don't know that one either."

"I'll show you. When we're done with all this. I'll take you home with me, and we'll watch *Spaceballs*. Of course, we'll have to watch *Star Wars* first, otherwise you won't get all the goofy references."

Her carefree amusement died as the reality of her situation doused her happiness like a bucket of ice water. She wouldn't ever get to watch those movies with him. Or do anything fun at all with Basil. And she didn't have the right to. She didn't have the right to enjoy his affection, didn't deserve to be the center of his attention. Oh, why couldn't she have met him under different circumstances? Why couldn't he have been someone else, someone she was free to like back, to care for?

Someone she didn't have to kill…

Pain more awful than what wracked her during the seizures raked through her, made her gasp.

How could she kill him now? Now she'd gotten to know him, now she'd glimpsed the warmth of his soul, the sunshine of his personality.

I don't want to take his life. A visceral thought, risen from the depths of her heart of stone, which yet had softened for this impossible male who so audaciously cared for her, who tumbled headlong into the challenges of life.

Survive, a voice whispered in her mind. *You need to survive at all costs.*

At all costs… But what good would it be to survive when what she had to do to stay alive would kill her inside?

"Hey." Basil's voice, breaking through her sinister thoughts. All laughter gone from his face, he studied her with concern in those eyes of myriad earth tones. "What just happened? You look like someone died."

Her breath hitched. "I need to go…take care of nature's call. Don't wait up. You can go ahead and settle down to sleep."

She jumped up and sprinted off before he could reply.

Whatever was tenuously budding between them, it was cursed, just as she was. No matter which way she turned it, she'd never be able to be with him. Either she snuffed out the flame of his life, or her own would fade into eternal darkness.

~~~

Basil watched Isa rush away from him as if fleeing from a soul-sucker demon. The rustle of the brush died down as she got farther away, leaving him alone with the silence of the night and the crackling fire.

Well, hell. That escalated quickly.

What in the world had gotten into her? One minute she was doubled over with laughter, her gray eyes alight with such infectious humor, his heart had filled with joy, and the next she looked so crestfallen and in pain, as if she'd lost everything dear to her.

Was it something he said? He frowned, poked the fire with a stick. What could have set her off like that?

Shaking his head, he leaned back against the cave wall. Just when he thought he'd made progress with her, she shut down and ran off. If only she'd tell him why she felt she had to keep her distance, maybe they could work on it together and figure it out. He'd love to help her with whatever made her hesitate to relax with him.

He loved seeing the glow on her face when she listened to him talk while they hiked during the day, the spark in her eyes when she asked him questions about his life. That was real interest.

When his high school buddies had regularly complained about not understanding girls, Basil was the one to point out subtleties and complexities in the females' attitude and explain them to his friends. To Basil, these things were clear as day, and he'd always been stumped when guys he hung out with acted like women were an enigmatic, irrational alien species.

Perhaps he understood the nuances of female behavior because he grew up in a community dominated by women—witch families were notoriously matriarchal—and the women in his life had always played a bigger role than men. But in any case, he never had a problem understanding females, their body language, and behavioral cues, just as well as men's. He knew when a woman was truly interested in him versus just making nice conversation or being friendly, and he picked up on even the subtlest nonverbal hints of a female rejecting him, which he always respected.

Isa, however… She was sending mixed messages. No clear rejection yet, rather she was vacillating between attraction and retreat. As if she was waging some kind of war with herself about whether to give in to whatever was growing between them.

He'd be only too happy to help her tip the scale toward giving in.

13

"Merle."

Hazel's voice yanked Merle out of the book she'd been buried in for the better part of the night. Pages upon pages of witch genealogy, archived history, and accounts from communities all over the world. This was the third tome she'd gone through today, all of them from the Murrays' family library. She already flipped through the archival records at home, had then joined Hazel at the mansion to spend the evening scouring whatever books the Murrays had on witch history.

"Hm?" she asked in noncommittal exhaustion, rubbing her closed eyes with both hands.

"I found something," Hazel said.

It was the odd tone of the Elder witch's voice that caused Merle to sit up straight, foreboding skittering down her spine like a centipede.

"There is one account here of a witch your age who had to assume the position of head of her family, and then became pregnant."

Merle swallowed, her stomach cramping. "And?"

Hazel lowered her eyes, a pained look on her face.

"Let me read it." Merle sounded raw even to her own ears, as raw as her throat felt.

With trembling hands, she took the book from Hazel, focused on the page. The more she read, the more her chest caved in and her breathing flattened out. *No.*

Rhun's presence brushed up against her skin as he entered the library, his concern flowing along the mating bond. "What is it?"

"We found—" Hazel began, but Merle cut her off.

"She lost it," she whispered, the heat of tears prickling in her eyes. "The only other witch who became pregnant while head of her family. She lost the baby because her family members continued to use magic and she had to uphold the balance." Her lungs seized, her heart shattered. "She stayed childless for the rest of her life." She stifled her sob with both shaking hands over her mouth, closed her eyes, and wept silently.

Warm darkness enveloped her senses, Rhun's power stroking over her mind, her heart, soothing the firestorm within her. He pulled her into his arms, held her head against his chest, his hand on her hair.

No words. He had no words for her this time, neither out loud nor in the intimacy of their shared mental connection. She knew why he remained silent. Anything he had to say had already been said, and repeating it now, with her soul in tatters and her emotions bleeding, would only send her tumbling further into despair. For there was nothing to say from his standpoint but to state the only logical step and do what had to be done to save their baby.

And yet the thought of pushing Maeve into the claws of the Demon Lord, of severing their family connection and ceding magical custodianship over her to Arawn was so inconceivable, so utterly sickening. How could she do this to her baby sister? After what she'd been through?

Merle cried until there were no more tears in her, until her chest ached, hollow and arid, the fiber of her soul so brittle it might crumble at any moment. With a last sniffle, she pushed away from Rhun, shook her head at the question in his eyes.

Please don't, she sent along the connection to his mind. *I need more time.*

Because the fiercest, most stubborn part of her clung with bloody fingers to an impossible hope.

I've always loved your stubbornness, Rhun replied mentally, *but there are things I will not budge on, either.* Such torment in his eyes, twisted pain in his soul—and the promise of steel in the tone of his psychic voice.

Understood, she whispered in his mind.

And she did. Time was running out, and she was racing far behind.

Hazel had silently left the room some time ago, and they found her in the kitchen when they went to say good-bye. She hugged Merle tight, a thousand loving, encouraging words in the warmth of that gesture, and accompanied them to the front of the house.

They were crossing the foyer underneath the massive chandelier when the doorbell rang. Hazel stopped short, glanced at the clock, which showed one in the morning.

"At this hour?" she murmured.

Since Merle and Rhun had been on the verge of leaving anyway, they followed her out to the main gate, where the nighttime visitor waited just beyond the perimeter of the magical wards protecting the Murray property. Rhun stepped in front of Merle as they approached, subtly reminded her to stay back—where normally he had no issue acknowledging that she was more powerful in terms of magic, he'd now firmly assumed the role of her protector, since she needed to use as little magic as possible.

Hazel stepped up to the gate, opened it with a flick of her hand. The wrought-iron fence was mostly for show anyway, for human eyes and perceptions. Any otherworld creature worth its salt would be able to scale a barrier like it; the *wards* kept out intruders of the supernatural sort.

And those protections remained in place, making sure the fae who waited on the sidewalk didn't take a step closer.

"Good evening," the female said, and inclined her head.

Light brown skin, blond hair flowing over her shoulders, and age-old fae power rolling off her, the visitor looked expectantly at Hazel, who stood frozen in place. Her energy pattern fluctuated wildly, and

Merle wished she could read auras as well as Lily just so she could figure out what was going on with Hazel.

"You…" the Elder witch whispered.

"I have come for the changeling."

A second, a heartbeat, of utterly speechless shock, which was written plainly on Hazel's face—and then she lost it. With a move almost too fast for Merle to follow, Hazel struck, her magic pulsing in the night air. Merle flinched when Hazel's spell hit the fae, bound her to the spot with a powerful paralysis charm.

Whoa, Rhun said in Merle's mind. *What's gotten into Hazel?*

I don't know, Merle replied, frowning. Given that Hazel had been eager to find a fae to take her into Faerie, and that, apparently, this was the fae who had brought Basil here all those years ago, such an aggressive move on Hazel's part didn't make sense.

The head of the Murray family advanced on the fae, twisting her hand to jack up the paralysis spell. Power crackled around her like an electric charge.

"I come…in peace…" the fae choked out.

"The hell you do." Hazel flashed her teeth, and Merle almost stumbled back at the fierce expression on her usually sweet face. "You have picked the wrong time to play with me. I have been worried sick about my daughter in Faerie, and now about my son, too, after he left without a word, while I have been stuck here waiting, waiting, *waiting,* when I should be out there protecting my children…and then *you* show up out of the blue, so convenient, so fitting, but I am done playing your game. I have no patience left to hear whatever lies you want to spin now, and you will find I am no longer the witch you coerced to do your bidding twenty-six years ago!"

With a primal, rage-filled scream, Hazel hurled another spell at the fae, her hands weaving in the air to form the most powerful truth charm known to witchkind, used to nullify even the strongest enchantments.

The fae gasped, jerked, and fell to her knees. Eyes widened in shock as Hazel renewed the paralysis spell again on top of the truth compulsion, the fae coughed, wheezed—and then her features changed.

As if melting under great heat, the lines of her face sagged, blurred, as did the rest of her body. Her appearance dissolved, gave way to another form. A male fae emerged in her stead—no, not a fae. Merle inhaled sharply as the unmistakable energy of a demon brushed her senses.

Now I have seen everything, Rhun muttered in her mind.

Merle couldn't agree more.

Golden blond hair, light skin with just the hint of a warm tan, the youthful look of a male in his prime, the demon's features reminded her of... Before Merle could make the connection, Hazel spoke.

"Who are you?"

The demon obviously struggled, trying to not to reply, but the truth spell pulled the answer out of him like a dentist yanked out a tooth. "The changeling's father."

Merle grabbed Rhun to steady herself. His shock vibrated along their mating bond, a mirror of her own. Nothing compared to Hazel's reaction. Her face blanched, her energy so palpable it felt like a whip.

"But you're a demon," she whispered.

"Yes," he ground out.

"What kind?"

"Hæmingr."

Frowning, Hazel looked at Rhun.

He cleared his throat. "Power-stealing shapeshifter demons."

"What is your name?" Hazel asked of the hæmingr.

He panted, his effort not to answer straining all the muscles in his neck, transforming his beautiful face into a hard mask. "Tallak."

"Tell me everything," Hazel rasped.

"Let me go," he grunted, "and I will explain."

"No." Hazel's voice sliced through the air like a blade. "You will remain under my spell until I am satisfied you have told me all you know. You are in no position to negotiate, and you better not try my patience, demon."

Well now, Rhun said mentally, *Hazel's not messing around, is she? Never thought I'd see her with zero fucks to give.*

You truly have a way with words, my darling demon.

She felt his grin more than saw it.

"Speak," Hazel growled. "Start at the beginning. How come you had a child with a fae?"

The demon—Tallak—grunted, then succumbed to the force of the truth compulsion. "I saw her—Roana—when she traveled outside of Faerie. I fell for her, courted her, and we became lovers, but she had to return to her people. She was part of the royal court, was called back to serve. She didn't want to leave me, so she brought me with her. Since demons are forbidden in Faerie, I had to conceal myself. When I couldn't hide, I would kill fae to take their powers and mimic their auras. It went well for a while. She became pregnant, and we made plans to flee Faerie. We were almost ready to leave when I was caught."

He panted, pain etching lines on his face. "Demon-fae offspring are a sin, an abomination to the fae. They do not permit them to live. Roana and I had an agreement—she was to run if my cover was blown, in order to save our child. Roana managed to escape before they got to her. They imprisoned me, for they do not know how to kill my kind, and they sent someone after her to bring her back. When the bounty hunter dragged her into the palace, they brought me out to watch before they locked me away again. She was almost at full term, and…"

A heaving breath, darkness pooling around him like a dismal cloak. "Even in my prison cell, news about the delivery reached me. She died in childbirth, and the babe along with her. At least that is what they told me —it wasn't until I escaped, after preparing it for twenty long years, wanting to take revenge on the whole rotten lot of them, that I learned the baby had survived.

I had slaughtered the damned pack in their pompous room of marble and gold, but the last one I intended to kill stayed my hand with her revelation that she'd smuggled my child out. She told me where to find him. My son."

His voice turned to a rasp, and something fractured in his gaze. "I have come for...my son."

Silence boomed in the night, only interrupted by Tallak's heavy breaths.

Is anyone writing this down? Rhun asked. *This would make one hell of a story.*

Merle poked him in his ribs with her elbow. *Shush.*

"Where is he?" Tallak asked, focused on Hazel. "Where is my boy?"

"Not here," she croaked. "He's gone into Faerie."

"What?"

She swallowed. "He's looking for my daughter, Rose, the one who was taken from me in exchange for Basil."

"Basil..." He frowned, his voice turning into a growl. "You named him after an herb?"

Rhun laughed. Merle poked him again, hard enough to make him wince.

I'm sorry, he said in her mind, the humor in his mental voice belying his apology. *This is just too good.*

Hazel flicked her wrist, and Tallak uttered a pained sound. "I would expect the father of the bright boy I raised to be smarter than to insult a witch while in her grasp."

Tallak glowered at her.

I wish I had popcorn, Rhun said.

You don't even eat regular food. Merle graced him with her death glare.

I would for this.

"Do you know anything about Rose?" Hazel asked. "About where she is in Faerie and how she is doing?"

"No. The fae who told me about my son didn't mention a witch changeling."

The magic pulsing around Hazel darkened.

"How do your powers work?" Hazel demanded. "You said you can absorb someone's powers...after killing them?"

"Yes." Spoken through gritted teeth. Tallak's eyes glowed amber while he stared at Hazel. "Taking the life of an otherworld creature means I can steal their magic and their memories."

"Forever?"

He struggled some more, grunted, then said, "No. It will last anywhere from a couple of days to two weeks."

Hazel was silent, her forehead furrowed, her aura vibrating. "You said you slaughtered the royal court of Faerie. Did you take all of their magic?"

A grunt, then, "Yes."

Holy powers. Merle was glad Tallak remained under Hazel's spell and on the other side of the wards. If he were to roam around unchecked...

"This happened last night?" Hazel asked.

"Yes."

"So you'll have fae powers for at least another day?"

"Probably even longer." The annoyed look on Tallak's face left no doubt that he'd rather have kept that info to himself.

"You said you can steal someone's memories, too. Did you steal those of the fae you killed?"

"Yes," he hissed. "It happens automatically when I absorb their powers."

"Then you know how to take non-fae into Faerie?"

"I do."

Hazel studied him for a few seconds, her resolve settling over her like the finest armor. "You will take me into Faerie, and together we'll search for Basil, and when we find him, we'll look for Rose. I will bind you to me, Tallak, so don't think you can skip and run. Try to harm me, and it will backfire on you. Understood?"

"Yes." The amber of his eyes glowed in the night as if lit with an inner fire, the harshness of his features promising Hazel retribution.

"Will you take Lily?" Merle asked Hazel.

She shook her head. "We don't know how long the trip will take, and Lily can't be away from Alek for more than one night, since she needs his *prana*. And Alek can't come along with us."

Right. His job as Arawn's enforcer would keep him here. If he wanted to take some time off to go into Faerie, he'd have to ask Arawn...and none of them wanted Alek to be forced to ask Arawn for anything else after he bargained his freedom away to the Demon Lord in order to help Lily.

"I'm sorry I can't go with you," Merle said.

"Don't worry, it's fine." Hazel gave her a reassuring smile. "Even if you can't use your magic right now, your presence here should keep Juneau and her witches on their toes. If she finds out I left, at least she'll think you're still here to hold down the fort, and she won't be as tempted to try an attack. Although it's best if she doesn't even find out. You need to make sure word doesn't get out that I'm gone—or that you're holding back on using your powers. Let her think our ranks are still strong."

Merle nodded.

Hazel turned to Tallak again, who was still on his knees outside the wards' perimeter, looking pissed as hell. "Let's go find my children."

"He's not yours," Tallak snarled. "He's *my* son."

Merle had never seen Hazel as cold as when she looked at Tallak now, her eyes narrowing. "I nursed him, I bathed him, I rocked him to sleep. I wiped his tears and heard his first laugh. He took his first steps on my hand, and ran into my arms when he was scared. I have loved him as much as my own flesh and blood daughter, and he is *mine* in every way that counts. You'd do well to accept that, demon."

Please tell me we can plant a camera on them when they go, Rhun said mentally. *I'd pay money to watch this unfold.*

Merle pinched him.

What? he asked, his face oh-so innocent. *This is better than any telenovela.*

~~~

Calâr retreated farther into the shadowy bushes across from the Murray mansion while continuing to watch the surprising scene playing out in front of the house. His disappointment over arriving just after Tallak— even though he'd raced to make up for the head start the demon got when he left the throne room— morphed into thrilling anticipation when he learned the young half-breed had already taken off into Faerie.

Such potential, so close to his grasp. He could still make it, could reach Roana's child—Basil—before the witch and the demon got to him. And then, if he played his cards right, he could win the boy's trust, and finally be able to test the limits of the possible.

Three hundred years he'd been waiting for an opportunity like this. That precious piece of knowledge in the annals of fae history, deliberately drowned into oblivion for fear of someone *using* it, and all that was left was the shallow hatred of demon-fae offspring to the point that any half-breeds—as rare as they were— were murdered on sight.

It still boggled Calâr's mind that not one of those once privy to the truth had ever entertained the vision and ambition to *use* this gift. How could they see this chance for greatness—and not grasp it?

Well, all the better for him that no one else had ever done it. He certainly didn't want to be on the other side of that equation when it came to pass.

Now he just had to make sure to delay the Murray

witch and Tallak while he raced into Faerie. But how? His mind worked furiously.

There was one major road into Faerie from here, the fastest route. He could take it but make sure to cause some sort of massive disruption behind him to block the road for a while. Tallak and the witch would either have to wait until the way cleared, or find an alternate route into Faerie. Both would buy him time.

Enough to find the half-breed first.

14

Pain.

Isa's body was on fire. Waves of needle-fine agony rolled through her, followed by torrents of twisting, crushing, stinging pain while her organs were being compressed to the point of exploding.

Yanked out of the depths of sleep, her mind blanked at the pain wracking her body. Thoughts and impressions and lingering images of a dream fizzled into nothingness in the face of such devastating torment that an involuntary scream tore from her.

Pain and darkness—and a taste of death, drawing ever closer.

Through the flaming ruins of her mind, a voice filtered, made it past the lightning bolts of agony shooting through her nerves.

…got you…here…fine…

Every cell seemed to tear apart, her skin dissolving in acid.

That voice again, breaking through her pain, fighting it back.

"It's all right. I've got you. I'm here. You'll be fine. You'll be fine."

Basil.

With a choked sob, she pried her eyes open, and the boundaries of her world began and ended with his face. Even in the dark of the night, the fire having long burned down, every contour and line of his features was so clear, so vivid, finely honed like the marble sculptures of ancient human civilizations, beauty set in stone.

Her hand shot up of its own accord, her fingers gliding over his cheek, his nose, his lips. His eyes widened. The flecks of light brown in them sparked, shone like crystals struck by the sun.

"You're so beautiful," she whispered.

Another wave of pain slammed into her, and she dropped her hand, balled it into a fist. Basil pulled her closer into his arms, buried his face in her neck, one hand on the back of her head, stroking her hair. He murmured words of comfort, a trembling edge of agony in his voice, as if he, too, was hurting.

She grabbed on to him, dug her fingers into his shirt, held on to him for dear life. He was her anchor, keeping her afloat in a sea of torment, making sure she didn't drown.

When the last sting of the seizure subsided, she found herself with her nose pressed to the crook of his neck, inhaling the warm earth of his scent. His heat seeped into her bones. He was still stroking her hair, his breath fanning against her ear. They both moved their heads at the same time, and in the next second, her lips brushed over his.

The fine cascade of pleasure that ran through her rocked her to the core, made her gasp. He studied her reaction, with his face so close to hers there was hardly any space between them, and slowly, deliberately, returned the soft kiss. Her nerve endings lit up again— this time with arousal.

Her mind still raw from the seizure, she wasn't thinking, her guard stripped away, exposing the hungry, primal creature underneath. She leaned forward, met his mouth again, with more pressure and urgency. More, she wanted *more*.

His fingers tangled in her hair as he obliged her request, thrust his tongue between her lips. Reason and sense nullified by the storm of pain that had wrecked her, she only craved, demanded, *needed*.

She rolled her body against his, seeking more touch to wash away the memory of pain. He half-groaned into her mouth, and gently bit her lip as he moved his hand down from her head over her back to her butt, pulled her against him—and his hardening shaft.

Feeling his desire for her fired off another cascade of sparks. She rotated her hips, rubbing against him, and moaned when he tightened his grip on her bottom. His mouth moved to her neck, where he kissed and licked along the lines of her throat. What would it be like to feel the heat of his tongue against her nipple? Within the flash of a second, nothing else mattered more than finding out.

She slid her hands to her front, unbuckled the clasps that held her reinforced tunic together, fumbled with the tie on her undergarment.

"Let me," he murmured and took over.

Less than a heartbeat later, he pushed aside the fabric covering her breasts, and the chill night air brushed her skin. Her nipples pebbled, anxious for his touch. And he didn't make her wait.

Tracing the dark ring of her areola with one finger, he pinched her tight bud between thumb and forefinger, just enough to make her back bow and her breasts strain toward him.

"Your mouth," she rasped. "I want your mouth."

The glint in his eyes mirrored the wickedness of his smile. "So demanding." He licked over her nipple, then blew on it. "So perfect," he whispered, and closed his mouth over her breast.

He sucked, let her feel his teeth, made her writhe under the zings of pleasure that arrowed straight down to the juncture between her legs. Molten lust flowed through her, centered throbbing in the spot she wanted him to touch above all others.

As if reading her thoughts, he brought his hand from her bottom to the front of her hips, cupped her over the fabric of her pants. She uttered a choked sound at the wonderful pressure of his hand on her aching core, and rubbed herself against his fingers.

Her nerves were on fire, for the best of reasons.

He moved on to her other breast, licked and nipped and sucked until she was strung tighter than a bowstring drawn back with an arrow. Her arousal had reached the level of dull pain, and she craved relief with a force that made her tremble.

Ever attuned to her needs, he made short work of the fastening of her pants and slid his hand inside, through her intimate curls to the swollen, sensitive flesh already slick with her desire.

Ye Fates.

Dropping her head back against the ground, she closed her eyes on a sigh, while she succumbed to shivers of pleasure at his touch. He slid two fingers inside her while he rubbed the heel of his hand over her mound, massaged the throbbing center of her arousal at the same time as he pumped his fingers in and out of her.

His teeth brushed over her nipple—and then he bit.

Starbursts of pleasure behind her eyes, an earthquake of lust and sweet, sweet relief rocking her body, warm bliss surging into every last corner of her soul.

He did something wicked, a twist of his hand, another finger added—and she came apart at the seams once more in a vicious, addictive high of an orgasm unlike anything she'd ever experienced.

She floated down from that rush of rapture, aided by hungry kisses on her cleavage, her neck, while the gleaming gold of Basil's hair became her focal point, the night air chill on her exposed skin…and those torn-down walls of reason and sense rose again. She blinked at the twisted reality she'd allowed to unfold.

Oh, no. She hadn't actually—

She bit back her sound of dismay. When her eyes met Basil's, she shook her head, pulling her garments together over her chest.

"I shouldn't have done that." She scooted out of his arms, struggled to her feet. With trembling hands, she fastened her pants. "I'm sorry. This can't happen again."

"Why not?" Basil sat up, his expression part lingering lust, part open concern, with a hint of frustration. "Talk to me, Isa. I'm sure we can work it out."

"Not this," she whispered, her heart twisting into a knot of barbed wire.

She shook her head again when he wanted to argue, grabbed her sleeping mat, and moved it over to another corner of the cave. Lying down with her back to him, she closed her eyes tight, gritted her teeth. Her body still tingled from his touch, her core throbbing with the aftershocks of the most exquisite pleasure she'd ever felt.

She wanted nothing more than to crawl back to him, to give him the same kind of pleasure, to see him come apart under her caresses. She yearned to fall asleep in his arms instead of five feet away from him, wrapped in the shame of her thoughtlessness.

Because thoughtless she'd been. She should have never let it come this far, should never have encouraged the passion between them to flare into a blinding blaze. It wasn't fair to him.

She needed to save his life soon, before her soul broke under the pressure.

~~~

Basil flopped down face first on his sleeping bag and stifled a groan of frustration. His cock was so hard and aching, he thought he might explode like an untried teenager. His fingers still carried the scent of Isa's arousal, driving him crazy with lust.

Gods *damn*, but she'd been so passionate, so unrestrained, demanding her pleasure, begging for his touch, and he'd been more than happy to deliver. After that first kiss, he'd known there lurked a fierce hunger underneath her composure, but this just now? It had blown his estimate of the level of her passion out of the water.

And, of course, now his desire to get her naked and riding him into blissful oblivion had only increased a gazillionfold.

Based on her retreat, however, that option seemed highly unlikely to ever become a reality. She'd apologized to him. *Apologized.* As if she'd done something wrong. What was going on with her? What was the reason behind her adamant resistance to give in to her attraction to him? How bad did it have to be that she couldn't even tell him? *I just don't get it.*

He thumped his forehead on the ground a few times and valiantly tried to convince his balls to just let it go and stop hurting. By the Powers, she was killing him.

15

"I think this is it." Isa stopped and pointed at something in the distance.

Basil stepped up to her side on top of the little hill and looked. Nestled into the trees across the clearing was a small cottage, seemingly fused with the pines surrounding it.

"Let me guess," he said, "wood fae?"

"Looks like it."

It had taken them all morning to hike to the lake and find the dwelling Rinnar had described, Isa's hawk keeping them company. At one point, the raptor had dropped a dead mouse at his feet, and Isa insisted he ought to take it as a compliment. Now the noon sun hid behind a layer of clouds, the rarely-changing winter sky of Oregon. They were lucky it hadn't rained while they'd been on the road.

Basil's lingering consternation about the status quo between him and Isa—they hadn't talked about last night, and Isa had gone back to treating him with friendly distance—dissolved in the face of his anticipation and the thrill buzzing in his blood. This was it. The house of the couple who supposedly took in Rose. She could be in there, right now. Luck willing, he'd be able to leave for Portland again today, with Rose.

And Isa?

Damn, there it was again, that sting in his chest, that cramping in his guts. She still owed him a life debt, so she'd probably have to come with him, but how would things go on between them? How could he help her resolve what forced her to keep her distance to the point that she wouldn't even let him in emotionally?

He rubbed a hand over his face and sighed. First things first. *Find Rose, get her out.*

"Let's go," he said to the fae who had become his own personal addiction.

Isa nodded, unfastened her bow, and drew an arrow.

"Good idea," he murmured while he did the same, nocking his arrow on the bow's string without pulling it yet. He'd be ready to shoot within a second.

They advanced on the house while keeping to the cover of the trees surrounding the clearing. He scanned the area for any signs of movement. Squirrels rustled in the leaves on the ground, the branches of the trees. Here and there a bird startled, flying from its perch on top of a pine.

Not a hint of magic in the air, neither witch nor fae. Which didn't have to mean anything—Rose and her captors might simply not be using any of their powers right now.

Isa stopped about a yard away from the cottage, her forehead furrowed.

"What is it?" he whispered close to her ear.

She shivered, inclined her head toward him the tiniest bit. "Even for wood fae architecture," she whispered back, "this looks almost too overgrown."

She indicated the facade of the cottage with a nod, and he saw what she meant. Creeper plants covered the walls of the house until the windows were barely visible. The intricately carved wooden front door stood a foot ajar, and vines twined around it in a way that made it clear the door had been open for quite a while.

His heart sank. "You think it's abandoned?"

"Let's find out."

With their arrows still nocked and ready to shoot, they approached the front door. When Basil wanted to go in first, Isa bumped him back with her shoulder.

At his glare, she said in a hushed voice, "Life debt, remember?"

He tightened his jaw, nodded, and stepped back. Isa pressed herself to the wall next to the door, her bow with the nocked arrow raised and pointed toward the opening of the front door. With her foot inching forward, she pushed the door open farther.

The loud creak of the old hinges made them both cringe.

Great. If anyone was there, they'd sure know someone was sneaking up on them now.

Isa apparently figured as much, for she rushed inside, her weapon at the ready. Basil followed her a second later. His eyes adjusted to the gloom within a heartbeat, and he took in the dilapidated state of the room.

Roots had grown through cracks in the wooden floor, vines crept in from holes in the ceiling and the walls, old furniture lay overturned, coated with dust. No one had lived here for quite some time now. Basil exhaled, lowered his bow halfway.

Isa checked all nooks and crannies, keeping her arrow ready to shoot, despite all signs pointing to them being alone. "Basil," she said quietly, her gaze on something on the floor.

He joined her, examined what she'd uncovered with her foot. A wooden doll, recognizable as a toy, even though it had been assaulted by time and neglect.

His pulsed raced. "She was here."

"It could be another child's."

"And how likely is that?"

She inclined her head, conceded his point. "It's been many years since a child lived here, though. Since anyone lived here."

He huffed out a breath. "Yeah."

A scratching sound came from the other room.

They both whirled around with their arrows ready to fly, aimed at the door. His pulse a fast drumbeat in his ears, Basil followed Isa as she approached the other room. Before she ever made it there, the door burst open with a bang—and a swarm of flying creatures poured out.

Isa's arrows swished as fast as the flutter of the fae's

wings, downing half a dozen of them. "Kill them!" she yelled at Basil. "They're flesh-eating."

The fuck?

But he was already jumping into action, firing one arrow after another, each one finding its bloody aim. The fae creatures screeched, the air filled with the click of their teeth and the sound of their beating wings.

Pain seared his left arm as one of the little monsters latched on to him. Basil grabbed the tiny fucker with his right hand, yanked him off, threw him on the ground and stomped on him. The fae crunched satisfyingly under his boot.

More of the bitey bastards swarmed him, and soon he was fighting them off at close range with daggers drawn and blades whirring. Isa was locked in a similar struggle, her bow at her feet.

An irate scream from Isa, and then the earth rumbled. A second later, a boulder the size of a desk smashed through the wall to their right, slammed through the swarm of fae creatures, and flattened them against the opposite wall. The few remaining flesh-eating creeps screeched and fled.

Basil blinked, looked from the rock missile embedded in the wall to the panting fae female who snatched up her bow. "Remind me to never piss you off."

One side of her mouth tipped up in a knee-weakening half-smile. "At least when there's stone nearby."

He wanted to reply when a faint noise drew his

attention to the ceiling directly above her—where a huge beam was coming loose from the impact of the rock she'd thrown.

"Watch out!" he yelled and launched himself at her.

He pushed her out of the way and against the wall a mere second before the massive beam crashed into the floor. Isa's breath hitched, her hands clutching the fabric of his shirt, and her mouth opened on a gasp as she stared over his shoulder. He turned his head and followed her gaze.

The beam had rammed through the floor exactly where Isa was standing a moment before.

She uttered a frustrated sound.

"What?" Basil asked, facing her again.

She graced him with a look that could have shriveled a lesser man.

He wanted to ask her about it when it dawned on him. "Oh. I saved your life again, didn't I? Wait, does that mean you owe me a double life debt?"

"No," she muttered with a sigh and pushed off the wall, out of his arms. "But you don't need to rub it in by repeating it." The wink she sent him undermined her grudging tone, made it clear she wasn't really annoyed.

Cocking a brow, he raised both hands. "Okay, okay. Next time someone or something wants to kill you, I'll let them have at it. Don't want nobody saying I'm disrespecting your wishes." He wagged a finger at her. "See, I'm a modern man, and I can absolutely hold back from gallantly saving a female's life if it offends her."

And with a decisive nod and amusement bubbling in his veins, he picked up his bow and collected his arrows.

~~~

Isa watched Basil retrieve his arrows, and her heart ached with how much she wanted to kiss him right now, kiss that barely-there smile on his face, inhale his humor, his sunshine, his light. Oh, and if she lived a thousand lifetimes, she'd always yearn for the brilliance of his smile, the warmth in his eyes, the way he could make her wonderfully dizzy with lighthearted joy just by looking at her. Could make her forget her troubles with a few funny remarks.

Light such as his should not be snuffed out.

The thought whispered through her mind, its roots growing into her heart. *I know,* she wanted to cry in answer, *and I wish there was another way.*

But there was none. She'd spent two decades searching for another way to break the curse, all in vain.

Her pulse thrummed in her head, her vision faltered. She balled her hands to fists, closed her eyes. *I don't want to die.*

She was a little girl again, clawing her way out from under the heavy body of the dead adult male who'd thought her easy prey...*survive*...living off insects and the carcasses of squirrels and birds during a particularly harsh winter before she learned how to hunt...*survive*...hiding in stone from the irate shop owner who caught her stealing a pair of shoes to replace the ones that fell off her feet...*survive*...breaking the water fae's hold on her ankle so she could struggle out of the lake and escape her death in the deep...

Survive. It was all she'd ever done, all she knew how to do.

Her breath hitched, burned in her throat. With a pained sound, she forced herself to move, to collect her arrows and follow Basil out of the cottage.

He stood with his back to her, his hands on his hips. When she stepped up to his side, he let out a heavy breath.

"It's a dead end, isn't it?"

She grimaced. "We can still ask around the nearby village, see if the fae there know anything about where Rose and her captors went."

He nodded, sighed, his sunshine subdued. "There'll be food, yes?"

~~~

Sitting with his back to the wall, Basil watched the patrons in the pub while he took another bite of his steak. So many different kinds of fae, their shapes ranging from bark-skinned, wiry creatures that could have been miniature ents from *Lord of the Rings*, over the more common human-looking beings with pointed ears—both the bigger-sized ones like him and Isa, as well as the tiny, winged variants also found outside of Faerie—to burly creatures who seemed to be two-legged boars.

As a member of a witch family, Basil was used to seeing nonhuman beings, but this group topped anything he'd ever encountered. The best kind of people-watching. Plus, the steak was delicious. The soup had been great, too. As were the bread, the salad, and the casserole.

Isa slid into the seat next to him, her eyes sparking. "I just heard—wait, you're still eating? How can you fit anything else in there?"

"I once won first place in an eating competition." He stuffed more bread in his mouth, chewed with relish.

"I don't doubt it for a second." She shook her head. "As I was saying, I just heard something." Her fingers drummed on the table.

Was she waiting for him to pull it out of her? He gestured with his fork, raised his brows while he chewed. "Spiff iff ouff."

She leaned forward. "One of the fae I've been talking to, she remembered something. She said she talked to the couple who used to live in the house, and they mentioned they were moving to a village called Ranagor. However, she doesn't recall if they had a child with them when they left."

He sat up straight. "That's still better than anything else we've found so far."

They'd spent the better part of the afternoon asking

around town, trying to find out where the fae who took in Rose went, or what happened to them, but nobody seemed to know anything. All they learned was that the couple had always been very reclusive, didn't mingle much in town, didn't have friends, so even in a village where everybody knew everyone else, no one had any information about where they'd gone.

"Ranagor," Basil muttered. "How far is that from here?"

"Another day's hike, at least."

He groaned. "Why don't you fae have cars?"

"Because we despise modern technology and prefer to stay fit?"

He threw a salad crouton at her.

16

The sunset's bold colors licked over the sky like fire, crowned by the velvet indigo of the impending night. Isa drank in the beauty of it, ever amazed by the splendor of the spectacle. No matter how old she got, she would never tire of gazing at a sunset, her favorite part of the day.

"Are we going to spend the night in another cave?"

Basil's question pulled her out of her trance. She cleared her throat. "Actually, we can sleep in a real bed tonight."

"Oh? Is there a village ahead?"

"Not quite. I've…taken the liberty of redirecting our course by about one hour so we can make a stop overnight."

"Where?"

"My house."

He blinked, obviously stunned. "You…you're taking me to your home?"

Why did she suddenly feel awkward? Her face heated. "I figured it would be nice to sleep there for a change, seeing as it's kind of on our way to Ranagor. You don't mind?"

"Not at all." His smile was blinding. "I'd love to see how you live."

And now her skin prickled, her heart thumped erratically, and her stomach had decided to try a somersault. *Great.* Why had she thought it was a good idea to bring him here?

Ten minutes later she led him toward the towering rock formation that housed her humble abode. Part of a sprawling landscape of forest-covered ridges, her own cliff featured natural caves which she'd expanded on and customized into her home. A stone staircase led up to an ornately carved wooden door, framed by floral patterns chiseled into the rock.

"Nice," Basil said from behind her as she unlocked the door. "Did you engrave these yourself?"

She threw a glance at him, at his hand stroking the decorations in the stone. "Yes."

He followed her into her house, studying the arched ceilings, the open doorways leading from one room into the other, the roughly-hewn, curved walls, the shelves worked into the rock, the strategically placed mirrors that reflected the light streaming in from the various skylights.

"Wow." Basil turned, craned his head, strolled through the rooms. "Don't tell me you did all this?"

"Well," she said, activating the crystals set in the walls to illuminate the house at night, "I do have a talent for working with stone, remember?"

"This is fan-fucking-tastic." Basil's voice came from her bathroom, muffled by the splash of water.

She peeked inside.

He gestured at the waterfall shower, his face alight. "Is this thing always running?"

"Yes. I rerouted part of the natural hot spring inside the rock formation and let it flow through here. The water's always warm enough for a shower."

"You have your own personal waterfall." He turned to her, all feigned offense. "I am so incredibly jealous."

She didn't quite manage to bite back her grin, instead walked out of the room before she did something fatal like kissing him silly. "I have a spare bedroom for you. Come."

He followed her, then paused and blinked at the nook she showed him. "That's...a room? Where's the door?"

"Uh, none of the rooms have doors. It makes for better air flow through the house." She shrugged. "Plus, I live alone."

He gave her a side-eye. "You don't often have guests, do you?"

"No." She looked down, turned away. "If you don't mind, I'll be going to bed. I'm really tired."

"Sure." Before she could walk away, he grabbed her hand, the touch an electric jolt throughout her body. "Isa."

She looked at him.

"Your home is beautiful."

The stone-cold part of her cracked, just a little.

"Thank you."

~~~

Damn it all, she hated waking up because she had to use the bathroom.

With a muffled groan, Isa swung her legs over the side of her bed—so soft, so inviting, calling out like a lover that she shouldn't leave just yet, but she knew she wouldn't be able to fall asleep again until she relieved herself. So she padded down the hall on silent feet, hoping not to wake Basil with her nightly wandering, and turned into the open archway to the bathroom—where she froze, her bladder's call forgotten, riveted on the breathtaking sight of one fine male in all his naked glory.

Basil stood under the waterfall shower, his back to her, the water splashing over the hard planes of his body, running down ridges and valleys of muscle and smooth skin. *Caressing* him.

She'd never been so jealous of water.

By the Fates, his form was delicious. Unadulterated strength poured into the shape of a prime male specimen, broad shoulders, tapered waist, narrow hips, and a butt that looked positively bitable. His muscles flexed and rippled as he washed himself, unaware of her presence.

She jerked herself out of the haze of lust. *You should leave. Now.* Her feet wouldn't move. Instead, her hand inched toward the arch of the doorway, touched the cool surface, and when the stone sang to her, she answered, allowed it to swallow her form, merge with the rock.

Naughty, she was so perfidiously naughty to be standing there ogling him. Shame heated her cheeks, while another emotion altogether warmed up wholly different parts of her body. *Only one more minute*, she chided herself. *Then you'll turn around and grant the man his damned privacy.*

Just then he slowed down, changing from efficient and passionless swipes and scrubs to a more languorous stroking when he reached his groin. His back was still turned, so she only saw part of his arm and elbow, his hand hidden from her by his hips.

Isa stifled a gasp. Was he—?

He shifted his weight, the new angle turning him more toward her so she saw him from the side, and...

Stars above and earth below.

He had his hand wrapped around his cock, stroked up and down in sinuous moves. The hard length of him jutted up from a close-cropped nest of dark blond curls atop his heavy balls, water sluicing around and over it, flashing images in her mind of her tongue taking that path.

Heat built in her lower belly, coiled and flared into a pulsing rhythm between her thighs. Her fingernails dug into the rough surface of the archway.

Up and down his hand went, gaining momentum and speed while he closed his eyes, parted his lips. His breath came faster. What was he imagining while he pleasured himself? A devious, selfish impulse wished it was her, even though she knew it wasn't right, wasn't fair. She didn't deserve to be his fantasy.

But the damage was done, and that wicked, oh-so-wrong, rogue thought of him picturing her turned her body into molten lust. She had to lean against the stone of the doorway to steady herself, her knees gone weak.

Breathing almost as fast as he did, her nipples sensitive against her nightshirt, she watched while he stroked himself harder, faster, working his shaft with practiced vigor and intent. She wanted to replace his hand with hers, grip him hard and make him thrust into her strokes. Wanted to kiss the powerful muscles on his chest that were bulging under the strain of his pleasure.

He threw his head back and uttered a hoarse, erotic sound that had her squeezing her thighs together against the throb of need. His bared throat invited her to lick along the column of his neck, nibble on the skin stretched taut over his veins.

She imagined doing this to him, giving him the pleasure she should have given him last night. *Like this*, she thought. *I want to make him come apart like this.*

His butt tightened as he thrust even faster into his hand, and the corded muscles of his forearm tensed. He braced his free hand against the wall of the shower, let his head fall forward again, water splashing around his neck and shoulders as he hunched over. A soft sound broke from his parted lips, his face contorted in pleasure-pain, and with a husky moan he found release.

His strokes slowed, became caresses again while the water washed away evidence of his orgasm. Panting, he laid his forehead against the rock wall.

A heavy knock on the front door startled Isa, and she almost lost the grip on the stone of the archway. Good grief, if Basil saw her now…

Another knock, louder. She frowned in the direction of the entrance.

"You should go open the door," Basil said.

With a gasp, she looked back at him. He was facing the archway, full-frontal, his still semi-erect shaft on open display, his eyes fixed on where she stood—but not quite directly locked on to her.

He can't see me, it's not possible. She checked her connection to the stone, found it solid. And yet—

More knocking from the front door.

She rushed away from the bathroom.

17

Basil's breath was still uneven while he used the towel he found on one of the bathroom wall shelves to dry himself off with quick, efficient moves. He was halfway back in his clothes the moment he heard Isa open the front door to whoever dared disturb her at this hour.

Dared interrupt what could have evolved into a *very* interesting encounter.

Gods have mercy, but that was *hot*. When he heard her padding into the bathroom only to stop dead in her tracks, he thought she'd turn on her heels and run back to bed. He hadn't faced her or signaled that he noticed her presence so he wouldn't embarrass her, but then she'd done the unthinkable—she stayed.

Even though he hadn't been able to see her, he knew she hadn't left. He would have heard it. So, he figured he'd give her something to watch.

He almost hardened again, just imagining what it must have been like for her. The fact that she stayed, had watched him...and now, as he crossed the threshold of the archway, his heightened fae senses picked up the lingering aroma of her arousal.

Yep, she definitely enjoyed the show.

With a grin on his face, he strapped on the rest of his weapons and walked toward the entrance area. Isa, clad in long, flowing pants and a loose, short-sleeve nightshirt, held the door open to a fae male, her posture defensive, her free hand half behind her butt, fingers twitching. Probably ready to draw a small dagger at her lower back.

He surreptitiously prepared one of his knives to slide quickly into his hand if need be. "What's going on?"

The male's attention flicked to him, his golden skin aglow in the light of the crystals, his long, silver hair braided above his temples. "Basil? Basil Murray?"

He paused. "Who are you?"

A smile lit up the fae's face. "I am so glad I found you. My name is Calâr of Air, and I have come to help you."

Basil frowned, his gut churning with suspicion. "With what, exactly? How do you know me?"

Calâr glanced at Isa. "May I come in?"

"No," Basil said. "Explain yourself first."

Calâr inclined his head. "Of course. I know you only recently found out about your fae heritage, because the glamour on you and the silence spell on Hazel Murray were lifted. The reason for that is that the fae who cast both has died, as I'm sure you suspected. I was a good friend of the fae who exchanged you, but even so, she kept your fate a secret until moments before she died. I was with her when she lay on her deathbed, and she told me of you and made me swear to find you and help you claim your powers."

Involuntarily, Basil had stepped closer, his mind racing with the implications of what the fae was saying.

"You see," Calâr went on, "half-breeds may have trouble connecting with their magic because of their mixed heritage, but there is a way to facilitate the emergence and claiming of those powers."

"Wait—half-breed? What the hell do you mean?"

"Oh, but of course." Calâr's eyes widened. "You wouldn't know, would you? You are not fully fae. Your father was a demon."

His words knocked the breath out of Basil. Dizzy, he swayed, his chest tingling, his stomach making a dive for the ground. He stared at the fae in utter speechlessness.

"That is why you were taken out of Faerie and hidden with the witch family," Calâr continued. "The relationship between your father and your mother was forbidden, and you would not have been allowed to live. They killed your father, and your mother died in childbirth. My friend managed to smuggle you out before they could kill you, too, because she had promised your mother to make sure you survived. When my friend's death drew near, she realized her magic would lift upon her passing, and you would find out you're more than human and might go in search of your identity. She thought it important for you to know the whole truth and learn to handle your powers. Thus, she tasked me to help you, and here I am." He bowed his head. "I am happy to have found you safe and sound, Basil Murray."

Basil's thoughts whirled, trying to catch up with these stunning revelations. "How *did* you find me?" he managed to ask, clinging to whatever sense he had left.

"My friend gave me the name of the witch family she chose for you, and I went there in search of you, only to find out you'd left for Faerie. I have been following your tracks for as long as possible, but when I lost your trace, I used this to find your location." He held up a compass. "It is bespelled by witches to point to someone's whereabouts if you know their name, an old charm that I've had in my possession for some time." At Basil's frown, he added, with a humble smile, "I am an archivist of treasures and knowledge for the fae court, and I was fortunate enough to collect some valuables of my own over time."

Basil studied him, his mind still piecing the puzzle together, his heart unconvinced. "If you met with Hazel, why isn't she here? She's been looking for a fae to take her into Faerie to join me, so why hasn't she come with you?"

"Ah." Calâr nodded. "You have a keen intellect. I understand your caution, but let me put your doubts to rest. Hazel was indeed eager to travel with me, but her witch friend—the redhead with the demon mate— mentioned a situation in the witch community with one called Juneau, and said the circumstances were too precarious for Hazel to leave and give Juneau and her witches reason to attack. Hazel was torn, for she wanted to find you and her daughter Rose here in Faerie, but I assured her I would take care of you, and that Rose was safe. I swore to bring both of you back unharmed, and she agreed to let me go in her stead."

"Wait...you know about Rose?"

Calâr nodded. "My friend explained where she is, and that she is well taken care of. She is in no danger, and we can go take her to Hazel after we connect you to your powers."

Basil was reeling, his thoughts a scrambled mess of *ifs* and *buts* and *maybes*, his feelings all over the place.

"Have you tried to connect with your magic yet?" Calâr asked.

Basil nodded numbly. "Didn't work. I feel a hum, the buzz of power coursing in my veins, and I discovered my element is earth, but I haven't been able to tap into it."

"I have read of this happening. It is because your dormant demon powers are blocking access to your fae magic. There is a way to activate all your magic...I assume you don't know your true name?"

"My what?"

"Every fae has a true name, revealed to them by the Fates at some point during their formative years, and that name holds all their power. There are rare cases of fae not learning their true name—as with you, probably because of either the glamour put on you, or your demon blood—and in these instances, there is a way to trigger that revelation. Once you know your true name, you'll be able to access your powers."

Calâr smiled. "I can help you with that."

~~~

That devious, shameless liar.

Isa stared at the male fae on her doorstep, the very one she'd seen in the throne room that fateful night—when he murdered the fae who'd exchanged Basil. Oh, but he didn't mention that, did he? No, he served up a bunch of lies half wrapped in enough truth to mask the deceit. Enough truth to whet Basil's appetite for more, judging by the gleam in Basil's eyes.

And who could blame him? Here he was, finally getting some more information about his heritage, as well as having the prospect of unlocking his powers dangled in front of him, something she knew he craved. This insidious male—Calâr—gave him these morsels of knowledge, gifted him with the insight into his past which Isa hadn't been able to divulge to him.

For if she had told Basil about his half-demon heritage, about the circumstances of his mother's death, he would have wanted to know how she knew. And how could she have explained it without giving away her involvement? No, it had been too risky, so she'd opted to keep her mouth shut and pretend she didn't know.

And now she couldn't even expose Calâr's lies—that the fae who exchanged Basil had been his friend, had asked him to help Basil, that Basil's father was long dead—because in order to call Calâr on his deceit, she'd have to reveal that she was there when Calâr learned about Basil, that she saw him murder the fae, and that Basil's father was still alive—and looking for him.

And it would expose her as a liar as well, because she had known, and kept these truths from him all this time. She couldn't afford to discredit herself in front of Basil, and she wouldn't be able to explain to him why she hadn't disclosed all she knew—not without telling him about the curse.

He couldn't know. He couldn't ever find out about her involvement in his past, that she'd dragged his mother back into Faerie, that Roana had cursed her... that she needed to take his life to save her own.

Which was why she hadn't even told him his father was alive, even though she knew it would be incredibly important to him. For if he found out his father lived and was searching for him, he'd want to find him, of course.

But any meeting with the demon would put Isa's life in grave danger—Basil's father saw her that day in the palace, when she brought Roana back. She'd worn her bounty hunter garb, her face half covered, but there was a chance he might still recognize her as the one responsible for surrendering his lover and unborn child to the king and queen. And considering the bloody revenge he took on the whole of the royal court, he might butcher Isa where she stood if he realized who she was.

The web of lies she'd spun now threatened to trap her as well. She choked on the irony of calling Calâr a liar when she was no better. But what did he want with Basil? Whatever his endgame, it couldn't be good, and he couldn't be trusted. She needed to warn Basil without exposing herself.

"How will you do that?" Basil asked, startling her. His gaze rested on Calâr, his brow furrowed. "How does this true name triggering work?"

"There is an ancient oracle," Calâr replied. "One of the facts it can reveal is a fae's true name. I will guide you there and show you how."

Isa narrowed her eyes. Was he speaking of the Nornûn? She'd heard of the temple, and how its worship had fallen neglected over time. Most fae didn't practice the old ways anymore, and many cult sites of old lay long forgotten. She'd never heard of the Nornûn being used for a true name revelation, but then again, she hadn't known of any cases like Basil's before now. Knowing one's true name since the early days of childhood was so natural, it hadn't even crossed her mind that Basil might never have learned his.

Basil's expression was thoughtful. "What about Rose? I set out to find her. I feel like we should check in on her first."

"I understand your concern." Calâr inclined his head again. "But rest assured, Rose is safe, and no harm will come to her where she is. There is no rush. You have ample time to claim your powers and your identity."

What a load of deer shit. She barely held back her snort. If Calâr truly knew where Rose was, Isa would grow a pair of fairy wings. No, there was no way he had any information about her whereabouts. Isa had heard what the fae who exchanged Basil told both Basil's father and Calâr, and it hadn't included anything about the witch changeling's location.

But once again, she couldn't tell Basil Calâr was lying without betraying her own duplicity.

Still, she had to try. "Basil, can I talk to you for a second?"

His eyes of myriad shades of brown met hers. "Sure."

She nodded at Calâr. "Excuse us for a moment." And with that, she closed the door in the male's face.

Basil raised his brows. "What is it?"

She signaled him to walk farther into the house with her. Once satisfied they were out of earshot, she said, "I don't think you should trust him. He seems insincere."

Basil blinked, jerked back his head. "Why would you think that?"

"I…" She closed her mouth, gritted her teeth. What could she say to convince him? "I'm just not sure he's telling the truth."

His brows drew together. "Everything he's said so far rings true to me. He knows all these things about me, my family, and my past. And it makes sense."

"I don't think he is who he claims he is."

"Okay, so who do you think he is?"

Again, she opened her mouth only to close it again.

She huffed out a breath. "I don't know. Someone with ulterior motives. Not someone who's on your side."

"Do you know him?"

She suppressed a sound of frustration. "No."

"Then how do you know he's false?"

"I don't, not for sure. He just…rubs me the wrong way. It's a…gut feeling. I sense he's not being truthful with you, and I think you shouldn't assume he has your best interests at heart."

The hypocrisy of her argument slammed into her with the force of the rock she hurled at the flesh-eating fae. Dear Fates, could she be any more duplicitous? She had no right to cry foul at whatever trickery Calâr had planned, considering her own nefarious agenda.

Her breath stalled, threatened to choke her for her deceit. Darkness crept in from the edges of her vision. Exhaustion settled over her like a mantle of stone, and suddenly she had no strength left to argue with Basil.

She shook her head, closed her eyes, her voice thin. "Just be careful with him."

"Hey." He cupped her cheek with one hand.

She looked at him, and drowned anew in the finely sculpted beauty of his features, the warmth of his concern for her.

"I'm not discounting your warning," he said, his voice velvet over her raw senses. "Right now, he's my best shot at claiming my powers, but I'll keep my guard up around him, okay?" His thumb caressed her cheek.

She nodded. He dropped his hand, and she wanted

to snatch it back up, lay it on her cheek again so she could snuggle into his touch.

"But," Basil went on, "is he right about the true name thing?"

"It's possible, yes."

"Every fae has a true name? You, too?"

"Yes."

A small smile played about his lips. "I'd love to know yours."

She bristled, straightened. "It's secret. You don't ever tell anyone else your true name."

"Why?"

"Like Calâr said, it holds all of your power. It is strong, age-old magic, and it could—" Pieces clicked together in her mind, and she gasped.

"What?"

"Basil," she whispered, "be *very* careful with Calâr. Knowing a fae's true name gives you power *over* that fae. He might be trying to learn your true name so he can control you."

He blinked in surprise, then frowned. "What for?"

"I don't know, but it can't be good."

"But he'd only learn my name if I *told* him, right?"

"Right..."

"So I just won't tell him." Shrugging, he smiled. "Thank you for the heads-up." He brushed his thumb across her cheek again, his eyes soft and warm. "I appreciate how much you care, Isa."

Her heart splintered.

~~~

Silence. *Finally.*

Calâr rose from the sofa in the living area of the female's house—Isa of Stone she'd called herself—and stole down the hall toward the nook in which Basil slept.

When Isa shut the door in Calâr's face, he thought that was it, that she'd try to keep the half-breed from him, and he'd have to resort to more desperate means to steer Basil toward the oracle. She'd introduced herself as Basil's protector, owing a life debt to him, though from the looks of it, there was more between them.

Whatever she was to the changeling—as long as she didn't get in the way, Calâr would tolerate her. It was easier for the time being to have her come along, and to use gentler methods on Basil to get him where Calâr wanted him. Once there, getting rid of the female would be child's play.

They talked for a bit when she allowed Calâr to enter her home, and agreed to start their journey toward Nornûn by the first light of morning. If it had been up to Calâr, they'd have left right away, but as it was only shortly after midnight, and Basil hadn't slept, Calâr had not argued too much against staying until morning.

Just as well. Casting a spell on someone was a lot less difficult if the person was asleep. He might not get a better opportunity than now.

Standing over Basil's bed, his pitiless gaze on the half-breed's slumbering form, he smiled and called on the intricate magic to weave into his mind.

18

Doing yard work, Rhun found, was a most excellent way to distract himself from a problem. Even one as large and looming as how to get Merle to cancel the fucking deal with Arawn and send Maeve to the Demon Lord.

That stubborn—he yanked out a weed—big-hearted —he hauled out another—damnably caring witch of his. He threw the weeds on the ground and trampled them for good measure. He'd have to hog-tie her after all, wouldn't he?

Blinking at the morning sun, he weighed the risk of Merle hating his guts for the rest of their lives if he forced her to surrender Maeve, versus losing their baby. Damn it, the entire mess didn't even make sense.

Maeve was promised to Arawn anyway, and sooner or later he'd claim her, and Merle would have to let her go. So why not give her up now? Keeping her around for a few months longer…it was *not* worth risking the life of their baby.

He jerked out another plant that didn't belong. He'd

always been a fan of ripping off a Band-Aid in one second instead of slooooooowly peeling it off over several minutes. *It has to be done, it's inevitable, so let's get it over with.*

"Uh, Rhun?"

He turned toward Merle's voice, saw her standing on the back porch, her eyes still red from crying. Fuck if that sight didn't punch him in the guts and shred them for good measure. If he could take her pain and make it his instead, he'd do it in a heartbeat. He enjoyed verbally sparring with her, but this? Fighting with her about Maeve bruised her soul, and he hated himself for it.

"You've got a visitor," she said.

Frowning, he looked behind her to the door leading into the kitchen—where Maeve appeared. She nodded at her big sister, and Merle kissed her on the cheek.

"I'll be in the library," Merle muttered and went inside.

Rhun blinked at Maeve, tilted his head. "You're here to see…me?"

In all the months since he helped rescue Maeve, had lived here in the old Victorian with Merle—Maeve having moved to the Murrays' because she hadn't been able to be around Rhun without having a panic attack, what with him being of the same demon species as the bastard who tortured her—Maeve had never truly talked to him, *especially* not alone. In fact, he couldn't recall that they'd ever been in the same room without someone else present.

He understood, of course. He'd seen first-hand what that fucker of a demon did to her, and in his darkest moments, images of Maeve's bloody, beaten, sliced-up body still flashed across his inner eye, rivaling the gruesome memories of his sister's death.

Maeve nodded and pushed her hair behind her ear, then froze. Looking down, she pulled her hair back over her face again. But it wasn't enough to hide the nasty scar running from one side of her chin and over her nose to the opposite temple.

Rhun gritted his teeth. He wanted to kill that motherfucker again so badly, his whole body hurt.

Taking a deep breath, he calmed himself, made sure his voice was gentle when he spoke. "What can I do for you?"

"Accept my apology." She still sounded so husky.

He raised both eyebrows. "You didn't do anything."

"Exactly." When he frowned, she elaborated. "It took me all this time to realize…I never thanked you."

"For what?"

"You saved me." Her tone indicated she was quite baffled about needing to explain it to him.

He shrugged, put his hands on his hips and looked to the side. "No need to thank me."

"But I want to. You deserve—" She took a deep breath. "I should have thanked you sooner. I was just… too much of a coward to talk to you. I'm sorry—"

"You're not a coward." It came out harsher than he intended, and he grimaced. "Look, I get it. You don't have to apologize to me. I never even expected any thanks—"

"Is it true you ripped his heart out?"

He paused, his chest heaving just from the memory of being in that blood-drenched warehouse. "His tongue, too."

The corners of her mouth twitched.

"Broke every single bone in his body."

Her eyes sparkled.

"Flayed the skin off his hands."

The smile taking over her face was an echo of the one he loved to see on Merle, similar, and yet different. The fire in her amber-gray eyes, however, flared with a ferocity born of ancient times, far beyond anything he'd ever witnessed in Merle.

"Thank you," Maeve said emphatically. "Thank you, Rhun."

"You're welcome." His throat felt thick and raspy.

When she blinked, that age-old glint left her eyes, and she was again the little sister of the witch he loved, reminding him so much of his own baby sister...the one he hadn't been able to save.

"I'm doing a lot better now," Maeve said, her hands in the pockets of her jeans.

"I'm glad."

And he was. He'd watched her make tremendous strides in her recovery, especially recently. She was able to go out more with her friends, could even stand to be in crowds despite her disfigurement—hell, he knew it couldn't be easy for her to brave the looks and reactions of strangers.

And yet she did, every single day.

She'd come so far since the night they pulled her out of that hellhole, and it was amazing to watch her take charge of her life again—and the realization was like a hot blade to his heart. *Gods fucking dammit.*

It had been so much easier to insist on sending her to Arawn when she'd been a distant concept, more present in his mind as the leverage they needed to use than as a real person. He'd barely seen her over the past months, much less spoken to her. And now here she was, come to *thank* him, while he was planning to hand her over to the monster who wanted to enslave her—

Hell, it made him feel like the shittiest person on earth.

He had trouble breathing past the ache in his chest.

After all the progress she made in her recovery, he could only imagine what surrendering her to Arawn now would do to the ember of spirit that had just begun to rekindle. If she had to leave at this point, it might very well send her straight back into a tailspin of despair and misery. And while she'd offered to go with Arawn when he first came to claim her—in order to prevent Merle from making that deal with him to keep her safe from him a bit longer—would she still be willing to surrender herself, now she'd just begun to piece herself back together?

"I was wondering," Maeve interrupted his dismal thoughts, "now I'm…better, would you mind if I move back in with you guys?"

Well, fuck. This couldn't be real. This was too cruel even for those fucked-up, sadistic Powers That Be.

"I think," Maeve went on, unaware of his inner turmoil, "I've reached the point where I can handle my anxiety and be around you without freaking out. I… miss home. I miss having Merle around. And…I'd love to get to know my…brother-in-law."

Eyes of fire and smoke met his own, and the sincerity in them slayed him. Inwardly, he cursed so hard it wouldn't have surprised him if his guts turned blue.

Don't show, don't show, don't show. He felt like fucking Elsa, what with how much he had to keep stuffed down right now, and it took everything he had not to smash something in front of Maeve.

He must have failed, however, because her face reddened and she took a step back. "I'm sorry. I mean, I don't want to impose—if it makes you uncomfortable —"

"No!" He flinched, gentled his tone. "No. It's all right. I don't—" He closed his eyes, dragged every last bit of his species' masterful ability to lie and deceive to the surface, smiled, and said, "I'd be happy to welcome you back home. I'll tell Merle, okay?"

She let out a breath, a small smile lighting up her face. "Okay." She turned to go inside, stopped, faced him again. "I'm looking forward to getting to know you, Rhun."

Her words clawed him bloody.

19

Isa had passed the point of being sick to death of Calâr's voice several hours ago.

They'd been on the road all day, hiking toward Nornûn, and Basil had begun a subtle interrogation of the suspicious fae. Calâr was forthcoming with information, glossing over the truth and possible holes in his knowledge with a skill that could have been admirable in another person.

She'd been forced to listen to his explanations and tall tales, all the while restraining herself from choking him. At some point she started whetting one of her blades while they walked, relishing the fantasy of driving it through his lying guts.

Thankfully, Basil seemed to keep her warning in mind. His attitude toward Calâr hadn't warmed much, and knowing what she did about him by now, she could clearly see his reserve in his interactions with Calâr.

With her, however, Basil displayed a wholly different side. He never mentioned what happened in the bathroom last night—and she'd been all too happy to avoid the subject, her body flushing with a potent mix of embarrassment and lust every time she remembered —but there was a deeper level of sensuality in the way he treated her. The looks he sent her way heated her insides, he regularly slowed down to walk beside her, his shoulder warm against hers, his fingers oh-so-accidentally brushing her hand, and he used just about any excuse to touch her.

And, despite her emotional turmoil, she couldn't scrounge up the will to tell him to stop. She knew she should. It would be the right thing. But by the Fates, she *couldn't*.

They were resting beside a lake, Calâr having wandered off to relieve himself, her hawk floating idly on air currents above, when it happened.

She was sitting on a boulder, face turned up toward the sun, as she heard Kîna's keen cry—indicating danger. Jerking her head up, she looked over at Basil— who'd taken off his boots, rolled up his pants to his knees, and was wading into the shallows. Her eyes widened. Her heart skipped a beat. What was he doing? Didn't he know—well, damn, of course he wouldn't.

"Basil!" she yelled.

He glanced up, his brows drawing together—and then he slipped and slid into the water.

No, he was *dragged*.

She'd grabbed her bow, had an arrow ready to shoot within a second, and jumped up.

Swish.

Her arrow flew, rammed into the body of the water fae who tried to pull Basil under. The beast was strong, had yanked him almost completely under the surface despite Basil's valiant struggle. The fae thrashed, bucked, its scaled body bobbing up and down. Basil's head broke the surface, and he hauled in air.

Isa fired another arrow, and another, both diving through the water to find their target, giving Basil cover as he hauled himself toward the shore. She kept another arrow nocked and pointed at the lake just in case.

It hit her when Basil heaved himself on the pebbled beach on all fours, breathing heavily. Magic tingled over her skin, grabbed her heart, her soul—and let go. Her arms began to tremble. Her lips parted. She shivered all over.

She'd just saved his life.

Turning, she looked at him, dripping wet and trembling, and time slowed to a crawl. *My debt is paid.* She was free to kill him now, to break her curse.

Involuntarily, as if drawn by an invisible force, her arms moved, her stance shifted, until the arrow she'd nocked pointed at Basil's head while he let it hang down, his eyes closed, his breathing choppy. Easy. It would be so easy. A clear shot.

The fingertips of her right hand brushed the feathers on the arrow's fletching as she pulled it back on the bowstring.

Clear…shot.

I don't want to kill him.

Her hands shook, made the bow and arrow quiver.

Survive.

Just one shot. That was all it would take. Straight to his head. Quick and painless. And her curse would break.

Her heart stumbled on its too-rapid rhythm, her head going dizzy.

Images flashed before her eyes, and sensory memories prickled along her nerves. Basil's blinding smile. The sparkle in his eyes when he looked at her. The warmth of his hand when he cupped her cheek. His lips on hers, hot, demanding, giving. His laughter, his humor, his love.

I can't. Ye Fates, I cannot take his life.

With a sob, she lowered the bow, let the arrow relax on the string.

Basil looked up at that second, smiled at her, and scrambled to his feet. Blond hair dripping water on his face, shoulders and chest, his clothes drenched, he came up to her, his eyes holding only half the knowledge of what had just transpired.

"Well," he said, oblivious to the raging storm inside her, "you did it, right? You saved my life."

She nodded, her throat making it impossible to reply.

He bowed, took her hand and kissed the back of it. "You paid your debt. That means you can now leave me and go on with your life. I bet you're glad you can finally get rid of me, hm?" The humor of his words was undermined by the hint of sadness in his smile.

Get rid of him... The pain in her chest was instantaneous, consuming, flaring out into all the parts of her heart, her soul. *I could never get rid of you.* She knew it then, knew she'd rather die than snuff out his light.

My life for yours, my love in death.

She closed her eyes, shook her head. "I think I'll stick around a bit longer."

The hope lighting his eyes speared her heart, yet poured love into her soul. "Oh, yeah?"

She nodded, swallowed. "You've...grown on me."

"Hopefully not like some cancerous wart," Basil quipped.

She choked out a laugh, wiped at her eyes. "No," she rasped, gathered herself to struggle through the maelstrom of bittersweet pain. "More like one of those stray chin hairs that keeps coming back no matter how many times I pluck it." She gestured at her face, her voice cracking. "Or this one abnormally long eyelash of mine. At some point I just give up and live with it, you know?"

Basil grinned from ear to ear, stepped closer to her. Putting his hands on her waist, he pulled her to him. "You've got a creepy long eyelash? Where? I've never noticed."

"Here," she croaked, pointing to her right eye.

Squinting, he tilted his head. "Hm. This one?" He grazed his finger over the one lash that extended past the others.

"Yes," she whispered, her heartbeat thunder in her

ears.

"It's white, too," Basil murmured, his voice intimately low.

His gaze locked onto hers, so full of warmth and everything good in this world, and—by the Fates, being at the receiving end of that look, being the person who made him glow like this, was the most beautiful thing that had ever happened to her.

Her heart broke with the knowledge that she wouldn't get to enjoy this beauty for long. Because soon she would meet her own death...so he could live.

She quenched the sob that wanted to break loose, and met his kiss instead. Hot, his lips burned hot, despite the chill water clinging to his skin, and she sank into his heat, his passion, his *love*. She cupped his face while she rose on her toes to kiss him with all the need and desperation she'd repeatedly beaten into submission.

No reason to deny herself this pleasure anymore. She would drink him in, become intoxicated from his sunshine, so she could tumble into death's arms later, buzzing with the bliss of how Basil made her feel.

"Oh, I'm sorry." Calâr's voice scratched over her nerves like a knife over a plate. "I didn't mean to interrupt anything."

They broke apart, and Isa shot a dark look at the deceptive bastard. Oh, she'd take him down now, would make sure to reveal to Basil what a mendacious rat he was. Not right this moment, though. No, she'd have to play her cards right, needed to first find out what the fae's true agenda was. An idea brewed in her mind, but she needed more time to work it out.

Until then, she'd watch him like a cat staking out a mouse hole.

~~~

"I really think we should keep going," Calâr said. "The Nornûn oracle is not much farther. We might even reach it tonight."

Before Basil could reply, Isa spoke up.

"And I think we should stop for a good night's sleep. In this inn." She peered at Basil from underneath half-lowered lids, and, now he knew, he always spotted that one extra-long, white lash. "In a nice, comfortable bed."

Her voice dropped to a sinfully low level on the last word, sparking an immediate response in him. He shifted to make room for his growing erection, and cleared his throat.

"Uh, yeah," he said. "Sounds like a terrific idea. I'm tired. Exhausted, actually. Let's spend the night here."

As much as he craved connecting with his magic, when weighed against the look Isa sent his way just now, the insinuation in her tone? If she wanted to do what he *thought* she wanted to do... To hell with his powers. The oracle could wait.

Whatever had gotten into her after she saved him from that water fae, it had smashed to smithereens any reservations she had about giving in to her attraction.

She'd been stealing kisses and touches from him ever since, and now this. Maybe it had something to do with paying her life debt to him? Who knew...perhaps there was some arcane rule about not hooking up with someone when you owed them a life debt?

Well, whatever the reason, he could explore it later—and he did plan to ask her about it—but first things first. He'd grab this chance with both hands and *gorge* himself on her. His mind already played a vivid selection of all the things he wanted to do to her, so he only half heard Calâr's protest, his gaze still on the temptation of the fine female in front of him.

"...less than two hours away. You must be eager to claim your magic. Why wait when you can unleash your powers tonight?"

Oh, he planned on unleashing something tonight. Did he *ever*.

Isa must have read his look correctly, because she snickered. *Snickered.* His serious Isa of Stone, giggling like a schoolgirl. Over *him*.

He cleared his throat, and still his voice came out husky. "I want to be well rested when I tap my powers. We've been on the road all day, and we need to catch some sleep." Not that he actually expected to get a lot of shut-eye...

He turned to meet Calâr's irate look, and he made sure the other male understood he wouldn't budge on this. "We rest here."

"As you wish," Calâr muttered, and stalked toward the inn.

Isa winked at Basil and followed the other fae toward the earth dwelling, which was charmingly reminiscent of a hobbit hole.

With most of his blood already happily rushing south, and his thoughts focused on one thing only, he waited for Isa to secure rooms—one for Calâr, one for Basil and her—and barely spared a glance at the bustle around him, or the kind of architecture he would have geeked out over at any other time.

They wished Calâr a good night, and then Basil followed Isa toward the second room.

"Basil?" she asked as she walked down the hall.

"Hm?"

"You're prowling behind me like an unfed lion."

"I *am* unfed."

"Right." She halted abruptly a few feet from the door, turned to him. "We haven't had dinner. Do you want to—"

He snatched the key from her, grabbed her around the waist, dragged her to the door, unlocked it, and shoved her inside. He slammed the door shut again, turned the key, stripped her of her bow, quiver, and pack within seconds, and then pushed her back against the wood, his hands on her waist, his mouth hot and hungry on hers.

"Priorities," he murmured against her mouth.

Isa gasped, caught her breath. "For once you do *not* want to eat? I can't believe it."

He kissed her jaw, trailed his lips down her throat, while he worked on the fastening of her pants. "Oh, I have every intention of *eating*."

He jerked the front of her pants open, hooked his fingers in the waistband, and dragged them down past her hips. With a few quick moves, he took off his bow, sling backpack, and quiver, and dropped them all on the floor, before he went on his knees in front of her, devouring the erotic sight of the dark curls between her thighs. The scent of her arousal slammed into him this close to its source, and a desperate, hungry sound broke from his throat.

"In fact," he said, running his hands up her muscled legs toward the vee of her core, "I plan to *feast* tonight."

Isa shuddered, her breathing ragged, and her hips shifted toward him. And yet, when he went to kiss those curls glistening with her desire for him, she pushed him back with her hands on his shoulders.

He glanced up at her, one eyebrow raised.

"Maybe I should wash up first," she said, her voice shaking.

His fingers dug into her hips as he held her in place. "If you make me wait for even five more minutes, I will spontaneously combust into a thousand pieces of blood and gore. You don't want that. I heard cleaning up the remains of an exploded person is quite revolting."

That earned him a choked-off giggle. "Yes, that sounds horrible." That glint in her eyes almost did him in. "It's not the kind of explosion I want from you."

He gave her a half-grin. "Good."

And with that, he yanked her pants down farther,

pulled the boot off her right foot, freed that leg from her pants, and then propped it over his shoulder. All within less than five seconds. His eagerness coaxed another laugh from her—which turned into a gasp when he dove in and put his mouth right where he yearned to be.

He flicked his tongue along her folds, lapped up her wetness, groaning at the heady taste of her. With his fingers stroking her intimate skin, teasing her clit, he thrust his tongue inside her.

"Ba...sil..." Isa's voice turned his name into a husky moan, an erotic prayer.

Her fingers dug into his shoulders, her hips bucked forward, met his touch. Pushing her right leg further to the side, he opened her even more, switched the action between his tongue and his hand. His fingers now slid down to her entrance, pumped into her while he licked up toward her tight bundle of nerves and circled it, before using the flat of his tongue to stroke directly over it.

Isa's breathing became erratic, her thigh muscles tensed.

He repeated the move, added a third finger to thrust into her, closed his mouth over her clit—and sucked hard.

With a keening moan, she came, her hands tangled in his hair, causing a delicious sting on his scalp. Her inner muscles contracted around his fingers, and all he could think about was how much he wanted to feel her squeeze his cock like that.

Soon.

He stroked her down from her climax, licked at her in languorous caresses of his tongue. She trembled, swayed on one leg, the other still over his shoulder. He set that leg down again, only to scoop her up in his arms, lest she collapse against the door.

"You wanted a nice, comfortable bed," he said as he carried her over to the big alcove, with its inviting-looking mattress. "I certainly don't want to deny you the fulfillment of your wish."

He laid her on the bed, pulled her boot and pants off her other leg as well, then crawled up her body to work on her tunic. She slapped his hands away, and he raised his eyebrows.

"I want to see you naked." She undid the fastening on her shirt herself, while she sneakily brought up her leg and pushed against his chest with her foot. "*Now.*"

He smirked at her. "And here I thought you'd already looked your fill of me naked."

A powerful blush rolled up her neck, darkened her cheeks. And yet her lips parted, her lids half-lowered over eyes gone quicksilver with desire. "How did you know I was there?"

"I heard your footsteps when you came up the hall. I never heard you leave." He moved off the bed and started divesting himself of the rest of his weapons.

"Maybe I tiptoed away." The playful hint of a smile made him want to kiss her, bite her, lick her, turn her laughter into moans.

"No. I know you were there the whole time." He

dropped the last of his daggers on the pile on the floor, grabbed his collar behind his neck and pulled off his shirt. "You breathe louder when you're aroused."

20

Isa inhaled sharply, partly in response to his comment, partly as a visceral reaction to the glorious sight of Basil bare-chested in front of her. With a wicked spark in his eyes. Ready to make her his.

Yes, please.

"What were you thinking about?" she asked, watching his hands as they unbuckled his belt.

"Do you really have to ask?" His voice scraped the line to delicious huskiness.

His belt was undone. The outline of his erection strained against his pants. She licked her lips.

"While I was watching," she whispered, her heart thundering, "I was imagining…you, imagining me."

He made a rough sound. "Of course I was."

Her eyes were glued to his fingers as they popped the button on his pants, lowered the zipper. His cock sprang free, proud and thick and long, making her mouth water. He grasped his shaft with one hand, pumped up and down once, then held it tight, close to the base.

"Isa," he ground out, sounding pained.

Her eyes flicked up to meet his burning gaze. "What?" she whispered.

"The way you're looking at me right now makes it fucking hard not to embarrass myself in front of you like a fumbling teenager."

Heat curled in her core, and she dug her fingers in the sheets. "I was just thinking about how I imagined putting my mouth on you while you pleasured yourself."

A sound from him that was half growl, half painful grunt. He stroked his cock, his eyes hooded with lust. "Exactly what I was picturing."

She took a slow, measured breath. "What if I want to now?"

For a heartbeat, he stared at her, his jaw turning hard, the muscles in his torso going rigid. Her bones melted, her blood turned to liquid fire, need throbbed in her still sensitive intimate flesh, and her lips tingled with the urge to sample the heat of his shaft...but she waited for his signal.

With one hand still wrapped around his cock, he raised his other one and crooked a finger at her in the universal *come hither* gesture.

Ready, so very *ready*, she crawled over to the edge of the mattress, knelt, and sat on her feet, while he lazily pumped up and down his erection. When she wanted to replace his hand with hers, he tsked and shook his head.

"Keep your hands on the bed." A hoarse whisper, a

dare.

An illicit thrill buzzed through her. *Well, now...* Sunny, lighthearted Basil had a darker side to him, and a deliciously filthy one at that. Who would have guessed? He always seemed so easygoing, not the type to take charge in bed. Then again, wasn't there a human saying that you should watch out for the quiet ones, and that still waters run deep? Not that Basil was the strong, silent type, but from what she'd learned about him, he didn't behave like the aggressive leader in his daily life.

Except, apparently, when it came to sex.

The knowledge shot tingles of excitement through her...seeing a side of him he didn't normally show, knowing he was willing to share it with her.

Bittersweet pain followed in its wake. *I won't get to share it for very long.* She pushed the thought away— quickly and vehemently—lest Basil see even a flicker of it on her face. She didn't want to taint this moment, didn't want the shadow of her impending fate to chill the heat of their passion.

Yes, she didn't have much time with him. Which was why she needed, *needed*, to savor every second, take whatever she could get.

With those maudlin feelings banished to the stone-cold corners of her heart, she sent him a sensual grin. Slowly, deliberately, she placed her hands on the mattress. She leaned forward, and he met her halfway, brushing the head of his cock over her parted lips.

Looking up at his face, she darted her tongue out,

flicked it along the vein leading up to the broad tip. His features tightened, then gentled in response to her touch, his multi-hued brown eyes glittering behind half-lowered lids while he watched her.

The enjoyment and desire on his face mirrored her own, and it drove her arousal even higher. She opened her mouth around the head of his erection, but didn't lean further forward to swallow it, instead curled the tip of her tongue to tease the underside of his shaft with slow licks, as if coaxing him deeper into her mouth. Still holding his gaze, she cocked one eyebrow in a dare of her own.

I see your wickedness, her gesture said. *And I raise it with mine.*

Understanding flashed across his face, and with a rough exhale, he tangled one hand in her hair, holding her head in place while he thrust into her mouth, tentatively at first. When she hummed her agreement against the heat of his cock, gave him the tiniest nod, he pumped faster, harder, though he kept a few fingers wrapped around the base of his shaft as a bumper to make sure he wouldn't ram deep enough to choke her.

The low, hoarse moan that broke free from him was so erotic, she had to clench her thighs together hard to counter the pressure building in her core. She wanted to see him lose it again, as he'd done in the shower, because of her—only this time not just imagining it, but knowing. *Feeling.* Making it happen.

She sucked him while he thrust into her mouth, knowing the pressure of it would drive him closer to his climax. His breaths turned to pants, and he closed his eyes, all his muscles so tight he resembled the finest sculpture, like a marble manifestation of sexual ecstasy. His orgasm shuddered along those magnificent lines of his body, his features slackening with bliss. She swallowed all he had to give, savoring his taste. His pumping slowed, his fingers in her hair relaxed their grip, stroked her head, then down to her cheek as he withdrew.

She leaned into his touch on her face, looked up at him, anticipation prickling along her nerves. His expression hovered somewhere between awe, satisfaction, and voracious hunger. His breath still ragged, he shucked his pants, then followed her as she scooted back on the bed.

"There are so many things I want to do with you," he murmured, "so many ways I want to take you and see you shatter with pleasure, I don't even know which one to pick next."

"Hm." She lay back, pulled him with her over her body, looped her hands around his neck and tugged him down to her mouth. "How about one of those kisses that are so slow and thorough and *focused*, they make me go insane with how much I *want* you?"

"Oh?" he asked with feigned innocence. "I do that to you?"

She cupped his face with both hands, her heart going quiet. "That and so much more," she whispered.

With a soft, tender gleam in his eyes, he brushed his lips over hers in the sweetest caress. "Isa."

Her breath hitched, and the words tumbled out of her. "I love you."

There. She said it, had bared herself to him as she'd never done to anyone else. And even sensing the depth of his feelings for her, in spite of all the signs of affection he'd shown her so far, her heart still hesitated with instinctive, irrational fear, anticipating a rejection.

But Basil had ceased breathing, as if his heart, too, had paused in its rhythm. He released a shuddering breath, laid his forehead against hers, his hand trembling as he stroked her cheek. "I love you, Isa of Stone."

He kissed her then, hard, fast, laced with fiery passion that could raze her soul. "I think," he said when he came up for air again, "I've loved you since the moment I saw you, that night I saved your life."

She exhaled on a soft laugh, shook her head. "How is that possible? You can't fall in love that quickly."

"I can. And I have." His eyes burned bright with an inner fire she wanted to wrap herself in, until all the parts still cold within her warmed and glowed. "It's never been this fast for me, but I'm not sorry for it. I could tell you it took time for me to fall for you, but it would be a lie. And why should I lie about something that is so true for me, it's the purest kind of pain wrapped in pleasure?" His breath caressed her lips. "I fell fast. I fell hard. And I love you with all I've got."

She swallowed past a throat gone tight and dry, tears prickling hot behind her eyelids. "You're right," she said quietly. "You should never be sorry for that. It's beautiful, and strong." *And I'll take it. I'll take it all, and hope the Fates will allow me to carry the memory with me into the eternal darkness.*

"Hey, now." He wiped a traitorous tear from her cheek. "Talk to me. Are you okay?"

Her conscience pricked her, almost made her flinch. She should tell him. Didn't he have a right to know? The irrevocability of her fate lay heavy on her soul, threatened to suffocate her. She opened her mouth, but the words stuck in her throat. Heat rolled out from the shame-filled corners of her heart into every part of her body.

If she told him about the curse, she'd have to explain her involvement in his past, and he would learn she'd been lying to him all this time. That light in his eyes, the warmth of his love, it would be dulled by her betrayal, and she'd lose the only thing that kept her afloat in the face of her impending death. *I can't tell him.* She swallowed the pained sound that wanted to escape.

"Isa?"

Live now, be in the moment. It was all she could do. Anything else would mean dying before her time.

"I'm all right," she finally said, her voice surprisingly calm despite her inner fractures, "but I'd be even better if you did one of those many things with me you mentioned. Like *taking* me." She wrapped her legs around his hips, bucked up to grind against him. Kissing a path toward his ear, she murmured, "I want to feel you inside me, Basil."

He shivered under her hands, his muscles flexing. Those gorgeous, finely hewn muscles she still hadn't had time to caress most thoroughly. She slid one hand down between their bodies, found his shaft already hardening. He thrust into her grip, nibbled at her lower lip—then froze.

"Oh shit."

She blinked. "What?"

He raised his head, his expression troubled. "I don't have any condoms with me."

Condoms... She frowned, then remembered. Ah, yes, the human contraception. With a smile, she ran her hand along his erection. "No need for that." He wouldn't know, not having grown up with fae, so she explained. "We're not fertile often. We live long lives, and I guess nature made sure we wouldn't be able to have children at the same rate as shorter-lived species. Females only have a fertile phase every couple of years, and outside of that, we can't conceive." She stroked him, that thick length she'd tasted a few minutes ago. "Mine is not due for a long while yet. We're safe."

His hips bucked as he pushed into her intimate caress. "Well then," he muttered against her lips, "in that case..."

He drew back, much to her protest, but grabbed her around the waist the next second, flipped her over onto her stomach. Her breath whooshed out of her, and excitement rolled through her on a wave of sparks at being *handled* by him. The heat and weight of his body pressed her onto the mattress while he pinned her down, skimmed one hand along her side. His hard cock was a welcome, enticing pressure against her upper thighs, so close to the point where her legs met her butt, and she pushed up with her hips, ground herself against him.

Just a little farther, and he would slide home.

He bit her neck. Pleasure arced through her, shot down to the juncture between her legs, to the spot already growing hungry and needy again. He half-balanced his weight on one arm next to her head, slid his free hand under her front, over her belly to her throbbing clitoris. His touch had her moaning into the sheets. Pinned like this underneath him, trapped between the pressure of his hand on her mound and the promise of his shaft at her upper thighs, there wasn't much she could do, nowhere she could go.

And it made the excitement building in her all the more delicious.

Basil kissed the curve where her shoulder met her neck while he played with her, let his fingers teasingly slide around her clit without rubbing it directly. Clever, he was so clever, knowing that touching anything *but* would make her writhe with growing need, panting for him to grace her with his caress.

By the time he grabbed her hips to haul her up to all fours, she was shaking with desire. His cock nudged her entrance, and she pushed back, eager to feel him. Before he could slide in, however, he wrapped one arm around her front, pulled her up until her back met his chest.

With his hand cupping her breast, his breath hot on her ear, he asked, "How hard?"

It took a moment for her lust-addled brain to catch up. Before tonight, it might have surprised her that he would ask, as she'd assumed his behavior in bed would mirror the cheerful kindness of his personality —the one he usually showed. But now she'd glimpsed the other side of him, that private, precious part of his character he only revealed to a select few, she understood. Oh, he could be gentle, too, yes. And she enjoyed those moments.

But he was capable of more, was willing to give more, and he was asking how much of it she wanted him to unleash, how much she was able to take.

"I want all of you," she said. "Rough, hard, fast…" The image of him thrusting into his own hand under the shower flashed before her eyes, his muscles flexing with his powerful, uninhibited strokes. "I'll take everything you have to give."

Behind her, his breath caught, and his hand on her breast squeezed, pulled her closer against him. A fleeting, *gentle*, kiss on her cheek…and then the pressure of his hand on her back, guiding her to all fours again. She bit her lip in anticipation as she set her hands on the mattress, as he grasped her hips, angled her just right.

His hand stroked over her butt, down to her sensitized, aching, intimate flesh. With one knee, he nudged her legs wider while he caressed her slick folds. The heat of his cock at her entrance—and he thrust into her with a powerful shove.

Pinpricks of light burst behind her eyes, her nerves overfired with pleasure-pain. As aroused and wet as she was, his size still stretched her, and those first few seconds stung in the most erotic way. He drew back and thrust in again, intensifying that sensual ache, until it turned into liquified fire in her veins.

"More," she whispered. "Go."

His fingers dug into her hips—and then he fucked her.

There was no other word that could describe the ferocity and primal roughness with which he took her. She grabbed the sheet in her fists, her weight on her forearms while he pumped into her with powerful strokes that set off fireworks of lust in her belly, streaming out into her limbs, erasing all thoughts, every hard thrust launching an avalanche of the most primitive thrills along her nerves.

The sound of their bodies slapping together, flesh on flesh, of Basil's moans and her own noises of helpless pleasure, drowned in the roar in her ears as she careened on the precipice of rough-edged bliss. Her legs and arms tingled, her vision flickered, the need in her building to a crescendo.

His finger on her clit, rubbing hard.

Then—a full-body detonation.

Pleasure hurled her high, high, high, out of the heat of her skin and Basil's grip, before she slammed back into the physical reality of a climax that left her gasping for air in a shuddering body, thoroughly taken, ravished, *destroyed*.

Basil rode his own release with sharp, quick thrusts into her throbbing core, then bent over her back with one hand braced next to her on the bed, his breath heavy and fast. He rocked against her a few more times, drawing out the pleasure for them both.

They stayed like this for several thudding heartbeats, their bodies fused in the most intimate union.

He placed a kiss on her shoulder, stroked along her spine as he straightened back up again, and pulled out. The loss of his heat, of the hardness of his shaft, made her shiver. She collapsed on the bed, closed her eyes, floated in the haze of her sensual bliss.

The mattress dipped as Basil returned. "Here," he said, his voice low and hoarse.

Opening her eyes, she turned to him, took the rag he held out to her, and quickly cleaned herself. He hauled her into his arms as soon as she tossed the rag aside, pulled her into the heat of his embrace, his love. That fire of his she wanted to wrap herself in, he'd thrust it straight into her, branding each and every one of her cells. She glowed with his warmth, his light.

Inhaling his scent of rain-kissed earth, she snuggled into him. "Basil?"

"Hm?"

"Isannarî," she whispered.

"What's that mean?"

She swallowed, drawing tiny circles with her fingers on his chest. "It's my true name."

His muscles tensed under her hands. He pushed her back just far enough to look at her, his face a study in disbelief. "Why are you telling me this? I thought you should keep that a secret?"

"I want to share it with you," she said, and made sure he heard the emphasis and determination in her voice.

"Why?" His expression bordered on panicked. "If it's so powerful, why would you trust anyone—"

She laid her hand on his mouth. "Not anyone. You. I trust *you*." She caressed his lips with her thumb. "It's a gift. I know you will honor it."

The greatest intimacy she was capable of, the most precious part of herself she could give him—besides her life. If she had to go, she wanted to do so knowing she had shared what was a prerogative between fae mates, bonded for eternity.

He clasped his hand around hers, so much emotion written into the sculpted planes and angles of his face, into the earthen shades of his eyes. "I will. I swear on my life, I'll never use it against you."

She smiled, kissed his hand. "It makes me happy, knowing you'll carry my true name in your heart." *Even after I'm gone.*

Her conscience stung her again, and made it difficult to breathe. She damned her softened heart for not locking away what had no place here between them. And yet, doubt soured her happiness.

She struggled again with the urge to tell him, if not all, then at least that she was cursed to die. She failed miserably. Explaining it to him was an exercise in pain and futility, because there was nothing he could do to break it. Nothing she would *allow* him to do. For the only way to save her life was to take his, and even if he knew, if he were to offer, or worse yet, insist, she'd never let him make the sacrifice. No, sharing her fate with him would do nothing but break his heart twice— once now, when she told him, and the second time when death took her.

Would it have been fairer not to have sex with him, not to return his love? Maybe. She could have made it easier for him by continuing to refuse his advances. Her death would hit him harder now. It would have been the truly selfless thing to do, to push him away, to not further encourage his love…

Ah, but wasn't she already selfless enough, giving up her life for his? This one thing, she wanted for herself…these few, fleeting moments in his arms, to be his true lover for the precious time they had left.

21

The key jingled in Maeve's hand when she unlocked the massive door to the Murray mansion. Stepping inside, she made sure to close the door carefully—she hated the loud bang when someone let it fall shut.

As she made her way through the foyer toward the kitchen, she heard them and smiled. Alek and Lily were home. After Basil went into Faerie, and Hazel left as well, Lily and Alek had moved in temporarily to keep her company. The house *was* awfully big for one person alone, and she appreciated having someone else around.

The door to the kitchen stood a little ajar, and Maeve was about to push it fully open when Alek's words made her pause.

"Why doesn't Merle just tell her? Maeve has a right to know."

Her breath caught. *I should go.* This clearly wasn't meant for her ears. Curiosity be damned—nothing good ever came from listening in on these kinds of conversations.

Lily replied before Maeve could bring herself to move. "She doesn't want to put her in that position. I mean, just imagine what it would do to Maeve if Merle tells her."

Tells me what? Closing her eyes, she shook herself. If Merle was keeping something from her, there had to be a good reason, and she should trust her sister's judgment. *Go. Now.*

And yet her feet remained glued to the tiled floor.

"Maybe there's still a chance to fix it," Lily added.

"But there's not much time left, right? What did Merle say, how long until she has to uphold the balance next?"

"A couple of days, depending on how much of her magic Arawn will use."

A frustrated sound from Alek. "That fucking rat bastard. Knowing him, he'll keep draining her for stupid shit, and then before you guys can find a solution, the payback will hit, and Merle—"

What? Merle what? Maeve wanted to scream.

"You know," Lily said so quietly Maeve had to strain to hear her, "having a baby is already so risky. Like, there's so much shit that can go wrong, and miscarriages are so common in the first three months. And I know how much Merle and Rhun wanted this. They've been trying for over half a year." Lily took an audible breath. When she continued, her voice was thick with tears. "I know how much this means to them. Merle wants to be a mom so bad—" Her sentence ended in a sob.

Dizzy, Maeve grabbed the wall so she wouldn't collapse. There was no blood left in her head. Couldn't be. Her heart wasn't pumping anymore.

"And now this," Lily continued, her voice paper thin. "Gods, Alek, this is so unfair. I thought it was bad that my mom had to decide which one of her babies to give to the fae, but Merle having to choose between keeping her sister safe from Arawn or saving her baby? This is so fucked up."

Her heart chose that moment to come back alive to thunder in her chest, to rush blood so fast through her body, her vision swam in red. Pieces snapped together in her mind.

Merle pregnant...upholding the balance...risking the baby...because of her deal with Arawn...

...to keep him from claiming Maeve.

Gasping for air, she pushed off the wall, walked back into the foyer, up the staircase and into her room, locked the door and sank to the floor, feeling so much that she felt nothing at all.

22

Now or never.

Isa watched Basil step off the path into the underbrush to "go water some tree," as he put it, giving her the precious opportunity she'd been waiting for. Ever since she paid her debt to him, she'd been racking her brain, trying to remember the correct spell to cast on Calâr. She still wasn't entirely sure she had it right, but time was running out. She needed to act.

They'd left the inn at dawn, and with the midmorning sun peeking out from behind a layer of clouds, they were so close to Nornûn now she could sense its magic. This might be the last chance she'd get before they reached the oracle. Now Basil had left them alone for a few minutes, she could turn on Calâr and find out once and for all what, exactly, he planned to do—and how to stop him. If she managed to extract the details of Calâr's agenda from him this way, she'd never need to reveal her own duplicity to Basil...she could sink into death's arms without having tainted the bond she shared with him.

Leaves rustled as Basil disappeared in the bushes. As soon as he was out of sight, Isa glanced at Calâr out of the corner of her eye, her muscles tensing. He was righting his tunic, looking in the other direction. One deep breath…and she muttered the words that would hopefully shatter his mental shields, penetrate his mind, and reveal his thoughts and memories.

"*Arîmai koyun'or tarhâ,*" she whispered, forming the complex hand gesture to unlock the magic of the spell, and praying to the Fates she got it right. There was a reason witches studied *years* to learn this craft—it was tricky, complicated, and dangerous if done incorrectly.

Power charged the air, then struck and slammed into Calâr. He gasped, swayed, stumbled against a tree. Isa staggered as well, as affected by the magic as he was, drawn to the object she'd cast her spell on. She tumbled into Calâr, her thoughts whirling, sights and sounds of the outside world fading in a storm of mental images as she was sucked into the other fae's mind.

Darkness, light flickering to and fro, shadows rising and falling like mist. Murmured voices echoed as if reverberating in a great hall. Colors and shapes formed out of the haze.

…unparalleled power…rare half-breed magic…

Basil's image flashed, faded.

Make them kneel, make them weak. I'll make them fear me.

Greed gripped her, so strong she shivered from it.

Voices whispered past, vicious and cold.

…not of royal blood…never ascend to the throne…keep

your nose in those dusty books…

Anger roared like a violent, red-tinged storm.

They drown in their decadence, unambitious and without vision. Now is my time. None of them had the gumption to even try, and it will be their ruin.

Basil's face again, his beauty like a knife to her heart. More images, thoughts, memories rushed around her, and she saw, *felt* the horror he planned.

"What's going on?"

The male voice punched through the swirling mist of Calâr's thoughts. A hand grabbed her shoulder, pulled her away from the other fae, broke the connection of their minds. Isa staggered against Basil, blinked at the light of the real world filtering back into her consciousness.

"Isa and I were just—" Calâr began, his chest heaving as if he'd run a mile, but she cut him off, her heart racing.

"He's set a trap, Basil."

Basil frowned, snapped to attention. "What?"

"Don't listen to her," Calâr said, taking a step towards Basil, his face set in such reassuring lines, his whole demeanor that of an honest, well-meaning male. "She seems to have had another of her seizures, and it confused her mind."

Isa gritted her teeth, looking daggers at the other fae. "My mind is *fine*." She stood, turned to Basil. "He cast a spell. While you were sleeping the other night. Some sort of mind mirror. He bound himself to you, so when you trigger the true name revelation at the oracle, he'll see what you see, hear what you hear in your head, because your thoughts are mirrored in his mind. Once he knows your true name, he'll be able to control you."

Basil tensed, glancing between Isa and Calâr.

"You have no proof," Calâr said, the calm of his voice betrayed by the twitching of his facial muscles, the murderous glint in his eyes as he glared at her.

Isa turned back to Basil. "I broke into his mind just now. I had to know, had to find out what he's planning to do with you. Remember my warning? This is it, this is the part that I was missing—why he'd want to control you. As a demon-fae half-breed, your powers —"

Calâr made a move, but froze at the sight of a nocked arrow pointing directly at his face, ready to ram into his eye. The muscles in Basil's arms flexed as he pulled the arrow back farther on the bowstring.

"Don't even think about it," Basil said to him. Looking at Isa, he added, "Keep talking."

She gave him a grim nod. "Your powers are a direct threat to all living fae. Used maliciously, your magic can weaken and hurt every single fae in Faerie...even kill them. Calâr wants this power for himself. Half-breeds like you are rare since the fae consider them abominations, and they're normally killed at birth, so he's been waiting for one for hundreds of years. Most fae don't even know about this anymore, because demon-fae relations have been forbidden for so long that all but a few of us have forgotten *why*. I had no idea. But he—"

She jerked her head at Calâr, curled her lip in disgust. "As keeper of the fae archives, he came upon this information. He found out about you, and now he's on the verge of a power grab the likes of which Faerie has never seen.

"And he's been lying to you beyond that." She focused on Basil again. "That story he told you about how the fae who exchanged you at birth told him on her deathbed about you, and asked him to take care of you? That's a bald-faced lie. Oh, he did learn about you and your identity from the fae who exchanged you... right before he murdered her. And he hasn't told you about your father."

"She's the one who's lying," Calâr hissed. "She hasn't mentioned that she—"

"He's still alive," Isa added, in a rush to distract Basil from whatever Calâr was going to spit out. "Basil— your father is still alive. He wasn't killed back then, he was imprisoned, and he managed to escape just a few days ago. He slaughtered the entire royal court to avenge you and your mother, and he injured the fae who exchanged you. She told your father about you, and he immediately left the fae in the throne room to go searching for you. Calâr was there too. He survived the slaughter, and he pressed the fae for more information and then killed her. He's been lying to you from the start, just like I warned you. He's been leading you here to the Oracle so you can learn your true name, but with the mind mirror he's set up, he'll learn it, too, and he'll enslave you."

The fae sneered. "Why should you trust her to tell the truth—"

"I trust her with my life." Basil's voice was deadly quiet.

"Oh?" The vindictive glint in Calâr's eyes chilled the blood in her veins. "The same life she needs to take to break her death curse?"

Basil frowned, but kept his bow and arrow trained on Calâr. "What?"

Isa trembled, her pulse a roar in her ears. *This is it.* Her precarious house of cards was going to collapse and scatter to the four winds.

An evil smile sneaked across Calâr's face. "She hasn't told you about that, has she? Not even in those intimate hours she spent in your arms..." He clucked his tongue. "How disappointing. Then again, it makes sense she'd hesitate to tell you that she needs to kill you if she wants to live."

The bow shook in Basil's hands. "Isa?" he ground out. "What the *fuck* is he talking about?"

She opened her mouth, her stomach cramping, but her voice fled. Words failed her.

"Now, look at this," Calâr said on a sigh. "She still won't tell you. Well, I guess that leaves me to explain her deceit to you. Mind you, I've taken this straight from her thoughts. When she attacked me just now, trying to break into my mind, her little spell backfired and allowed me to see inside *her* head. So much in there she hasn't told you, so much guilt and shame..."

Calâr shook his head. "You see, twenty-six years ago,

she was cursed to die a slow and painful death, and the seizures she's been having are the symptoms of that curse progressing. She's stalled it with magic for a while, but death has been catching up with her. And you—" His smile was sharp like a blade. "—you're her only hope to break the curse. For that, she needs to kill you."

No, Isa wanted to scream, *it's not true*. Not anymore. The bastard was twisting the truth, and yet her heart raced so fast, her breath came so uneven, she found herself incapable of uttering a single word.

Basil stood as still as if turned to stone, his widened eyes fixed on Calâr.

The nefarious fae weasel continued, his expression displaying more confidence than mere moments ago, apparently buoyed by the obvious impact of his revelations. "You're probably wondering why she would need to kill *you* to break her curse. Know what else happened twenty-six years ago?" He made a dramatic pause. "When your mother ran from the royal court to save you, she was brought back...by a bounty hunter."

Basil jerked, and the bow almost slipped from his grasp. His eyes flicked to Isa.

"Yes," Calâr whispered. "It was Isa. Your mother pleaded with her, *begged* her to spare her and her unborn child. And what did your beloved do? She dragged your pregnant mother back to Faerie anyway, to collect her reward."

Isa couldn't see through her tears, but even so, she

felt Basil's look spear her like a physical weapon.

"Your mother," Calâr went on, "realized the bounty hunter didn't have a shred of compassion or decency, so she cursed her."

A gasp broke from Isa's throat. *Air*. Where was the air? Her lungs tried to haul in breath.

"When your lovely Isa later learned that the only way to break the curse was to kill the one who cast it, or end her bloodline, she despaired. Roana died in childbirth, and her babe as well, from what she heard. Now, imagine her joy when she found out Roana's child was alive all along—she only needed to find him, kill him, and her curse would shatter.

"And guess how she found out about it? She was there the night your father slaughtered the royal court. She was present in the throne room, hiding in stone when the massacre began. She heard the fae tell your father about you." Calâr lowered his voice to a vicious snarl. "She knew your father was alive all this time. She knew, and she kept it from you, even though she understands how much it would mean to you."

Her chest constricted at the look on Basil's face. At the pain etched into his features. "Isa," he rasped. "Is this true?"

Shaking, she was shaking so hard she barely got the word out. "Yes."

Something broke in his eyes, and her heart splintered along with it. "You saw my father? You knew he's looking for me?"

"Yes." Her voice, it was a hoarse whisper.

"And you were the one who brought my mother back to Faerie?"

"Yes." Her heart, it could not hurt more than this.

"She cursed you to die?"

"Yes." Her soul, it could not be any more stained.

His voice was barely more than a croak. "You want to kill me?"

"*No.*" She shook her head, frantically, and took a step toward him. "No, I don't."

He frowned. "But you just said—"

"I *wanted* to kill you." The words tumbled out on a sob. "To break the curse. It's the only way, but I don't want to anymore. I can't take your life. I just can't. And I won't, I swear to you."

"But all this time," Basil ground out, "you've been lying to me." He exhaled roughly. "That's why you were so mad when I saved your life. Because owing me a life debt meant you couldn't kill me, right? There I was, falling in love with you, while you were biding your time until you could *turn around and kill me.*"

He shouted the last part, and she flinched.

"Please," she whispered. "Please understand… I've been suffering from this curse for more than *two decades*…when I met you, all I cared about was survival. I didn't *know* you. To me, you were the one thing left between me and an end to my curse, my suffering. But the more I got to know you, the more I —" She tried to draw in breath, and her lungs stung. "Basil, I could already have killed you, right after I paid my debt. I didn't. I *can't.*"

Sniffing, she wiped at her eyes. Her chest burned from the pressure of suppressed sobs. "You won me over, you stole my heart, you changed *everything*. I love you. More than my own life, which is why I changed my mind. I'll rather die than take your life."

"And yet," Calâr chimed in, his voice insidiously smooth, "she never told you the truth until now. She would have kept all this from you, would have gone to her death, leaving you to mourn her, without ever warning you that you were going to lose her. A fine lover you have there." He clucked his tongue again. "Betraying you until the very end."

~~~

The pain piercing Basil's heart spread through his chest, through his veins, like corrosive acid, until everything, *everything* hurt. His arms trembled as he held the bow and arrow still trained on Calâr, though he looked at Isa. "Why? Why haven't you said anything?"

"Basil…" Tears trailed down her cheeks, her face contorted. "I didn't want to spoil what we had. I know I'm going to die. I can't change it. You can't change it. And I…I just wanted to enjoy you, wanted to enjoy what little time I have left…"

"And you *kept* this from me."

Her chin quivered, her eyes liquid silver. "And what was I supposed to say? How should I have told you about the curse, and your mother, your father, about

—" A sob visibly destroyed her. "I was ashamed. I was afraid of how you'd look at me, that I'd lose your love if you learned how I betrayed you—"

"*You should have told me you're going to die!*"

She jerked as if he'd slapped her.

"What the *fuck* do I care about the things you had to do to survive—I fucking care about you *not dying*. I had a right to know I'd lose you!"

"I know," she choked out. "I'm sorry. I'm so s-sorry…"

A stealthy movement in the corner of his eye. Basil whipped back toward Calâr, who'd drawn a dagger out of nowhere, his face set in harsh lines. Basil raised his bow again—which he hadn't been aware he was lowering—and pointed the arrow at the duplicitous male fae once more.

"You," Basil growled. "Do not even dare to *breathe*. I'll get to you in a minute."

Calâr narrowed his eyes but stayed where he was, both hands half-raised, his right one holding the dagger in a non-aggressive way. Basil ground his teeth, his blood on fire with too many poisonous emotions he didn't even have a name for.

Isa's strangled cry startled him. His attention shot to her, and his stomach dropped. She was doubled over, jerking. *No.* Another seizure?

Symptoms of her death curse progressing…

His heart froze, along with the blood in his veins. His chest knotted, locked in his breath.

Isa convulsed and collapsed on the ground. Without

thinking, on instinct, Basil lowered his weapon and rushed forward. The same instant, Calâr jumped to the side in a lightning-quick move, grabbed Isa off the ground and hauled her up in front of him, the blade of his gleaming sharp dagger held under her chin.

"Stop right there, or I'll cut her throat."

Basil stumbled to a stop, his heart racing.

"She's convulsing heavily, and shaking hard, and I'm doing my best to keep her still, but if you take one more step toward me, my hand might just slip."

Reflexively, Basil raised his bow again.

"Uh-uh." Calâr increased the pressure of the blade until it nicked her skin, and a rivulet of blood trickled down her throat. "Lay down your weapons. Now."

Gritting his teeth, Basil lowered his bow, relaxed the arrow, and laid both on the ground.

"*All* of your weapons."

With a curse, he complied. One dagger after another clattered on the growing pile in front of him, until he was done, and held up his hands, palms outward.

Calâr sneered. "Good. Do what I say, and I won't harm her. If you come along and trigger your true name revelation, I will hand her over to you, unspoiled."

Basil fisted his hands. His muscles tensed with the instinct, with the urgent need to lunge at Calâr and free Isa from his grasp. But he knew, he fucking *knew* he wouldn't be quick enough. Calâr would slit her throat before Basil ever reached him.

A keening cry floated down from the breeze,

followed by the flap of wings. Basil looked up, as did Calâr, and the next second a bird of prey shot out of the stretch of sky between the trees lining the forest path.

Kîna.

Claws outstretched, the hawk launched herself at Calâr. He ducked his head and lost his grip on Isa, who slumped to the ground.

Now.

Basil grabbed a dagger from the pile and ran toward the other fae. Calâr had shaken off Kîna, but she came back at him immediately in a quick flight maneuver, distracting Calâr while Basil charged him.

With a roar, a mighty wind rose up out of nowhere. The squall hit Basil full-on, shoved him back with the force of an oncoming truck until he slammed down on the ground. The violent gust also hit the hawk, whipped at her in the middle of her attack, and hurled her away. The raptor crashed into the bushes several yards into the forest.

No. Not Isa's beloved bird. Rage boiling in his gut, Basil glared at Calâr. That fucking air-manipulating bastard.

Breathing hard, Calâr hauled Isa up again, set his dagger once more at her throat. "Now," he snarled, "we walk the last bit to Nornûn."

A thought flitted through Basil's head, unwelcome and devastating in its implications. He didn't even want to entertain it.

But it must have shown on his face, for Calâr quietly said, "You don't know if she's really going to die. There may be a cure yet, one she hasn't found. If you comply with my demands, I'll hand her over, and there will be time for both of you to search for a cure. Aren't the witches in your family especially talented? I'm sure they will find a way to break her curse, and then both of you will be able to live happily ever after. But if you don't do as I say, I will cut her throat, and she *will* die, right here, right now. Don't gamble your chance at a future with her for the uncertainty that she might die anyway."

Shit. No matter how he turned it, Basil was well and truly fucked. Give in to Calâr's demands, and he'd enslave Basil and use his powers to begin a reign of terror in Faerie, or refuse to obey in the belief that Isa was doomed to die anyway, and watch him kill Isa right in front of him.

But the bastard was right—Basil wasn't completely convinced her curse could only be broken by killing him. Maybe there *was* another way. If he only had more time with her…

Dammit, he would *not* risk Calâr killing Isa on the off chance that she was right and her impending death was inevitable. He really didn't have a choice.

With a grim nod at Calâr, he resumed his trek toward the oracle.

23

Merle was once again in the old Victorian library when the doorbell rang. With a sigh, she pushed her chair back from the desk piled with dusty books—none of which held any clue as to how to stave off paying back to the Powers That Be—and trudged over to the front door.

The dark power seeping through the cracks in the wood and stone clued her in as to who was standing on the other side even before she opened the door. Her stomach dropped, nausea swamped her—a different kind than the one caused by the tiny spark in her belly. This one went down to her soul.

When she unlocked the door and Arawn strolled in as if he owned the place, unperturbed by the wards set around the property, Merle's knees almost gave out. *No.* He couldn't be here. Not now. She wasn't ready yet, hadn't found a way to minimize the consequences of her magic use.

Hands in the pockets of his black suit pants, he scanned the foyer with eyes the color of shadowed moss. A finely tailored dress shirt of dark ruby red stretched over his broad shoulders, hugged his strong frame. He was built to put berserkers to shame. His skin glowed a dark bronze, his face all harsh angles and hard planes, the black of his hair swallowing the light. Standing there in her family's foyer, he not only dwarfed her, he claimed the very air that touched him, his sinister power creeping into all the nooks and crannies of her home.

Her *home*.

He dared come here, into her refuge, her house, sauntering in as if he had a right. That rotten, evil, impertinent son of a—

"Where is your demon, fire witch?" The deep bass of his voice boomed in the foyer, even though he had spoken in what were his quieter tones.

"Gone to run an errand," she gritted out.

She had a sudden craving for pistachio ice cream, and her darling of a demon jumped to get it for her as soon as she mentioned it.

"Good," the Demon Lord said, facing her. "I find his yapping presence rather annoying when you and I do business. Now"—he produced a rolled-up bundle from the gods-knew-where—"for today's order, I require you to put a spell on this." With a flick of his hand, the bundle unrolled.

"A rug? You want me to bespell a *rug*?"

He tilted his head, gave her a look that clearly said he wouldn't deign to answer such a redundant question.

She inwardly rolled her eyes. "What kind of charm would you like?"

"A truth spell, forcing whoever stands—or kneels—on the rug to be incapable of lying."

Merle sealed her mouth shut and breathed through her nose to keep her temper. It was going to be a damn powerful charm, difficult to weave, and requiring a huge amount of magic. Magic she couldn't afford to draw upon.

"And make it undetectable," Arawn added.

She barely held back her sound of frustration. *Like a fucking cherry on top.* Concealing a spell was often even harder than the charm itself, which was why it mostly wasn't done. She might as well slit her skin now and bleed out for the Powers That Be.

She snatched the rug from the Demon Lord's hand. "Anything else?"

The hint of a terrifying smile ghosted over his face. "Where has the Murray witch gone?"

She froze. He'd noticed. Her heart raced. Cold sweat broke out on her skin.

Well, of course he'd learn that little tidbit, wouldn't he? Considering he had the mansion staked out to watch Maeve. And then there was Alek, Lily's mate... Arawn's enforcer.

Merle narrowed her eyes. "I thought you already knew? Or don't you wring every last drop of information about what's going on with us out of Alek?"

Arawn tsked. "Aleksandr only reveals what he

wants to reveal, and I do not pressure him for more."

She raised her brows. "I find that hard to believe."

That ghostly smile again. "I do not bend a knife until it breaks. A fractured blade is of no use to me."

She frowned, blinked. *Devious, perplexing bastard.*

"Where has Hazel Murray gone?" Arawn asked again, the shadows in his eyes deepening. "And why would she leave when Juneau Laroche watches you and yours like a hawk, waiting for the opportune moment to strike?"

Damn it, but he honestly shouldn't be able to rattle her any more with anything he said. She should already be used to him having his fingers in every pie and his spies in every corner. And yet, here she stood, trying not to breathe noticeably faster so she could hide just how much his knowledge shook her.

She swallowed past her anxiety. "Didn't you once say you don't involve yourself in the affairs of witches?"

His smile this time dripped with condescension. "Obviously, my interests have changed."

A shiver ran down her back. And not the good kind of shiver.

"Tell me where she went."

"I am *so* not—"

"Tell me."

"Seriously, if you think—"

"Tell. Me."

"SHE'S GONE INTO FAERIE TO FIND BASIL, OKAY?" Uncharacteristic rage lashed out of her in a wave of sparks—visible, real sparks that settled on the rug and glowed bright before she extinguished them with a flick of her hand, her heart pounding. She hadn't lost it like this around Arawn since he'd come to claim Maeve right after her rescue.

The Demon Lord's attention pinpointed on her with laser-like focus. With narrowed eyes, he stalked forward, prowled around her, leaned in and sniffed at her. Growling, he drew back.

"How long?" he demanded.

"I don't know, a couple days?" She gestured with her free hand. "A week? I have no idea how long it'll take her to find him."

"Not that," Arawn snarled. "How long have you been with child?"

If lightning had struck her right then and there, it would have been less of a shock. She virtually *felt* all blood leaving her face, her head.

"I don't know what you're talking about," she whispered.

"You should know better than to think you can lie to me."

Her mind scrambled back into order. "This is none of your business."

Arawn paced a few feet away, turned back and advanced on her until they were almost nose to nose. Or nose to chest, considering their height difference. "Why have you not informed me of this?"

She jerked back her head. "Ex*cuse* you?"

"You should have told me, fire witch."

"Why? What's it to you?"

"It changes things," he said gruffly and turned away.

"Wait—what?"

He strode toward the door, was already outside on the porch when her brain caught up and she ran after him.

"What about the rug? Do you still want me to bespell it?"

He halted, glanced at her over his shoulder. "No. I have no need of your services for a while."

"Do you want the rug back?" she asked stupidly.

"Keep it."

Again, her thoughts took a few seconds to come up to speed. "Wait...wait. You're not canceling our deal, are you?" Her heart threatened to beat out of her chest. Dread curdled her stomach.

Arawn tilted his head. "Consider it...paused. I will not call on you to use your magic until after your babe is born. Then we will resume our cooperation."

And with that, he left as he so often did—he changed into the shape of a huge black eagle and surged skyward.

Merle stood on the porch, clutching the damned rug, her mind a huge blank. It continued to be a bottomless void for several heartbeats, while her body was numb.

Then it hit her. Slammed into her like a tidal wave into a small vessel, flooded her until she drowned, drowned, drowned in joy so pure, so overwhelming, it spilled forth as tears.

Rhun found her on her knees on the porch, weeping

into the rug.

24

Basil entered the sacred realm of the oracle, his eyes adjusting to the dimness of the room. Moss covered the circular walls as it did the stairs outside leading up to the entrance. Tree roots had broken through the stone here and there, and were growing up and down the walls, forming a hauntingly beautiful yet natural pattern. In the middle of the gym-sized room loomed a dais built of multiple slabs of slate. On top of it towered the larger-than-life statue of a man with a stag's head, complete with antlers. The imposing stone figure radiated the same mood as the intimidating portraits and statues Basil had seen in the only Catholic church he ever set foot in, back when he was a child.

He stopped at the feet of the dais and cast a look over his shoulder. "What now?"

Calâr dragged Isa with him into the temple. Her convulsions had finally subsided, leaving her limp and unconscious in that damned fae's arms. Anger boiled in Basil's very cells, and he gritted his teeth. He had no right to touch her.

Still holding the dagger to Isa's throat, Calâr said, "Your blood is needed to wake the oracle. Cut your palms on the sharp edge of the stone there, ascend the dais, and lay both hands at the statue's feet. Close your eyes and loudly say, *Yar nîm cata'or.*"

"What's that mean?"

"*My true name reveal.*"

"And then?"

Calâr lifted the dagger off Isa's throat and waved with it. "And then…the Nornûn will show your true name to you, and you should see it in your mind."

And because of that fucking mirror spell he'd done earlier, Calâr would see his true name as well.

His thoughts raced and spun again with the desperate need to find a way out of this. Endanger the whole of Faerie for a chance to save Isa, or watch her die… Nausea swamped him at the vision of her lifeless body sinking to the ground. *Never.*

Taking a deep breath, he rolled his shoulders and laid his hands on the serrated edge of the slate in front of him. He braced himself for the pain and slashed his palms open on the sharp slab. *Son of a bitch.* He steeled himself against the vicious sting shooting from his hands along all nerve endings in his body.

He'd just set one foot on the stair-like dais when Isa's gasp caused him to freeze mid-step. He whirled around.

Her eyes fluttered open, and the glorious, luminous gray of her gaze locked onto him. "Basil…" She jerked in Calâr's grasp. "Please, please don't do this. I'm not worth it. My life is forfeit already. Don't let him use me to manipulate you into—" Her sentence ended in a scream that curdled his blood.

He turned on Calâr. "Stop it! Don't hurt her. I'm doing what you want, okay? Just stop it."

Calâr frowned. "I'm not doing anything. She's just —"

Isa's convulsions were worse than any Basil had seen so far. Spittle frothed at her mouth, and she was shaking so hard Calâr had to lower the dagger so he wouldn't accidentally slit her throat. The stone walls of the oracle rumbled, as if stirred in the deep. Her skin turned ashen, her chest rattled.

Instinctual premonition arrested his breath, spread tingling dizziness throughout his limbs. *No.* It couldn't be...

Calâr lost his grip on Isa, and she crumpled to the ground. Her back bowed, and with a strangled gurgle that broke everything good inside Basil, she exhaled and then collapsed. Her chest ceased moving. Her head tilted to the side, her eyes open yet motionless, her face a mask of stillness. The rumbling of the stones stopped. Silence filled the temple.

His soul fractured. *No. No, no, no.* She couldn't be— there had to be more time.

Basil's thoughts were a mess, his mind unwilling to comprehend, to process what just happened, when a violent gust of wind slammed him down, hurled him up the dais. He hauled in a breath, grabbed a hold of one the edges of the slabs, pain piercing his cut palms.

"Well," Calâr sneered from the foot of the dais, "now your pretty fae is dead, it seems I've lost my leverage over you. Which means we'll have to do things a different way. It will be a bit harder, but I'm sure you'll be just as willing to cooperate with enough incentive." His voice dropped low, barely audible amid the whooshing of the wind. "It's all a matter of how much pain you can tolerate."

A tornado-strength torrent of air lifted Basil off the dais, broke his grasp on the slab, and catapulted him against the wall. Pain exploded in every nerve, the breath knocked out of him. He was still gasping for air when another violent gust hurled him across the room again, slammed him against the opposite wall. More fierce agony pierced his battered mind and body.

He sank down to the ground, caught sight of Isa's still form as he struggled to breathe.

She's not dead. The thought surfaced in his mind, buoyed by an impossible hope. Maybe, maybe she wasn't gone yet, and he just had to get to her. If he unlocked his powers, he might be able to help her— after killing Calâr, of course. He couldn't risk triggering the true name revelation with that bastard still alive, but once he was gone...

"Are you going to be a good sport and cooperate?" Calâr strolled toward him.

"Yes," Basil croaked. "I just need...a hand. Not sure I can make it up the dais."

If only he could get close enough to the fucker—the weight of the dagger he'd kept hidden in a sheath strapped to his calf felt damn good right about now. One well-timed strike, and he could incapacitate the asshole, then kill him.

"Sure, I can help you with that." Calâr's smirk said he wasn't fooled by Basil's request for assistance.

With a flick of his hand, he called the wind again, hauled Basil up to his feet, and pushed him toward the slate slabs. *Dammit.* Against the force of the whipping wind, he managed to grab the dagger from his ankle sheath, twisted around and threw it at Calâr.

Its flight path changed by the wind, the blade rammed into the fae's shoulder instead of his chest. Still, Calâr grunted from the impact, and his grip on the air slackened. Enough for Basil to charge down the dais and launch himself at him.

With a roar, he tackled the bastard, punched him in the jaw so hard, the fae's head snapped back. Calâr retaliated with a strike to the side of Basil's face, making stars burst in front of his eyes, and sharp pain shoot down his neck and spine. The next second, a line of fire slashed across his chest, followed by the cold kiss of a blade against his throat.

Calâr loomed over him, the dagger in his hand nicking the skin below Basil's chin. Breath heavy, the fae snarled at him. "You leave me no choice, half-breed."

A nasty, brutal force slammed into Basil's mind. He wheezed from the impact, his weak mental shields assailed by Calâr's powerful magic.

"I was hoping I wouldn't have to do this," Calâr

whispered, his face contorted as if struggling with lifting a heavy weight. Sweat beaded on his forehead, his eyelids twitched. "Cooperate with me, and I will refrain from causing you more pain."

Whatever mind control Calâr was trying to achieve, it had to take one hell of a toll on him. *Good.*

Basil gritted his teeth. "Fuck...you."

Trembling, he fought against the foreign force invading his mind. His vision flickered in and out, darkness closing in from the edges of his sight. He tried to pull up mental shields the way Lily and Hazel taught him, but each barrier he attempted to build shattered under the onslaught of Calâr's growing power. The fae smashed through Basil's fragile shields as if they were made of porcelain. Pain radiated through his limbs, flowed and ebbed in his blood. Calâr's mental control was as cold as ice, penetrating Basil's bones. He couldn't shake him.

Crawl to the platform.

Calâr's command echoed in the corners of Basil's mind, hammering at him with an imperative that was so powerful, so overwhelming, his body moved without his conscious control. Screaming inside his head, he crawled up the dais toward the statue.

No. He struggled, gathered all of his force of will just to lock his muscles and remain still, disregarding Calâr's booming command reverberating in his head.

Crawl to the top. Lay your hands at the statue's feet.

Basil's muscles trembled from the force it took to stay motionless, to disobey Calâr's order. How much longer could he keep it up? The tenuous hold he had on his own body snapped when Calâr boomed another command in his head. With a gasp, Basil crawl-stumbled forward until he reached the top of the dais.

Sweat broke out all over his skin, and his jaw was clenched so hard the pain of it zinged throughout his entire body. *Have…to…resist.*

Lay your hands at the statue's feet.

Shaking as hard as Isa used to do when caught in one of her seizures, Basil laid his hands on the platform at the feet of the statue.

Close your eyes.

His face hurt from the struggle to resist Calâr's command to close his eyes. To no avail. His lids fluttered closed.

Say out loud, Yar nîm cata'or.

Basil gritted his teeth even harder. And yet, his mouth opened of its own accord and he ground out, *"Yar…nîm…"*

A blast of white-hot magic lit up the dark of the temple like lightning. Calâr's brutal grip on Basil's mind snapped like a wire being cut.

"Don't you dare touch my son," an unfamiliar male voice growled.

Jerking back, Basil withdrew his hands from the feet of the statue. Fae magic sparked in the air as a dark shape slammed Calâr to the ground and began a merciless butchery.

Behind the struggle between Calâr and his attacker, a witch rushed into the temple. Black hair swept up in a ponytail, clad from neck to toe in dark combat gear, Hazel scanned the room—and then her brown eyes locked onto Basil. "My baby…"

She scrambled up the dais, knelt beside him, her hands on his shoulders, his face, his chest, checking him for wounds. "Are you injured? Are you okay?"

Basil shook his head, struggled to get to his feet. "Isa. We need to help her."

Hazel followed his gaze to the crumpled shape of the female who held his heart. Together they ran down the dais, crouched next to Isa's body. Hazel spread her hands over Isa's chest, and a glow emanated from her palms. Golden light flowed down into Isa. Hazel closed her eyes, frowned. Her lips parted. Her face fell.

The glow faded, she balled her hands to fists and let them fall at her sides.

"What are you doing?" Basil grabbed Hazel's hands, pulled them back over Isa. "Heal her. *Please*."

"Basil…"

"Mom, please."

"Baz." She cupped his face, shook her head, her eyes shimmering. "She's gone."

"*No*. Bring her back."

"Sweetie, no one can bring back the dead. Not even witches."

His breath burned in his lungs, heat prickled behind his eyes, and his stomach cramped. He heaved, but nothing came.

A crunch, a strangled scream, followed by sudden silence, and the sounds of struggle close to them abruptly ceased. The shadowy attacker who had launched himself at Calâr now rose from what remained of the male fae he had all but ripped to shreds. When he looked over his shoulder at them, the resemblance struck Basil like a blow to his guts. Uncanny, unsettling—undeniable in its implication.

Even if he hadn't heard him yell something about *my son* earlier, Basil would have known. From the blond hair, its shade and nuance exactly like his own, to the facial features that were an eerie mirror image of Basil's face, the family relation was indisputable.

Power poured off the demon like steam. His breath heavy, he stood there over the body of the slain fae and stared at Basil.

But Basil's mind was too preoccupied with something else to even begin to acknowledge the emotional consequences of this. Calâr was dead. His threat to Basil eliminated.

I can unlock my powers.

His eyes flicked to Isa's still form, then to the statue atop the dais.

He ran.

Breath coming in quick bursts, he scaled the slab stairs, slammed his hands at the feet of the statue. Eyes closed, he murmured, "*Yar nîm cata'or.*"

A blinding flash of light in his mind, a force that nearly made him stumble down the dais. His lungs seized, his muscles spasmed.

Sarômtanhâr.

The name whispered through his thoughts, burned

itself into his soul—and unlocked a thousand seals within him. Magic blossomed in his cells, fused and merged and surged until it rolled into every last atom of his body, his mind. The hum he'd heard before grew to a deafening crescendo, in sync with the rising melody of the earth.

He gasped for air, half staggered, half slid down the dais, buzzing with a heady rush of power. With his eyes on Isa, he swayed forward.

Only to freeze in place, his muscles locking against his will.

Along the pathway forged by Calâr shortly before, a new presence sneaked into Basil's mind. This one dark, much darker than the fae's had been. It tasted familiar and yet strange, full of hot, age-old wrath.

Basil glanced toward the source of the new mind control, to that face which bore an uncanny resemblance to his own. His father's eyes glowed amber in the dim of the room as he stared at Basil.

So much power, whispered his voice inside Basil's mind. *I've seen it in the fae's thoughts. What you can do.*

Basil grunted, struggled against the control.

I've seen what he planned. You could kill them all. They deserve it.

"No," Basil ground out.

In his peripheral vision, he saw Hazel rise from her crouch, magic vibrating around her. "What's going on?"

If you won't do it, I will. A terrifying smile stole across the demon's face. *Sarômtanhâr.*

Basil gasped, jerked as if hit with an electric charge. *Shit*. Somehow, his father had taken over Calâr's mind mirror after he killed him, and now he knew Basil's true name.

Basil struggled, pushed against the control to get to Isa.

Stop.

He froze as if paralyzed.

"Don't do this," Basil choked out. "Let me help her."

His father tilted his head forward, his gaze never leaving Basil's face. *She's dead. You can't help her.* He spit on the ground and added, *She deserves her fate, after what she did to Roana. She deserves to die.* His mental voice dropped to a tortured whisper. *They all do.*

"No!" Basil struggled against the invisible force holding him in place, against the insidious demand to use his powers to connect to, to find, to touch all living fae's minds…

Witch magic rose in the air, its buzz like that of an enormous swarm of bees. "Basil? What is he doing?"

"He's accessing my mind." Basil panted. "He's got a lock on me, on my powers. He's trying to use them to slaughter every fae in Faerie."

He'd barely finished his sentence when Hazel lashed out with her power, and slammed his father against the wall, holding him there in a magical vise grip. She advanced on the demon, stopped a few feet away from him. The air around her cracked and sparked with electricity, her face as harsh as Basil had never seen her before.

"Let. Go. Of. My. Son." She bared her teeth at him. "If you want to have any kind of meaningful relationship with him—and I *know* you do—then release him. Do *not* use him this way. He will never forgive you."

His father tensed, looking daggers at Hazel. Then, with a shuddering breath, he relaxed, closed his eyes.

Basil gasped as his father's influence receded. With a start, he raced to Isa's side and pulled her into his arms, cradling her lifeless body against his chest.

Maybe, just maybe, if there was a spark of life left for him to grasp, he could pull her back... On instinct, not really knowing what he was doing, and yet *knowing*, he closed his eyes, dove in, deep into his new powers, into the humming, swirling, iridescent darkness within him. It grew, stretched and rolled out, spread into a black field as far as his mind could reach.

Blips of light in the dark velvet surrounding him, blinking, sparking, moving... So many minds, so many thoughts and sensations, memories and images in a cacophony of light and darkness. And there...the fading ember of a flame that touched his soul. *Isa.*

He grasped at it with his mental fingers, and it almost, *almost* held—before her light slipped away, ran through his hands like softly glowing sand. He had to keep her. He knew he had to grab on to her to...*what?*

An idea brushed his mind, and on an impulse, he followed it.

Again, he reached for that elusive, fading light—and spoke into the darkness.

Isannarî.

25

Slipping, slipping away.

Here to there, now to then, through velvet and darkness and time beyond time.

A voice, calling through the layers of all that was and will be. Calling *her*. Back?

Death's arms cradled her with so much care. *Infinite* care.

Where was Back? And when?

She floated.

That voice again, piercing the darkness.

Isannarî.

She jerked, electrified, called forth by a power she could not resist. All the parts of herself that were eternal, the fabric of her soul, her mind, the tapestry of her being, were ripped open, apart, *unraveled.* A million threads of possibilities, unwoven, untangled…knitted together again, forming the pattern that was Isa.

Come back to me.

And, lovingly, Death let her go.

26

Isa's mind and soul slammed back into her body with enough force to make her convulse again.

Her back arched, her heart started—its rhythm a staccato beat—and her lungs contracted. She opened her mouth, hauled in air with a strangled wheeze. She flailed, flailed, her arms and legs twitching, every single nerve overloaded with too much sensation.

"Isa."

Darkness still, this one harsher than the stygian velvet she'd just floated in. Colder, except...for the heat of the arms that held her.

"I'm here. Isa, baby. I'm here. I've got you. You're okay." His voice broke. "You're *okay*."

She opened her eyes, and the world was gold and light and sunshine, finely honed beauty, and myriad shades of brown, and love in the tears that ran down his cheeks.

Basil.

Her hand rose to touch his face, trembling fingers brushing his lips. "I was..."

"I know." Hoarse, his voice was so hoarse.

"But you brought me back." She frowned. "How?"

A jerky shake of his head. "I don't know. I don't care."

She blinked, remembering, her frown deepening. "You...*unmade* me." A tiny gasp. "And wove me back together..."

"Whatever I did," he whispered, "whatever it was, I don't care, as long as you're here, you're back..." His throat worked as he swallowed. "I couldn't lose you. You're my life. You're *everything*. I need you here, with me. When I saw you die..." He shook, shook so hard he made her tremble as well.

"Shh." She brought her other hand to his face, too, cupped his cheeks, stroked up into that hair of spun gold. "You came for me. You brought me back. I'm here now."

He clutched her to him then, his embrace speaking of despair in the face of death, of an abyss of loss in his soul that gaped so devastatingly, it threatened to drag her down into the void of his excruciating pain. She inhaled on a shudder, grabbed onto him with all the force of her newly sparked life, to let him know, down to his bones and the marrow of his soul, that she was going to hold on to him as hard as he did to her.

"I will *always* come for you." A harsh whisper against her ear, a vow that was a balm to her battered heart. "I'll never let you go, Isa. You're mine, and I'm yours, and not even Death will take you from me."

It broke out of her on a sob. All the fear and the

anger, the guilt and the despair, the greedy, insatiable, selfishly selfless *love*, the hope for the impossible, the rush of disbelieving joy, it poured out of her with the waning of adrenaline in her veins, and she was left shaking in Basil's arms, crying into his neck.

He held her, and rocked her, and together they cried, for what could have been minutes, or hours, or eternity.

Only when Basil eventually lifted his head and spoke to someone else did Isa realize they weren't alone. With a start, she twisted in Basil's arms, glanced around.

Calâr's lifeless body—or what was left of it—lay several feet away, but two other people stood in the temple—a demon and a witch. The male she recognized immediately, her stomach dropping with acidic fear. The way he glared at her...he, too, remembered how they met before, and under what circumstances.

"It's okay," Basil said. "He won't harm you. Aren't I right...*Father*?"

Those amber eyes sparked in a face so similar to the male she loved, and yet so very, *very* different. Slowly, the demon inclined his head. "Since you...care for her."

Basil gave him a sharp nod. "Isa," he then said, "meet my mother, Hazel."

A flash of warmest joy crossed the witch's face when he introduced her—and Isa noticed, too, the fact he hadn't said *adoptive*—before she stepped closer, smiled at Isa. "It's good to meet you. Basil will have to tell me all about you."

"Later," he said. "First, we need to get Rose."

Hazel's expression tensed, the air around her darkened.

"Mom," Basil rasped. "I know where she is. I've seen her."

"How? Where?"

He shook his head. "I'm not sure how to explain it. When I...went for Isa, I kind of...connected with all fae in Faerie. It's like I had a direct link into their minds, their thoughts, their memories. There were so many of them, so much information, but I saw...Lily, just different. Someone who looks *exactly* like her, and—" He frowned. "*Witch.* I picked up on the word, and it was connected to her."

Hazel's lips trembled. "That has to be Rose." She inhaled sharply, her eyes hardening. "Think you've seen enough to lead us to her?"

Basil gave her a grim nod.

"Then let's go."

27

Merle wiped the latest tears off her cheeks and checked her reflection in the mirror of the passenger side sun visor.

"Is the crying going to continue?" Rhun asked from the driver's seat. "Because I have to tell you, it'll make me uncomfortable. I thought after He-Who-Shall-Not-Be-Named pulled that surprise act, there'd be fewer tears. If this is going to be the new normal, we'll have to stock up on tissues, little witch."

She punched him in the shoulder, laughing at the way he undermined his flippant comments with a surge of love along their mating bond. Sniffling, she said, "I'll be fine. I'm just...I can't wait to tell Maeve. I hadn't realized how much it hurt me that I had to keep this from her. She's going to be an aunt! Oh, gods, she'll be so thrilled."

He took her hand, squeezed, and shot her a smile that was an echo of the relief flowing through their shared connection. She felt his burst of happiness when she told him Arawn had paused the deal, and Rhun's entire soul had brightened as if a crushing pressure had been lifted. Rhun hadn't *wanted* to surrender Maeve, she knew that, and he was just as relieved as she to know they wouldn't have to make the decision now.

Taking a deep breath, she nodded at him, opened the car door, and got out. Rhun joined her, and they walked to the imposing gate of the Murray property. She unlocked it with the spare key she always carried, and they stepped through the wards onto the grounds. The magical protection was calibrated to allow Rhun to pass even though he was a demon, just like Alek and Lily.

Lily's car was parked in the wide, circular driveway, right next to Alek's truck.

When they entered the lofty foyer, silence greeted them. Lily and Alek might still be sleeping; as *pranagraha* demons, they were nocturnal, spent the day indoors due to their species' sensitivity to sunlight. Maeve was probably up in her room with her nose buried in a book.

"Lil?" Merle called out. "Maeve?"

"Merle!" Lily's head appeared over the banister of the landing platform above. "Merle—oh, gods. I was just about to call you."

"What's going on?" Merle was already racing upstairs, Rhun hot on her heels.

When she reached Lily, the expression on her best friend's face made her blood ice over with foreboding.

"What is it?" She grabbed Lily's hand. "Are you

okay?"

"It's not me," Lily croaked.

With a trembling hand, she held out a piece of paper. Merle's pulse thundered in her ears as she took it.

"I got up just a bit ago," Lily went on. "Maeve didn't mention she planned to go out, so I thought she'd be in her room as usual, but when I went to say hi to her, I found her room empty, and this note on her bed."

Merle was barely able to make out the words written on the paper, her hand shook so hard.

I know about the baby, the letter read. *I know you didn't want me to find out, but I'm glad I did. Merle, maybe you don't want to put me in this position, but it is where I need to be. This is my choice, my responsibility. I never wanted you in that position, never wanted you to have to make these tough decisions because of me. You've already done so much for me, risked so much, and I am so, so thankful. Which is why I can't allow you to risk anything else—anyone else— on my behalf.*

I'm surrendering myself to Arawn, so he will stop using your magic. Your baby will be safe.

Please, don't come after me. By the time you read this, I'll be well on my way to his lair. It's long overdue, and it's what I should have done weeks ago.

Merle, I love you. You deserve to be a mom, and I'm so happy for you.

Rhun, I would have enjoyed getting to know you.

Lil, I love you, too. Please hug Baz and Hazel for me when they get back. I haven't known Alek long, but I'm so glad you found each other.

I'll keep you all in my heart. Maybe one day I'll get to see my niece.

— Maeve

Rhun caught Merle as the world around her collapsed into darkness.

28

"How much farther?" Hazel asked.

"Five minutes at most," Isa replied. "It should be just around this bend."

Basil had given her as much information as possible based on what he gleaned from the faeries' minds about Rose's location, and Isa had pieced together that it had to be a cave dwelling on the outskirts of Angûn, a town just a couple of hours from the oracle.

They made the trek in record time, the urgency of what Basil saw happening to Rose driving them on. He wouldn't tell them details of what he'd glimpsed, just that they needed to get her out ASAP. Every time either Hazel or Isa asked him to explain, he shook his head with a pained look on his face and said, "Don't ask me to describe it."

Tallak would glance his way, darkness shadowing his face, and then walk on ahead.

A hawk's cry pierced the silence of the woods. Isa shielded her eyes from the sun while she looked up, smiled at the beautiful sight of Kîna in full flight. To think she'd almost lost her… Her breath hitched.

After they left the oracle, Basil insisted they check on something. He wouldn't say what, and ordered Isa to stay back while he led Hazel off the path into the brush. Of course Isa had gone after them, only to sink to her knees next to the twisted shape of her beloved hawk, her heart in pieces.

But Hazel simply pushed Isa aside, laid her hands on the bird, and muttered, "She's alive. I've got her."

And when Kîna flapped her wings not a minute later, then shook herself and looked around, as if she'd never been harmed, Isa hugged Hazel so tight the witch gasped for air. If she hadn't already appreciated Hazel for having given Basil a childhood full of love and shelter, this alone would have earned her Isa's undying love.

She grasped Basil's hand, squeezed it, and whispered, "Thank you for thinking of her."

Basil followed her gaze to the idly circling hawk above, then gave her his dazzling smile. "Of course."

The path curved around the cliff set in the forest, trees growing up above and below, on whatever ground the plants could cling to on this rocky terrain. To the right, the wooded floor sloped steeply down into a fern-covered ravine, and to the left rose the cliff, covered in parts by moss and yet more ferns.

And up ahead, a mere yard away, gaped the opening to the cave dwelling Basil saw in the minds of the fae who held Rose.

Basil stopped and nodded, his face grim. "That's it."

Hazel took a deep breath. "Okay. We need to know how many fae are in there, and where exactly they keep Rose. Can you check for that?"

"I'll try." He closed his eyes, muscles in his jaw rippling, mouth pressed into a thin line. A harsh inhale, all color leaving his face.

"Have you found her?" Isa laid a hand on his arm.

He gave a jerky nod. "She's..." He swallowed, his voice rough. "They're..."

"Taking her blood," Tallak said, his expression impassive.

Isa tilted her head in surprise before she remembered. Basil explained that his father took over Calâr's mind mirror when he absorbed the fae's powers. Tallak saw what Basil saw.

Magic thickened the air, like pressing summer heat. "How many fae?" Hazel hissed.

Basil's forehead furrowed as he concentrated. "Fifteen...I think. Including guards."

"Kill them." Tallak tilted his head, his intense amber eyes on Basil.

He blew out a breath. "I'm not sure I can pinpoint my powers to kill only these few. I don't have a handle on it yet. I could end up slaughtering every other fae in Faerie, too."

Tallak's raised brow clearly said he didn't see any problem with that.

"No," Basil said emphatically.

"Okay." Hazel cut through the air with her hand. "We need to go in carefully, kill them one by one, without making a fuss, until we get to Rose and—"

"Uh, guys?" Isa interrupted.

Hazel and Basil both looked at her.

She pointed at the entrance to the cave dwelling, where Tallak disappeared inside, his sword drawn.

"Shit!" Basil took off after him.

Hazel followed him at a run, leaving Isa to catch up.

Inside, they both stumbled into Basil, who stood staring at the trail of blood and guts leading deeper into the caves. No sound but the swishing of a lethal blade and the thunk of bodies hitting the floor.

They followed the evidence of Tallak's slaughter, their weapons drawn, and found him in a dungeon-like room lit by few flickering torches. Standing over a pile of dead fae, bathed in their blood, he looked up at them with glowing amber eyes, his breath scarcely a touch faster in spite of all the killing.

He raised a brow at their shocked silence, gestured to the bodies at his feet. "What? I wasn't supposed to let one of them live, was I?"

Hazel inhaled sharply, shook her head. She studied the room, her attention snagging on a crumpled form in the corner. With a choked sound that broke Isa's heart, Hazel rushed forward, sank to her knees next to the young woman dressed in rags. Chains clinked as she gathered her in her arms.

Basil walked closer, haltingly, his face a picture of silent horror. Isa grabbed his hand.

"You can heal her?" he asked his mother, his voice but a rasp.

Hazel's breath hitched. "She's not injured, she's anemic. I need to get her home, brew a potion to replenish her blood."

Her hand trembled as she brushed the greasy hair off Rose's face—a face which so closely resembled the older witch's that there could be no doubt about their relationship.

Rose woke with a start, twitched, opened her eyes and hissed. Sluggishly, she struggled in Hazel's arms, clearly panicked. Magic whispered through the air, although it was barely more than a breeze.

Hazel uttered a pained sound and let go of Rose. The young witch scrambled away from her, into a corner, dark hair hanging into her face, muscles in her bare arms and legs tensed.

"It's okay," Hazel said, her voice soothing. "You're safe, Rose. We're going to get you out of here…"

Rose spoke, and it took Isa a moment to realize she'd done so in Fae.

"She doesn't understand English," Isa whispered.

"What?" Hazel stared at Isa.

"It makes sense." Isa swallowed. "She's been raised here. They never taught her English. Why would they?"

Power crackled around Hazel, and Rose flinched, cowered lower in the corner. With a gasp, Hazel gentled her energy.

"I'm sorry." She took a tentative step toward her daughter, who stared at her with an expression Isa hoped she'd never have to see again. "Rose," Hazel said. "I've come to take you home."

Isa translated, then listened to the young woman's reply. "She's asking who Rose is," she whispered.

Hazel exchanged a glance with Isa, and nodded. So Isa told Rose. Told her all about how she'd been born to a witch, taken from her mother, swapped for Basil, how they'd come searching for her, ready to take her to freedom.

The young witch listened, her eyes darting back and forth among them, and when Isa finished, Rose peered at Tallak.

"Did he kill them all?" she asked in Fae.

"Yes," Isa said.

"The mistress, too?"

Isa frowned, glanced at Tallak.

He tilted his head. "Tall, green hair, gray skin, and blue eyes?" he asked in Fae.

Rose gave a shaky nod.

"Dead."

A shudder went through the young woman, and she closed her eyes, sagging against the wall.

Isa translated the exchange for Hazel and Basil. At the mention of Rose's "mistress," Hazel's expression hardened, clearly indicating she'd get to the bottom of the story behind that. *Later.*

She nodded at her daughter. "Isa, please tell her I'm going to use magic to take off her chains."

Isa relayed that to Rose, and the young witch nodded her consent, holding out her arms with the heavy cuffs around her wrists when Hazel approached her. Metal clinked, the chains clanked on the stone floor, and Rose was free.

She eyed Hazel's outstretched hand for a moment, as if unsure whether to take it. As if she was looking at a dog, trying to decide whether it would lick her hand— or bite it.

With an unsteady breath, she grasped Hazel's fingers, let the older witch pull her to her feet. She swayed, and Hazel steadied her with her hands on her shoulders. Rose cringed, pulled back just a little.

Enough to make hurt flash across Hazel's face, visible even though she tried to hide it the next second. "It's all right, Rose," Hazel said, nodding at Isa to translate. "I understand. I don't expect you to trust me yet. You don't know me, and it will take time. But please know I'm here for you. I've been waiting to take you back into my arms for twenty-six years." Her voice dropped to a hoarse whisper. "I can wait a bit longer."

Rose listened to Isa's translation, studying Hazel with wide eyes, mapping her face—undoubtedly rattled by the resemblance.

"Rose," the young witch said, as if trying the word. She looked at Isa, spoke in Fae. "That is what she named me?"

Isa nodded.

"What does it mean?"

"*Karûn*," Isa said, naming the flower in Fae.

Rose considered that, tilted her head. "That is better."

"Than what?"

"*Nem.*"

Isa exhaled roughly, her heart cringing.

"What?" Hazel asked.

She translated, finished with, "They called her *morsel.*"

Isa had to hand it Hazel. The witch kept her temper under tight control, despite the murderous glint in her eyes.

"Here," Tallak said in Fae, and threw a bundle of clothes at Rose, including boots.

She caught them, clutched them to her.

Isa raised her brows at him. She hadn't even noticed when he left the room, but apparently he'd searched the other parts of the house.

At the curious looks directed his way from everybody, he huffed. "Unless you want her to walk out of here like that?" He gestured at her shabby garments. "She won't make it half a mile without shoes."

"Good thinking," Hazel muttered, then ushered them all out of the room so Rose could change.

Isa followed Basil to the entrance of the cave dwelling, found him staring down the ravine, his hands on his hips.

"Hey." She slung her arms around him from behind, pressed her cheek against his back next to his quiver.

"We found her." His voice was a low rumble she felt as a vibration on her skin.

"She'll be all right." It might take time—lots of time —but Rose's future looked infinitely better than even a few hours ago.

He let out a rough breath. "I hope so. I've seen Maeve come back from worse. I'm just glad we got her out."

She squeezed him. "Well, I'd say your mission into Faerie was a success. You found Rose. You unlocked your powers. You even found a father you believed dead."

He turned, grasped her face with both hands, laid his forehead against hers. "I found *you*."

She wound her arms around his neck and pressed her body closer to his. "That you did."

"Finders keepers," he murmured against her mouth. "Marry me."

She laughed into his kiss. "The human way?"

"Human, witch, demon, fae...I don't care which one. As long as I can claim you as mine."

Her fingers tangled in his hair. "Then we'll do them all."

"So that's a yes?"

She looked up into those mesmerizing eyes of multihued brown, let the love and warmth of his gaze wash over her. "A thousand times yes."

EPILOGUE

"This is *so* unreal," Lily muttered, staring out the kitchen window into the backyard of the Murray mansion.

Basil followed her look to where Rose lay on the lawn, face turned up toward the starlit night sky, her fingers twined in the grass. She'd been like this for an hour already, Isa keeping her company and talking to her in Fae, while Rose soaked up sounds and sights and sensations like someone criminally underfed. Which she was, in a lot of ways, not just in terms of nutrition. From the bits and pieces about her captivity that Isa had gotten out of Rose so far, she'd mostly been kept indoors and underground, had only been allowed out on rare occasions...when she'd been "good."

She was so starved for nature and fresh air that, even after the journey here from Faerie, which had taken several days, she still couldn't seem to get enough of the outdoors.

"So. Unreal," Lily said again, gaping at a twin she'd

never known existed.

Their first meeting had been…interesting, to say the least. Lily, who always seemed to have a comeback for everything, who had a witty or sarcastic remark for every situation, and who tended to indulge in running commentaries about what was happening—even when it was in her best interest to shut up—just stood there in shocked silence for a full five minutes when they presented her with Rose.

Basil had to pinch her to snap her out of it. And Rose…indigo eyes wide, slack-jawed, marveling at the sight before her, raised a hand to Lily's face, as if to trace the features that so resembled her own, only to draw back with a flinch. She started to apologize in Fae —translated by Isa—when Lily grabbed her hand, raised it to her face, and let Rose touch her.

That moment still gave Basil goosebumps.

"Seeing her next to you," Basil said from his seat at the table in the breakfast nook, "drives home just how frail she truly is."

Compared with Lily's strength—not only from her demon nature, but from years of exercise and martial arts training—with the healthy glow of her skin, the humor in her smile and the sparkle in her eyes, Rose was a wraith, a haunting specter of what Lily might be if faced with years of neglect and starvation. It was unsettling, *infuriating*, this stark reminder that Rose should be just as healthy, her magic just as strong, her spirit unbroken.

"I wish," Hazel whispered, "Tallak had left them

alive." Her brown eyes bore a hard glint, and her nostrils flared, as she looked out at her daughter. "So I could deliver the slow and painful death they deserve."

"I second that." Lily narrowed her eyes—which had started to show red specks, a sure sign she was getting demonically pissed—then took a deep breath and exhaled roughly, her eyes returning to deep blue once more. She was getting better at controlling her new otherworldly instincts. "So this kind of treatment was okay with the fae who swapped her? Didn't she say Rose was going to be well cared for?"

Basil and Hazel were still in the process of bringing Lily and the others up to speed on everything that happened—as much as they knew, at least. Some details were missing yet, and it would take time to piece it all together. Rose needed to adjust, and they didn't want to pressure her into a *bare-your-soul* therapy session.

"From what she told Isa so far," Basil said, "it seems those fae we freed her from were not the ones she was originally placed with when she was brought into Faerie. The fae couple whose tracks Isa and I followed had Rose for the first few years. Rose mentioned that the fae who gave her to that couple did check in regularly for some time, but stopped doing it after some years. By the time Rose's powers kicked in when she was seven, the couple hadn't heard from the fae in a while, and they assumed she wasn't interested in Rose anymore. Apparently they didn't know how to handle Rose's awakening witch magic, and were glad to get rid of the burden when another fae approached them and asked to buy her."

The room darkened, the windows rattled.

"Mom." Lily turned, sat next to Hazel and took her hand.

The magic charging the air relaxed, lost its menace.

"I'm all right." Hazel squeezed Lily's hand, closed her eyes briefly. "It's just…"

"I know." Lily's eyes glowed again with fiery sparks, her banked outrage at the fact Rose had been sold probably stoked by the memory of how Lily, too, had only recently been auctioned off among demons. Like Rose's captors, those demons had met a bloody and painful death.

"She'll get stronger again," Hazel said. "I'll make sure of it. There's no irreparable damage. Given enough food, rest, exercise, and time, she'll become what she was born to be."

Lily startled. "Mom—I just realized." She clapped a hand over her mouth, then let it fall back on her lap. "Our line hasn't ended, has it?" Her eyes glistened with unshed tears, and her voice grew husky. "After I was turned into a demon, I was so worried about it. I felt guilty when I decided to stay demon, but I thought —hey, at least Basil might keep the bloodline going. If he has kids, they might inherit the magic, right?" She paused, inhaled sharply. "Now I know why you were so reserved when I mentioned how I hoped Basil could carry on the line. You knew he couldn't." She uttered a choked laugh, then sobered. "But now...with Rose... The Murray magic lives on. She'll continue our line."

Hazel's face was tight with silent pain. "I wish I could have told you."

"So," Basil chimed in, "Rose's magic... Isa said Rose never actually used it. They didn't let her. When they started taking her blood, it was enough to reduce her powers to a level where they could easily control her."

Rose's captors had apparently been privy to a well-kept secret among select fae—that ingesting witch blood enhanced a fae's own magic temporarily and acted as a potent drug. They'd kept her as a living source of intoxication and stimulants, keeping her at the edge of death for long stretches of time, providing just enough food and other essentials to assure she was able to bleed for them. The mere thought of what the better part of her adult life must have been like turned his stomach and heated his skin with a primal rush of rage.

Hazel proved why she deserved a place among the ranks of Elder witches with the icy control she maintained on her powers, since the wrath she surely harbored had to be a thousand times hotter and more devastating than what Basil felt. Unleashed, that wrath could, without a doubt, raze their entire mansion to the ground.

As it was, the flicker of the lights and the electric buzz in the air were the only signs of her ruthlessly restrained rage. "Her magic will become more powerful as she regains her strength. I will be there with her, every step of the way. I'll teach her how to control her powers, and how to wield them."

"It'll still be hard for her to adjust." Lily looked out at Rose again.

"It's too bad," Basil said, his voice gone quiet amid a surge of grief, "that she never got to meet Maeve." He swallowed hard, his throat tight and hurting. "I'm sure Maeve would have taken to her right away. They have a lot in common."

The silence that descended was heavy with loss and heartache, the hole ripped in their midst still raw and gaping.

"Has Alek heard anything?" Hazel asked, her voice thin.

Lily shook her head, the lines around her mouth tensing. "Nothing."

And with their only link into Arawn's network— Alek—unable to gather any intel about Maeve, they were all left to drown in a sea of uncertainty about her fate.

Basil couldn't keep thinking about it, not when he wanted to maintain a functioning brain, so he switched to a subject he'd been meaning to broach ever since they traveled back from Faerie.

"Mom," he said, deliberately using that name, "now we're back… There's something I want to ask you."

"What, honey?"

"Since I found out I'm not your son…" He took a deep breath. "I've been wondering—if you ever—" He balled his hands to fists, gritted his teeth.

"If I ever what?"

"Resented me."

The air stood still at Hazel's palpable shock. "Why would you think that?" she whispered, her expression stricken. "Did you feel unloved?"

He swallowed again, this time past a lump that formed with unsettling speed. "No. Not really. I mean, I *thought* you loved me. But knowing you had to give up your daughter and got me instead, I was wondering…if maybe sometimes you looked at me and thought—"

"That you were to blame?" Hazel's voice trembled with quiet outrage.

He shrugged and looked out the window, his chest constricted, his stomach one fucked-up knot.

"Baz." Hazel grabbed his hand and held it so tight he faced her again. Her expression was drenched in such raw pain, it struck him deep. "I have *always* loved you, Basil. Yes, I wanted my daughter back, and I cried for her when no one would see me. But—here is where I am selfish. I wanted the fae to return Rose…but I didn't want to give you back. Even knowing we had a deal, knowing you'd belong with your kind if they ever came for you—I would have fought to keep you. I would have bargained for you. *That* is how much I love you, as my son."

Her lips quivered, and she squeezed his hand. "I never resented you. Not for one second. You were a *baby*, Baz. A sweet, innocent child. *My* child. You stole my heart the moment I took you in my arms, and you will always be my son. I'd give my life for yours, without even thinking about it." She curled his fingers around his. "I love you, sweetie."

"I love you, too, Mom." Basil blinked to clear his eyes, inhaled on a shudder, and turned to the sobbing mess of a sister sitting next to him. "Want me to fetch you the entire roll of tissues from the counter? We have ten more in the garage. You look like you might need them all."

Lily uttered a keening wail of unintelligible sounds, smacked him upside the head, then lunged for him and sobbed against his shoulder. He hugged her, patted her back, and laughed until the tightness in his chest eased and Lily started pinching him in the side.

"Mom," he said when Lily eventually went to get the roll of tissues. "There's something else I've been thinking about. You said you think the fae magic changed Robert, that it poisoned his mind somehow, and made him turn on you like that."

Hazel stiffened.

"I don't think it's true," he went on. "I mean, it's possible, sure, but what if he was just an assh—a narcissistic jerk all along?"

"But he wasn't like that in the beginning."

"Well, that doesn't mean he changed because of magic. He could well have been a narcissist all his life and simply managed to charm you for a while. That's what abusers do."

Hazel opened her mouth, closed it again. Basil could see her mind working behind her warm brown eyes.

Before she could say anything, he added, "Think about it. For years now, you've been beating yourself up because you believed the whole thing with the changeling swap and the spell being put on him was the reason he treated you like shit."

"Language," Hazel said, but her rebuke was mild instead of sharp this time, her expression thoughtful.

"What if he just managed to hide his dark side from you until after the delivery? If you look at it this way, it means you don't have to feel guilty about anything. There's literally *nothing* you could have done. He would have shown his true colors sooner or later anyway, with or without anything 'triggering' him." He met Hazel's eyes as she focused on him again. "It really wasn't your fault, Mom."

Her voice was barely audible when she whispered, "Thank you, baby."

"So," Lily said as she plopped down next to him and sniffed in a most dignified Lily kind of way, "what's the status quo with your demonic father? Oh, and by the way, knowing you're half-demon explains *so many* things—" She dodged his mock swing and grinned.

"Well." He grasped the nape of his neck. "We're sort of...friends? It's a bit weird, to be honest. We talked on the way here from Faerie. We both missed out on so much time we could have spent together, and he never saw me growing up. I think it eats at him that he didn't get to have the experience of being around me while I was a kid. And it's strange for both of us to meet as adults." He shrugged. "I mean, I have a hard time relating to him as my father."

"Yeah." Lily frowned. "He looks like he's your age."

Basil grimaced. "Apparently, hæmingr demons live pretty long, and can stay young for most of their lives."

Lily raised a brow. "Good for you. Plus, there's that nice shapeshifting power y'all got. Have you tried it yet? Can you do it?"

He gave her a slow smile, leaned back in his seat—and morphed. Power rippled over his skin, through his cells, and with a feeling of being folded and turned over in a million tiny ways, he changed his shape.

Lily shrieked and jumped back from the table. "Oy!" She pointed a finger at him. "Stop that. It's weird enough seeing just *one* other version of me walking around."

He laughed and let go of Lily's form, shifting back to his own appearance.

Hazel smiled. "Impressive. Although without having absorbed the magic of the person you're changing into, you can't imitate their aura, can you?"

"Right. Which means this kind of power is only good for fooling beings with dull senses, like humans."

"Or for shocking unsuspecting relatives," Lily muttered.

Basil grinned and winked at her.

"I still think," Hazel interjected, crossing her arms, "that Tallak should be punished for slaughtering the fae court."

"Mom…"

"It wasn't right." She shook her head. "No matter

how nasty some of them supposedly were."

Basil exhaled through his nose. "He spent twenty-six years in their dungeon. I think that was punishment enough, even if it was before the fact."

"And what about the fae he killed before he was imprisoned? The ones whose powers he stole to conceal himself in Faerie. He's a murderer."

"He's changed."

Hazel gave him a look that spelled out *Oh, really?* in an extra-italicized, sarcasm-dripping font. "It's been less than two weeks since he butchered the royal court."

"Who tortured him for a quarter of a century." He rubbed a hand over his face. "Mom, please. I only just found him. Leave him alone. He just wants to get to know his son and enjoy his newfound freedom."

Hazel arched a brow, the move so reminiscent of Lily's best withering glare. "It's the latter one I'm especially concerned with."

"He promised he won't cause any trouble."

"Well, you tell him I'm holding him to that. I'm *watching* him. If he takes even just one step out of line, he'll find our dungeon to be as cozy as the fae court's."

Basil swallowed. "Got it."

He looked out toward the lawn, where Isa stood up next to Rose. His mate's movement inexorably drew his attention to her sleekly muscled body, to those gray eyes—incandescent with the inner fire he'd actually, *literally* touched while he unmade her—and everything else fell away.

He inhaled on a rush of need that set his blood ablaze, and got to his feet to follow the invitation in the sly smile she sent his way while she strolled toward the second backyard entrance to the mansion, which was around the corner...and happened to feature a staircase leading up his room.

"I've...gotta go," he murmured to whoever else was in the kitchen with him, his feet already carrying him into the foyer.

He barely heard the snickers that followed him out, his mind and body focused on the sole reason his heart was beating. And when he intercepted her as she sprinted for his room, when he caught her around the waist, shouldered her amidst her giggling protests, and dumped her on his bed so she bounced off the mattress with a gasp, that heart of his, the one he'd fused inextricably with hers when he wove her back into life, threatened to burst with too much love.

"Never too much," she whispered, and held out her hand.

He smiled—and pounced on her instead.

AUTHOR NOTE

Enjoyed *To Stir a Fae's Passion?* Sign up for my
newsletter on my website www.nadinemutas.com to
receive my novella *To Caress a Demon's Soul* for free,
and to be notified of new releases, and get more
newsletter-exclusive goodies in the future.
My newsletter is low-volume and won't spam your
inbox. I'll never share your information, not even with
my demons. You can unsubscribe at any time.

Reviews are any author's lifeblood. Even just a few
lines help spread the word, so other readers can find
the books they'll love. Consider leaving a review on
Amazon, Goodreads, or another platform of your
choice. You're also welcome to contact me via email:
nadine@nadinemutas.com
I love to hear from readers!

Books in the *Love and Magic* series by Nadine Mutas:

Novels:
To Seduce a Witch's Heart (Love and Magic, #1)
To Win a Demon's Love (Love and Magic, #2)
To Stir a Fae's Passion (Love and Magic, #3)

Novellas:
To Caress a Demon's Soul (Love and Magic, #1.5) **Sign up for my newsletter on my website www.nadinemutas.com to receive this novella as a free read!**

ABOUT THE AUTHOR

Polyglot Nadine Mutas has always loved tangling with words, whether in her native tongue German or in any of the other languages she's acquired over the years. The more challenging, the better, she thought, and thus she studied the cultures and languages of South Asia and Japan. She worked at a translation agency for a short while, putting to use her knowledge of English, French, Spanish, Japanese, and Hindi.

Before long, though, her lifelong passion for books and words eventually drove her to give voice to those story ideas floating around in her brain (which have kept her up at night and absent-minded at inopportune times). She now writes paranormal romances with wickedly sensual heroes and the fiery heroines who tame them. Her debut novel, To Seduce a Witch's Heart (first published as Blood, Pain, and Pleasure), won the Golden Quill Award 2016 for Paranormal Romance, the Published Maggie Award 2016 for Fantasy / Paranormal Romance, and was a finalist in the PRISM contest for Dark Paranormal and Best First Book, as well as nominated for the Passionate Plume award 2016 for Paranormal Romance Novels & Novellas. It also won several awards for excellence in unpublished romance.

She currently resides in California with her college sweetheart, beloved little demon spawn, and two black cats hellbent on cuddling her to death (Clarification: Both her husband and kid prefer her alive. The cats, she's not so sure about.)

Nadine Mutas is a proud member of the Romance Writers of America (RWA), the Silicon Valley Romance Writers of America (SVRWA), the Rose City Romance Writers (RCRW),   and the Fantasy, Futuristic & Paranormal chapter of the RWA (FF&PRW).

Made in the USA
San Bernardino, CA
06 June 2017